Search

more kate killoy mysteries

Fashion Goes to the Dogs
Book One

Puppy Pursuit
Book Two

National Security
Book Three

Search

a kate killoy mystery

Suspense for the Dog Lover

by

Peggy Gaffney

Kanine Books

Peggy Gaffney

Kanine Books is a division of Kanine Knits Books & Patterns
877 Marion Rd, Cheshire, CT 06410

This book is a work of fiction. Names, characters, places, and incidents are products of the author's imagination or are use fictitiously. Any resemblance to actual events or locales or persons, living or dead, is entirely coincidental.

Website - peggygaffney.com

Cover design by the author

ISBN 978-0-9993878-0-1

Acknowledgments

I would like to express my thanks to friends in the world of Samoyed dogs who have made my life full and happy, especially three very special ladies: Lisa Peterson, Cheri Hollenback and Judy Mears, who made it possible for me to bring the wonderful Dillon and Quinn into my life.

I also want to thank Sandy McDonough for her keen eye as editor in helping me create the best book possible for my readers. It was nice to work with someone who knows the world of dogs.

I want to thank my son Sean for his support and encouragement, as well as my fellow members of Sisters in Crime New England and The Connecticut Authors and Publishers Association.

But most of all I'd like to thank my wonderful readers who encourage me, write complementary reviews, and stop me at dog shows to tell me how much they enjoy the books and ask for autographs. You make this worthwhile.

Dedication

For Dillon, Quinn and all my Samoyeds down through the years.

Search

CHARACTERS IN ORDER OF APPEARANCE

A faithful reader suggested that with so many attending the wedding, this guide would be helpful.

CHARACTER	WHO THEY ARE
Kate Killoy	Owner of Killoy Boarding Kennel, dog breeder of her line of Shannon Samoyeds, dog trainer in everything from obedience to police dog training, fashion designer and owner for Kate Killoy's Fancier Fashions and THE BRIDE
Man with a gun	Mob killer who is trying to kill Kate
Billy Albert	Connecticut State Trooper works with canine officer Belgium Malinois 'Rosco'
Alan Waller	Connecticut State Trooper works with canine officer German Shepherd Dog, 'Luther'
Danielle DeFelice 'Dani'	Connecticut State Trooper works with canine officer Bouvier des Flandres 'Jake'
Sal Mondigliani	Kate's kennel manager and co-instructor in dog training, retired police chief
Roger Argus	Connecticut State Trooper with canine officer Labrador Retriever, 'Moren'
Agnes Forester	Recently retired #1 fashion model, now bank president, Kate's cousin and the MAID OF HONOR who is coordinating the wedding
Dillon, Quinn, Liam, Rory, Shelagh, Kelly, Dedre, Teagan, Maud, Dermod, Brendon, and	Kate's Samoyed dogs. Some are showing in breed, some obedience,some agility, some do search and rescue, and some

Shannon	therapy work
Harry Foyle	Former math geek for the FBI, Owner of a successful cyber security company, searching for his father's murderer and THE GROOM
Deshi Xiang 'Des'	Special agent at the FBI, friend of Harry and Kate
Sarah Mondigliani	Harry's sister who is married to Sal's son. BRIDESMAID
Ellen Martin	Manager at 'Kate Killoy's Fancier Fashions' and former manager at Killoy and Killoy Forensic Accountants
Sean Connelly	Connecticut State Trooper with canine officer Golden Retriever 'Patrick', and Agnes Forester's fiancé
Richard Carsley	New York Bank President, member of Kate's search team whose dog is a Chihuahua named 'Spike'
Sgt. Konrad Gurka	Canine Coordinator Connecticut State Troopers with canine officer German Shepherd Dog, 'Teddy'
Cora Benson	Member of Kate's search team whose dog is Bernese Mt. Dog 'Hugo'
Kathy King	Member of Kate's search team whose dog is Landseer Newfoundland 'Tenney
Alice Simmons	Member of Kate's search team whose dog is Golden Retriever 'Lucky'
Mr. Windom	Father of the missing child
Jennifer Windom	Second grade girl who got lost on a field trip

Search

Cathy Harrison	Samoyed breeder and dog show judge, friend of Kate who is dating Harry's best man. BRIDESMAID
Seamus Killoy	Kate's younger brother, math wiz, and twin of Tim, senior in high school
Tom Killoy	Kate's older brother and CEO of Killoy and Killoy Forensic Accountants
Satu Mituzani	Seamus' girlfriend and math wiz, senior in high school
Doc Walters.	Killoy family physician
Will Killoy	Kate's younger brother, a math wiz, finishing his final year at the Massachusetts Institute of Technology and will soon become part of K&K as Tom's partner. Outstanding chef
Tim Killoy	Kate's younger brother, a math wiz, twin to Seamus and a basketball and baseball star, senior in high school
Maeve Killoy Donovan	Kate's great-aunt, math wiz, former MI-5 agent
Padraig Donovan	Maeve's husband
Randy Mackowsik	Connecticut State Trooper with canine officer Golden Retriever, 'Walt'
Eric Chaffin	Connecticut State Trooper with canine officer Bloodhound, 'Fingall'
Gaetano Campanelli	Mob hired gun who tried to kill both Kate and Harry, who is injured when trying to escape, part of the Zuccarello Crime Family in Philadelphia

Peggy Gaffney

Fr. Joe	Priest at Killoy family's local Catholic church
Sgt. Pete Foyle	Harry's murdered father, former Boston policeman
Rory Killoy	Kate's cousin married to Sharon
Sharon Killoy	Rory's wife who gives Kate a bridal shower
Mrs. Foyle	Harry's mother, a difficult woman
Denise Marshall	FBI Agent who is undercover as a reporter in Kate's knitting studio, keeping the knitters safe
Rufus Blackburn	Harry's friend from his time at Caltech, dating Cathy and the BEST MAN
Jordy Blackburn	Rufus' 12 yr. old son, a math wiz, in a special program at Massachusetts Institute of Technology
Bob	Electrician working on Kate's security system
Malcolm Bullock	Agent in Charge at the D.C. office of the FBI
Sadie	Harry's assistant and former FBI agent
Andy Sibowitz	No. 1 fashion photographer in the country, friend of Kate's and here to photograph the wedding
Ann Killoy	Kate's grandmother
Lily Peters	Quinn's breeder, a Texas District Attorney
Joyce Marks	Samoyed breeder working for the Denver P.D. and dog show judge

Chapter One

"How are you doing there, Kate?"

"Well, let's see. I'm standing around in a sweaty camouflage bite suit which makes me look like a combat Michelin man, five large dogs have mauled me so far today, and I'm more than ready for lunch. To tell the truth, Sal, hiding is boring enough to make me look forward to Agnes nagging me about the wedding. Have you sent out Billy yet? I'm visualizing a sandwich and a cup of tea with my name on it as I wait for his Malinois, Rosco, to find me. Honestly, filling in as the criminal on these search and capture practice runs stinks. I prefer being on the right side of the law searching with Dillon."

"Billy left three minutes ago. He's trying to beat everyone's time so it won't be long until you eat."

"I hope he remembers to use his release word this time. I don't want people saying the bride wore black and blue. Agnes should be here soon and she'd freak."

"Hang in there, kid. Billy's should arrive in four minutes. You and I both know you can't keep the diva waiting. She's already upset that we scheduled this test run so close to the wedding."

Kate put her phone back in her pocket and put back on the protective mask she'd ditched to make the call. Agnes, recently retired as America's favorite supermodel, was not only her cousin and maid of honor, but a whirlwind who kept people hopping and was lovingly referred to as Hurricane Agnes. The wedding was one hundred and sixty-eight hours away and thanks to Agnes and her family, everything was ready. Everyone invited was coming. The food, which her brother would cook, was ordered. The reception venue, which was her barn, would be converted on Wednesday, and her grandmother had even made her a spreadsheet to ease the job of sending thank-you notes for the presents. So instead of working on the wedding, the bride -to-be was hiding in the woods in a sweaty bite suit.

Leaning against a hemlock tree, she crouched, as she listened for signs of movement. A half dozen state troopers with their search dogs had previously found her, but she wasn't making it easy for this last one, hunting her. She maneuvered around the tree, making sure not to break the silence. Not breathing, she heard only two blue jays squabbling, and a squirrel shouting profanity at her for infringing on his space, but other than that, nothing.

She snagged a branch, steadied herself by transferring weight onto her right foot as she stepped out to the left and was about to ease out from behind another massive hemlock tree when a snap of a twig made her freeze. The noise had come from behind her. She waited but instead of nature's chorus, this time she heard only silence. Seconds went by, but still nothing. She began to chalk it up to her imagination when a twig snapped again.

Billy couldn't be that close this soon plus he and Roscoe would approach from the east, not the southwest. Another twig snapped, proving she wasn't alone. Whoever it was, they had stopped using stealth.

A man wearing a camel hair topcoat, city shoes, with a silk scarf around his neck, and soft leather gloves on his hands walked into the clearing. His attire may have been Fifth Avenue, but his face looked pure prizefighter. He strode along the trail until she lost sight of him behind the curve of the hill. To find a better way to see him, she eased herself forward, her camouflage clothing blending with her surroundings. He had gotten much closer when she spotted him again.

Mr. Big City did not belong in her woods. She almost laughed out loud when he walked right through a patch of poison ivy. He was going to itch for at least a week. He glanced left and right as he moved, and seemed to be looking for someone. Unfortunately what he wasn't watching was the ground. An exposed root caught his foot making him stumble. He caught himself just short of wiping out. Kate thought about warning him, as he plowed through still another patch of poison ivy, but didn't, since his furtive behavior gave her an uneasy feeling.

He had reached a spot just below her when Kate realized that Billy was due in two minutes. A man standing between Rosco and his search quarry would throw off their score to say nothing of being a surprise for the stranger when the Belgian Malinois burst out of the underbrush. If this guy was having trouble dealing with the trail and poison ivy, he would completely freak out when faced with an aggressive pursuit dog in attack mode.

Kate braced herself to stand but then stopped as he pulled a gun from his pocket. It was an automatic like the one in her fiancé's gun cabinet. This man's weapon had a larger magazine than Harry's. It was a gun designed to kill people — lots of people.

She had to do something. Billy was barely a minute away and completely unaware of his danger. She squatted again, putting out a hand out for support. The hand connected with a rock. With more instinct than thought, her fingers tightened around it, prying it from the ground. She saw the man swing the gun left, then right holding it steady then he twisted to check behind, looking away from her. At that second, Kate stood and threw the rock is far she could toward the ravine. Then she dropped as shots rang out. The gun had a hair trigger. She'd counted at least 10 rounds in rapid succession.

Search

The silence, which followed the shots, gave way to the noise of barking. Billy must have noticed the shots, but from the sound of movement in the brush, he was still coming.

Kate pulled her phone from her pocket, and sent a fast text message to Sal telling him to warn Billy of the shooter then she switched off her phone so its ring couldn't give her position away, and searched for another rock. Tim, her brother who loved baseball, had taught her to throw. He said she had a hot arm and she prayed he was right.

The man hurried toward the ravine but stopped when dog barks began sounding closer. He pivoted, lifted his gun and gripping it with both hands, aimed it toward the sound.

Kate acted. She snatched up the second rock, adjusted her grip, focused on her target, and as Tim had taught her, drew back her arm, let out a breath and let fly. Three shots went off as she knocked the gun out of his hand and watched as it slid across the ground and fell over the edge of the ravine.

The shooter shook his hands in pain. He whirled around trying to spot his attacker but abandoned that to head toward the ravine. He had only taken two steps when the woods filled with the sounds of approaching dogs. With more speed than she imagined he had, the gunman whirled and raced back toward the main trail.

Kate didn't move until Rosco sprang from the underbrush followed by Billy Albert. Kate rose and pointed to the trail. "Shooter! He ran toward the logging road." As Billy, raced in pursuit, he was followed by Alan Waller, and Dani DeFelice with their dogs Luther and Jake.. Sal came up right behind them, but he veered off in her direction. Kate sank to the ground, her legs no longer supporting her. The bite suit, which had seemed hot, felt icy and chills traveled through her body. She shivered as Sal came up behind her. Noticing her shaking, he lifted her from where she'd been hiding.

"Kate, what's going on here?"

She fought for control of her body then said, "I don't have a clue. I was hiding from Billy, when this idiot, dressed for Park Avenue, came strolling through my woods. He pulled an automatic and fired. I knocked the gun from his hands with a rock and it slid into the gully over there. We've got to retrieve it before some kid finds it."

Eyeing the spot where she last saw the gun, she started for the gully, but Sal pulled her back.

"Wait a minute, Missy. Somebody shot at you and you want to climb down a gully to find up a gun? Kate, I need information here." She kept going. "Can you stop, please?"

"Sal, we've got to locate that gun."

"I know we do, but first talk to me. You said someone went walking in your woods and shot at you."

"Yeah, a Park Avenue guy with an ugly face, though he didn't shoot me. He ran down the trail and the troopers are after him. We've got to get that gun, Sal."

"Tell me more." Sal grabbed her arm and spun her around to face him but she kept looking over her shoulder at the edge of the gully.

That was when her hands began to shake hard, and soon the shaking took over her whole body, causing her to have trouble standing. He lowered her to the ground as she lost her balance.

Search

"Kate, say something," Sal yelled. He pulled out his phone and hit speed dial. "Roger, bring the ATV out here now. We're out at the far end of the trail just before the big turn. Kate needs help."

Sal took the helmet from her head and unzipped the top of the bite suit so that Kate could breathe. He checked her pulse then took her head and held it trying to force her to focus on his words. Her teeth were chattering as though they might break, so he pulled the strap off the helmet and forced it between her teeth. Then he held her tight.

With a screech of brakes, Roger Argus arrived, with his Lab, Moren, in the back. Sal pulled Kate to her feet, as Roger grabbed her helmet. Once she was standing, he picked her up and placed her in the vehicle and climbed in behind. Roger turned in a tight circle and headed back towards the barn. Sal wrapped his arms around her, holding her while she shook. Bypassing the barn, Roger drove straight to the door of Kate's cottage. Sal lifted Kate from the ATV, set her on her feet, and with Roger's help, unzipped her from the bite suit and pulled the strap from her mouth, then holding her tight, half-walked, half-carried her toward the door.

Once inside, he settled her in a kitchen chair and turned on the kettle to make tea. Roger grabbed bread, meat, and cheese, from the fridge and began to make a sandwich, Sal ducked into her room and pulled the quilt from the end of her bed and wrapped it around her. Then he made her tea and placed it as well as the sandwich in front of her as Roger left to take the ATV and go to fetch the troopers.

The shaking had lessened. He took her face in his hands and said, "Now you sit here, Kate, and eat." Holding the tea mug, he kept it to her mouth until she drank. Then he put the sandwich in her hand, lifted it to her mouth and said, "Eat. We need to put food into you to counteract the blood-sugar drop. You're in shock, but you'll be okay. Finish that sandwich. When you're done, we'll talk this out."

She clutched the cup seeking warmth as she drank the tea. After she'd finished the 1st cup, Sal took the cup to refill it and placed some more of the sandwich in her hand. Once she was eating, he refilled her mug, and she'd finished the sandwich by the time the state troopers arrived. They crowded into the kitchen and Billy passed something to Sal.

Kate scanned the serious faces surrounding her then asked, "What's going on?"

The looks that passed between the troopers had her uneasy, but Roger stepped forward and said, "The shooter got away Kate. But, when he reached for his car keys, something fell out of his pocket."

"What? What did he drop?"

Kate glanced from Roger to Sal who was holding a scrap of paper and looking furious.

"What is it? What does it say?" Kate demanded.

Sal sighed and placed it in front of her. Her eyes traveled from his face to the white piece of paper which lay beside plate. It contained only three words — Kill Kate Killoy.

Chapter Two

Kate stared at the note as ice again flowed over her. She shook her head. The tingle began again in her fingers. Then a new mug of hot tea materialized between her hands and larger hands surrounded hers guiding the warm liquid to her mouth. One sip, then two more and the warmth began to melt her chill.

Sal told her, "Finish that cup and I'll make another. Roger, get her some cookies. She needs sugar in her system to fight shock."

Without taking her eyes from the note, she said, "Sal, we need to get that gun. A child could get hurt."

"What gun?" Asked Roger.

"The shooter's gun. It flew toward the gully right before he took off running for his car."

"The gun flew?" Billy stared at her.

"No. It was knocked out of his hands when the rock hit them."

"The rock?"

Kate stopped and took a breath. Then, repeating herself one word at a time, she told him,"The rock I threw at his hands to stop him shooting you--which is what he was planning to do when you broke cover"

"A rock?" Billy and the other troopers stared open-mouthed at each other. "You threw a rock and knocked an automatic out of a gunman's hands? Those were the shots we heard before we reached the trail? God, Kate, you must have some arm."

"Tim says I do, but I think it's the mathematical adjustments my mind makes when I throw, which helps me hit a target."

"I for one want to thank you for saving us. I never thought the shooter would turn on us." The others nodded and smiled. Then Billy said, "Hey, Danielle. Isn't Jake trained in firearms detection?"

"Yeah, he qualified three months ago." She smiled.

"Good, let's you and I go find that gun. I don't want that guy coming back for it. You know, Dani, we all may need to get some help from Tim before we face off against the local police department's softball teams next summer."

Roger pushed himself away from the counter. "Sal, the rest of us will go clean up the barn, get things organized and put away. Kate, you stay here and relax, but keep practicing your pitching. I can't believe you threw a rock and hit his hands. I think we've got another skill we need to add to our training. Sal, take care of her and make sure to guard her arm," he said and left chuckling, as the troopers followed.

Sal sat down, and took her arm not letting her move when she tried to follow the searchers. "Kate, focus. Look at me. Do you realize someone went to the trouble of finding out where you and tried to murder you?"

"Yes," she said fighting against the thought.

"Someone walked into your woods, and brought a gun specifically to shoot you."

"I know, but how did he know I'd be there? Who told him?"

Sal sat up with a start, stared at her and pulled out his phone.

"Roger. Did any of you talk about the morning's test before coming here?" His expression darkened. "Dunkin' Donuts. Right. Got it."

He stood and grabbed a mug shoved it into the one-cup coffee machine. He silently thanked Harry for bringing this fancy coffee maker from Boston because right now he needed strong black coffee and lots of it. After his first sip, he looked at the cup, scowled and asked, "Kate, where is Harry?"

"What did Roger tell you?" she asked, stalling.

"The troopers spent the time before the test sitting with their donuts and coffee this morning, discussing who'd get the best score and which trails and hideouts you might use. I know they didn't think their fun might lead to getting you shot at, but they're trained officers of the law, they should know better than run off at the mouth in a public place."

Kate agreed and would work it into the training after she got back from her honeymoon if she lived so long.

"I answered your question, now answer mine--where's Harry?"

She couldn't lie to Sal, the person who brought the two of them together. He loved Harry like a son. Kate kept her eyes on the mug clutched in her hands trying to   avoid looking at Sal while she tried to figure out how to tell him that she couldn't tell him where her fiancé was. Harry had begged her to keep his whereabouts a secret, and she would. Marrying Harry meant he deserved her trust.

"I can't tell you."

"What do you mean you can't tell me?"

"When Harry left, he made me promise not to tell anyone. If anyone found out, it could endanger his life. That's not a chance I'm willing to take."

"When? When did Harry leave? I thought he was packing up his place in Boston prior to the wedding. Kate, how long has he been gone?"

"Three weeks."

"Wait a second. Your fiancé has been gone for three weeks, into a situation that is so secret that you can't tell me where he is, and you are walking around acting as if life is normal. Aren't you worried? What if something happened to him? Kate, you're getting married next week, and you didn't tell anyone?"

"He'll be here for the wedding. Of course, I worry but I trust him. You should trust him too. You've known Harry longer than I have. Would he not show up for his own wedding? Don't you have any faith in him?"

Search

"I have faith in Harry. But Kate, someone tried to kill you today. Don't you think your fiancé might like to know about that? How can I get in touch with him?"

"I don't know. He is out of contact. I've tried to get in touch with him. It didn't work."

The front door banged open hitting the wall and shut with a slam as Hurricane Agnes strode into the kitchen looking ready to kill. She reached down and grabbed Kate's chair, spinning it around and bending, so they faced off eyeball to eyeball.

"When in the hell did you plan to tell me that somebody shot at you?"

"How did you find out?"

"A firearm was discharged within Sean's jurisdiction and one of his fellow troopers reported it. He thought I might be interested in this nugget of information since the target of the shooting happened to be a bride for whom I'm going to be maid-of-honor. It happens I am interested. Very interested. How am I supposed to be your maid-of-honor, if you don't update me on the little details such as you being a target for a potential murder? Sean said the shooter got away, so is it still a problem?"

Kate stared back at Agnes. Her cousin seemed almost as beautiful as she was furious. But this wasn't Agnes the supermodel, nor Agnes the banker. This was Agnes the Valkyrie descending from Valhalla on the warpath and taking no prisoners. She sighed and turned away from her cousin toward Sal. "Sal, could you give us a moment to talk please, alone?"

"Okay girlie, I'm gonna trust you not to do anything stupid like walking around outside without protection. Do I have your word you'll stay safe?"

"Yes, you have my word I won't go anywhere without protection"

Sal stood and pushed in his chair. He stared at Kate, looking for a catch in what she had said, but for the life of him he couldn't figure out what it could be. He frowned at Agnes and said, "Watch her, I'll be in the kennel office."

"Fine, Sal's gone, now talk."

"I honestly don't know why someone shot at me. I don't have any enemies that I know of. It may be one of Harry's cases, but I have no way of knowing that. Anyway, why would somebody with a grudge against Harry, know about me."

"Have you asked Harry?"

Kate stood and walked to the kitchen door. Her dogs all lined up watching her. She opened the door and they flooded into the room. Dillon, Quinn, and Liam and the rest all pressed up against her. She reached out and buried her hands in their long white coats as she sank to the floor.

She leaned into the dogs, hugging all she could reach, then looked up at Agnes and said, "I don't know where Harry is. Three weeks ago he got a text message from a coded address. He told me it was vital he leave. When I asked him where he was going, he said he couldn't tell me. I lost it and threw a fit demanding to know where he was going, saying some horrible things about him not caring. I became a nasty bitch, a person I've never been in my life. Finally, I blockaded the door with my body and wouldn't let him go without knowing where he would be. I may have freaked him out because he finally gave in and told me, but at the same time, he asked me to keep it a secret. He said if anyone found out, it could mean his life. It's why I can't tell you."

"When did he pull this disappearing act?"

"Three weeks ago."

Agnes' shocked face stared down at Kate on the floor surrounded by a dozen Samoyeds. The Sams seemed to recognize her need for comfort, instinctively knowing she hurt. Agnes sat in the chair she'd vacated and reached out to hold Kate's face. "Tell me where he is. He's got to come home. Is he in Boston?"

Kate stared at her without answering.

"New York? Philadelphia? LA? You're not going to tell me, are you? Washington? Ah ha, that's it."

Agnes stood and hurried into the living room. Kate buried her head in Dillon's ruff knowing Agnes had forced her to betray Harry. This was a game she'd played with them as children. You couldn't lie to her because she could detect it when you blinked.

She hushed the dogs to listen to what her cousin said on the phone. She must have called someone, asking for a name but thanks to Quinn and Shelagh's barking, she couldn't hear her cousin's exact words. Kate tried to lean closer to the doorway, but Quinn decided it was time to play and soon the entire kitchen became involved in a game of bite everybody's feet and jump on everyone's back. The barking accompanying the game meant Kate heard nothing.

When Agnes shut the door to the living room, Kate got up, reached for biscuits and bribed the dogs back outside. Once gone, Kate raced to the door between the kitchen and living room only to hear Agnes say, "Thanks, I appreciate that. I'll see you soon."

Agnes strode back into the kitchen. "Why don't you go take a shower and get ready to try on your wedding dress. Sarah will be here in half an hour. Cathy won't arrive till later according to her text.

"Ellen and your knitters are anxious to see how you look in the dress considering all the work they put into it. Here are the foundation garments you need to wear under the dress. You might as well put them on now as well. I'm going to make myself a cup of tea. So get going."

"What have you done? Who did you call? Did you talk to Harry?"

"Don't worry about it. Nothing is going to stop this wedding. Not a shooter, and not the invisible Mr. Harry Houdini Foyle."

Chapter Three

Harry stared out through the crack in the drawn curtains, studying the gray sedan   parked across the street. It had been there for the last twelve hours, replacing the black sedan which been in the spot the day before. It worked as a perfect spot for the two men inside to see everyone who came and went from the hotel.

A woman left the hotel walking a white dog. A Poodle. That glimpse of white dog tore his mind from the case. He needed Kate, her touch, her laugh. He'd spent half his life searching for the killer behind his father's murder, but being away from his fiancée for three weeks brought home to him the truth that Kate mattered more than anything.

Peggy Gaffney

FBI agent Deshi Xiang became a good friend last month at the National Specialty Dog Show for Samoyeds, when they needed help to save Kate's life. It took the FBI and NSA, plus local police to keep them alive as he and Kate searched for a coded clue necessary to stop a threat against America.

The help from Des, this time, was personal. He contacted Harry when a thumbprint from his father's murder turned up in an FBI case. A reporter had supposedly committed suicide. But a conscientious CSI checked not only the gun but the bullet casings for fingerprints. She discovered a thumbprint which matched Boston PD's database and still open case of the murder of Sgt. Peter Foyle. Des made the connection and texted Harry.

This victim, a reporter working on a story about a locals syndicate, had caught his curiosity. Des found no trace of the reporter's notes on him or in his computer. However, he discovered a blind file hidden on the dark web, but neither he nor the crime lab experts had been able to decode it.

He contacted Harry. He knew his last case involved searching coded messages on the dark web. He passed Harry the link hidden in the overlay network. Harry opened the files, read them and immediately made a copy which he hid on his own server. After doing a quick read of the notes, he sketched out a gist of the information which he sent to Des. When Des told him about the connection to his father's case, Harry needed to go to Washington.

The reporter discovered the syndicate was in the process of finding talented men who could control investigations from inside, in local, state, and national law enforcement. These bad actors would be passed off as respected members of civil service. They would hide in plain sight. From what Des had found, somewhere in this group, existed the man who had murdered both the journalist and Harry's father. Harry needed to find him.

For three weeks, he'd been hiding in this hotel room studying endless piles of data from the Bureau, the Department of Justice, and Homeland Security. Harry was amassing a frightening pile of evidence about some unnamed event involving various organized crime families up and down the east coast. However, in spite of the vast collection of facts, he was no closer to finding the actual plan. Whatever it was, it was powerful enough to unite crime families after years of blood feuds. He suspected the cars in front of the hotel were part of it.

His eyes strayed to the bed. Driving while this tired was stupid, but sleep hadn't been a priority for weeks as he went through all the files. He managed to write a program, based on the data, which might help predict where their next move might be, but it needed more data. He'd used it a week ago to predict the next victim would be a state senator from Philadelphia. He'd sent his theory to Des, but by the time they checked, the senator's home had been firebombed. It turned out he'd voted no on a project put forward by a contractor connected to the crime family. The Bureau investigation found prints on a microchip in a cell phone found in a dumpster near the explosion. The phone had been the detonator--and the prints matched his father's killer.

Peggy Gaffney

Harry had been stuck in this room for 504 hours, his world since he left Kate. He felt he was close to the answer, but there was no time left. Somehow the mob had made him. He had to go back home. He needed Kate.

Everything had been scanned and uploaded to his server. He'd finished shredding the rest of the papers and filling the burn bags. On his way north, he'd swing by Langley to dispose of them. There was nothing left to do here and he couldn't wait to get back to Connecticut and Kate. He had pulled out his phone and started to call her, but then forced himself to stop. Calling meant a possible trace. He'd wait.

He stuffed his backup phone in the go bag and did a quick sweep of the room to make sure no trace showed he'd ever been there. As he picked up the bags, a knock sounded at the door. Without making a sound, he lowered the bags to the floor, pulled his gun and moved toward the door with his back to the wall. Next a quick look out the peephole. Des stood in the hall, looking left and right to make sure he was alone. Harry opened the door just enough for his friend to slip in.

"Do you really know the supermodel, Agnes Forester?" Des asked.

"God, yes, Agnes hates me. Why are you asking me about Agnes?"

"Hate you or not, she just called me and said if I knew where you were to tell you   to get your--let's just say I didn't know that ladies use language like that--she said to get back to Connecticut as fast as you possibly can because someone tried to murder Kate."

"Kate. I've got to go. Did she tell you what happened?"

Search

"No, but she said you needed to be there now. She also said something about an Oxford airport before she hung up. Harry, don't tell Kate I was part of the operation keeping you away these last weeks. She likes me and I don't want that to change. She told me she had a dozen dogs like Dillon at home and I would hate to have them turned against me."

"Quinn wouldn't hurt you, but if you hurt Kate, I would lay bets on any of the others letting you off lightly."

Des had become friends with Kate and her dogs at the Samoyed National. He'd investigated the murder of a former agent who been one of the Killoy's old family friends and was killed because of her involvement with spies and a threat to the country. It all came to a head while they were at the show and it almost cost Kate her life. He'd developed a soft spot for Dillon's puppy, Quinn, who'd built himself quite a fan club among what Kate called 'the long arm of the law club.'

Des held out a tiny flash drive."I'll take the burn bags. This is the latest we have on your guy. From what Bullock hinted, your man has taken a giant leap forward in his career. Also, I picked up some whispers that you're not as invisible as we hoped. So we're leaving your car here for two more days and will have it brought north.

You're flying into this Oxford airport and a rental car will be waiting. Bullock thinks both you and Kate will be safer together. I'll be joining you on Saturday. We won't have met since October. Do you think Kate will have said anything?"

"No, she may have told people I'm on a case, but not what it involves. Remember this is Kate."

"You sure got lucky finding her. She is one in a million."

Peggy Gaffney

"Don't I know it. And in a week, she'll be my wife."

Des checked the hall, then both men moved down the rear stairs and out the back way. They ducked through a break in the chain-link fence behind the hotel, and jogged up a neighbor's driveway to a street where Des' car waited.

They took a roundabout route, all the time checking for tails, and finally arrived at a gate which led into a private airport. A small plane was waiting with its engines already going. Des told him not to speak to the pilot because as far as the man was concerned, he was delivering a package as a favor to an old friend. Harry nodded and shook his hand. Dragging his cases, dashed from the car, and boarded for a quick flight to the airport nearest home. Home and Kate. He smiled at that thought but worried about someone trying to kill her. Possibly, this was only the start and he could be bringing danger with him. The plane took off immediately barely giving him time to fasten his seat belt.

Once they were in the air heading north, he stuffed the flash drive Des had given him into his briefcase. He could pull all the facts from it and put them together to find the killer after the wedding. But right now, all he could think of was Kate and the fact that somebody had tried to murder her. He needed to know what had happened. Was she hurt? Was she still in danger? Damn Agnes.

Chapter Four

Agnes leaned against the counter as Kate came out of the bedroom. She ran her fingers through her wet hair and tucked a shoe box under one arm. In contrast to Kate's somewhat damp, thrown together appearance, her cousin still looked like the Agnes Forrester who had been graced magazine covers and on billboards across the country—every inch a supermodel.

Agnes watched Kate gather up the teacup she had left on the table and move to the sink to rinse it. "How can you be so calm? You were shot at less than two hours ago? I realize that this isn't the first time it's happened to you, but come on. It's a week before your wedding for heaven's sake. You'd think the bad actors in this area would give you a break to get married. These wanna-be killers just have no respect for tradition. The last thing you need is to be upset before walking down the aisle."

Peggy Gaffney

The front door opened and Harry's sister, Sarah, walked in, headed straight for the kitchen and demanding a cup of tea while she collapsed into a chair. She shoved the next chair back and put her feet up. "That girl is going to put me in an early grave. Have you heard the latest, Kate?"

"The latest what?"

"I just had a call from my mother, and it seems that you and Harry won't be the only ones getting married. She and her boss have finally decided to do the deed. She's even selling the house. She told me to let you know that boxes of my father's things were on their way to Harry. Mom figured with you building the new house, you'd have more room for sentimental memorabilia."

"I wondered about the pile of boxes, which arrived yesterday, addressed to Harry. I stuffed them all into his room rather than have the dogs eat them."

Kate got up from her chair and moved to make Sarah some tea, then put some cookies on the plate, and placed both in front of Sarah. Just as Agnes went to say something, Kate's phone buzzed. She looked at the readout and answered. "Hi, Ellen we'll be over to the studio in about five minutes."

Ending the call, she asked,"What was the holdup with Cathy?"

"Something came up." Sarah said. Reaching for another cookie, she filled Kate in. "She called to tell me a new puppy owner couldn't pick up her puppy yesterday. This meant Cathy had to bring the puppy to the airport with her today to deliver it. Of course, their flight got delayed, and wasn't scheduled to land until two hours after hers was to leave. So, as things stand now, her new flight will get here about four-thirty, so she'll miss the grand reveal of the wedding dress."

"Do I need to pick her up?" Kate asked running her fingers through her hair as it started to dry and fluff up.

"No," Agnes told her. "Sarah and I will pick her up. This way we can have a planning dinner on the way back from the airport and go over the details of each person's responsibility as your bridal support."

"Sounds good. I'll leave it in your very capable hands." Kate hugged Agnes and high-fived Sarah whose arm shot up and then immediately collapsed as her phone buzzed with a text. "That child is like the Energizer Bunny. She doesn't stop for two seconds from morning till night. Pete is finding that his life in the Army was like a spa day when next to keeping up with his demon daughter."

Agnes chuckled. "I think it's great she has so much energy. My bank runs a program of math camps in the tri-state area for kids from preschool through grade 6. You could enroll her, and she could spend time learning as well as burn off some of that energy and which would make your life easier."

Sarah, who had perked up at the concept of her daughter burning off energy, flopped back and groaned. "Oh no. I forgot you were one of them, rather than normal, or as normal as a supermodel can be."

Agnes' eyebrows rose. "One of them?"

"Yeah, a math freak like my weird brother."

"Well, I'm not your brother's biggest fan, but it's not because he's a mathematician. What's wrong with being into math?"

"I suppose it's all right for some people, like old professors such as Kate's mom, But Harry was starting fourth grade when those people came to the house and fussed over his mega brain. Then talked my parents into sending him to college in California. Dad loved the idea because he knew he'd never be able to afford college for both of us, since it is so expensive. This way Harry would be getting his education with all his expenses paid. But I mean, he was my little brother, not bloomin' Harry Potter, and he went to Caltech, not Hogwarts."

Agnes studied her for a minute then said, "For some people, math is magic and I suspect Harry is one of them. But it had to have been hard losing your brother so suddenly like that." Sarah looked down. "Yeah. At school all my friends wanted to talk about was my super brother. Nothing I did could compare to the little genius."

Kate studied Sarah for a minute, then sat in a chair next to her. "You've never forgiven him for leaving you, have you?"

"He shouldn't have gone," Sarah whispered and turned away.

Kate studied the woman about to become her sister-in-law. This seemed to explain why she was so hard on her brother. Harry had issues about the separation as well, but she suspected that Sarah had never considered his side. Kate doubted she'd seen it from his viewpoint of being wrenched from his family and friends and sent across the country. She needed to talk to Harry when he got back. Thoughts of Harry had her glancing at the front door but it stubbornly remained closed.

"Now, ladies, let's go see how the dress turned out," Kate said as she shook off her longing and stood up. Agnes took the shoe box as Kate helped Sarah hoist herself from the chair. Mindful of what Sal had said, they took the inside route through the kennel which was the shortest route out to the studio.

"You know, the design for this dress only happened because of stress over a murder. I used it to calm down."

Agnes snorted. "Half the designers I know would love to have your calming skills." As they crossed from the kennel up the staircase to the second floor of the barn, Kate caught sight of what looked like a car behind a stand of maple trees to the left of the driveway. She stopped and as she watched, it started up, pulled out onto the highway and drove away.

"You coming, Killoy?" Agnes shouted.

She trotted up the wooden staircase but paused to glance over her shoulder every few steps. At the top, she checked the woods on either side of the barn before turning to go into the studio. Could it be the shooter? She didn't know what his car looked like. She wished that Harry were here.

The vestibule coat rack had one hook left for her jacket, so she hung it up and kicked off her boots setting them in the tray below. Pasting on a smile, she moved into the studio. She needed to focus on her dress. Harry often would tease her about her intuition. But the knowledge that the shooter was sneaking about her property terrified her.

Silence met her when she stepped into the studio. None of the machines were going. All the knitters along with Ellen, Agnes, and Sarah had gathered in front of the big West window which overlooked her woods. Kate walked toward them, squinting into the sun which lay low in the November sky. It flooded the room with light. When her grandfather had planned her studio, he consulted almost every designer in the business and light was absolutely vital. So he had them install massive windows with morning and afternoon light plus a line of skylights across the roof. She looked at all the women lined up before her. Then she realized their focus fell behind her. She turned and froze.

A raised platform stood in the center of the east window and on it was a dress form modeling her wedding gown. Her breath caught and the room receded. The reality of the gown had grown from her imagination into something far more beautiful than what she'd drawn. The dress drew her forward. She reached out, a single finger touched the delicate silky white stitches. The front of the dress fell in classically simple lines. Stockinette stitches made up the fabric of the floor length skirt which dropped straight from the waist. In contrast to the simplicity of the front, the back of the skirt was divided into six gores. Each section, widened like a waterfall as it descended in a cascade from the waist to the floor. Her mind immediately pictured how the gored skirt would swirl out behind her, when she and Harry waltzed, the wedding reception. Harry was a wonderful dancer.

The fitted bodice, knit of the same lightweight wool yarn as the skirt, had a simple scooped neckline in front. Over this simple background, a delicate knitted lace, so fine it looked like mist, rose from the waist to end with two bows at the shoulders. The lace was scattered with thousands of tiny knitted shamrocks gathered into bouquets, which made her smile and warmed her heart. The lace sleeves tapered to a point at the

Search

wrists. In contrast, the neckline of the back of the bodice was shaped as a deep V falling from the shoulders to the middle of the back. The lace overlay followed this V down from the shoulders to its point only then to be gathered into a massive lace rose. From this rose, the same lace swept out to form a train which swept to the floor and several feet beyond.

As Kate studied the train, she suddenly began to cry. Her eyes had followed the waterfall of shamrock bouquets down the lace train only to find they magically scattered, changing into hundreds of tiny paw prints instead. Kate dropped to her knees and reached her fingertips to touch the bottom of the delicate train as sobs shook her.

A hand gripped her shoulder. Ellen, her studio manager, leaned over and hugged her, saying, "You can thank your grandma Ann, for the paw prints. She said your father and grandfather would have suggested it if they had lived. The dogs are such an overwhelming part of your life, it seemed fitting."

"It's perfect," Kate choked out as she took tissues from Agnes and wiped her eyes.

"She said that one day you'd have a daughter who loved dogs as much as you do, and this could be her dress as well."

Kate looked at the faces above her through her tears and saw not a single dry eye. Sarah took a breath and cleared her throat. Wiping her eyes, she looked at her watch. "I've only got forty-five minutes until my husband ends up tied to a kitchen chair by his wild-child daughter, so let's get this show on the road." Everyone laughed effectively breaking the sentimental mood.

Kate scrambled to her feet and hurried to the restroom to change. Agnes opened her tote and pulled out an exquisitely made slip which would be perfect under the dress. "This will put the finishing touch on the outfit. I got it in the interest of bringing tradition into the wedding, but your dress has already taken care of that."

Kate hugged her, and quickly slipped the silky feeling fabric over her head and let it fall to the ground. A second later, Ellen appeared with two of the knitters holding the dress and as she stepped forward, they lowered it over her head easing it down her body. The knitted fabric molded to her making buttons or zippers unnecessary. She stepped into the high-heeled shoes from the box Agnes had brought and took a few tentative steps forward to get her balance. Agnes, Sarah, and all the knitters had their smartphones out and were snapping pictures.

The fit was perfect. Kate hugged her crew who had not only worked knitting the unique sweaters and accessories she designed in her business, but who had become her good friends as they built the business together. Ellen had, for years, been her grandfather's office manager at Killoy and Killoy Forensic Accountants. She retired when Kate graduated from fashion college and went to work for Kate to help her set up her business. Her business thrived because of the kinship among these women.

Kate heard a buzz coming from her phone which she'd left on the sink in the restroom telling her she had a text. Though she wondered about it, she told herself she'd check it in a minute. But a second later, she heard three more buzzes. She hurried to the restroom and grabbed the phone.

"I've got to go." She told them as Ellen lifted the dress off. "Agnes, help me out of this slip and fancy bra, it has too many hooks."

She quickly typed a response into her phone as she heard cars filling up the driveway below. Quickly she tugged on her jeans, pulled a turtleneck top and sweatshirt over her head, then stuffed her feet into socks as she raced from the restroom. Kate noticed the knitters were lined up at the front window staring down at the parking lot. The area in front of the barn had filled with cars, vans, and state police vehicles.

"Kate, what's going on?" Ellen asked.

She opened the door, grabbed her jacket, pushed her feet into her boots, and yelled, "I've got to do a search. A child is missing."

Chapter Five

Running from the bottom of the staircase across the parking lot and into the kennel, she paused only long enough to grab a tracking harness, search vest and tracking lead from her office, then raced to the door to the exercise yard. She opened it a crack.

"Dillon, come."

Tightly wedging herself into the opening so that only he could slip past the door, she said, "Sorry, Quinn, not this time."

At the sight of the harness, Dillon's body froze except for his tail which wagged a mile-a-minute, eager to wear the harness. In seconds, she had it hitched, had slipped the search vest over him, clipped on her tracking lead and raced down the hall, through the kennel and out to the barn.

The cars scattered about were filled with dogs. However, though several were highly trained police dog like the Malinois and German Shepherds she'd trained that morning and were now heading toward New York with their trooper handlers to take their certification tests. These were mostly dogs which made up her search team, They included a Golden, Newfoundland, Bernese Mountain Dog, and even a Chihuahua, all wearing search vests and all ready to go. The few police cars held a German Shepherd, a Belgian Tervuren, and a bloodhound.

The colorful leaves that covered the ground lent a festive air to the scene. Kate and Dillon pushed in through the side door of the barn. The building had once again been converted from a training venue to a command center. Folding tables snapped into place, cupboards, which lined the walls now stood open to display everything from climbing equipment and ropes to first aid kits.

Sean Connelly, a state trooper and Agnes' fiancé, followed her into the barn. Her search team was already assembled. Richard Carsley, a New York Bank President who lived a quarter mile down further down the road, coordinated everything. He passed out the walkie-talkies as Sgt. Konrad Gurka, who led the Connecticut State Police canine unit, stood leaning over a map with two troopers and their dogs. Gurka's German Shepherd, Teddy, and two others milled around getting to know Kate's team of trained search dogs. A trooper, Randy Mackowski, weighed down the corners of the maps as his Golden, Walt, watched. Richard's Chihuahua, Spike, sat on the table proudly wearing his search vest. He had passed the search certification, but, due to his diminutive size, rarely did any actual active searching. This freed Richard to coordinate everyone. Cora Benson, with her Berner, Hugo, sitting at her feet, had plugged wires from the big screen monitor by the door, into her laptop and now had the area to be searched projected onto the wall-screen using Google Earth.

Kathy King laid out and tested the communications equipment they'd need as her massive Landseer Newfoundland bitch, Tenney, stood at the table, nose-to-nose with Spike. Dillon ran immediately to join Alice Simmons' Lucky. The Golden Retriever leaned against Alice who was talking to Gurka as Kate arrived.

The plane no sooner landed than Harry dashed to the rental desk where a car waited for him. He left the airport quickly and in a few minutes headed up the on-ramp of I-84 west. At the next exit, he left the highway turning onto Route 6 North, and headed for Kate's. Though he didn't think anyone had tailed him from DC, he kept a constant check on his rearview mirror. Of course, if they knew who he was, they'd quickly figure out where he was. He worried that this case might be the reason someone had shot at Kate. He had to get to her, hold her, make sure she was untouched by the ugliness he'd been investigating.

"So what's the story?" Kate asked Richard.

"A second-grade class went on a field trip to gather leaves and pine cones for a Thanksgiving project and to study nature. All seemed to go well until they loaded up the bus for the trip back to school and came up one child short. Neither the teacher nor the four parent helpers saw the child wander off. According to them, she stayed with them during the gathering process though she got upset when one of the other children accidentally squashed her bag full of leaves. The teacher told her there wasn't time to gather more and the other children would share. Five minutes later, when they lined up for the bus, they realized she was not with the others. The child's name is Jennifer Windom, and she's six years old almost seven. She has brown hair, blue eyes, about forty-eight inches tall, outgoing and adventurous according to her parents. I think we can all agree with that, and she wore a light blue short sleeved tee shirt, jeans, and a pink jacket. She is also had on pink sneakers."

A blue Chevy sedan pulled up to the door and a man carrying a paper bag jumped out. He rushed to the center of the crowd and pushed the bag at the Sargent. "I did just what you told me and got her pj's into the bag without touching them. Has anybody seen her yet?"

"Not yet, Mr. Windom," Gurka told him, "but we're just starting out. This will help the dogs find her."

"Oh no, Jenny's afraid of dogs. If she sees them, she'll run away. My brother has a Rottie mix. It chased after her one day and scared her badly. She wasn't hurt, but she's been afraid of dogs ever since."

"Well, the thing about the search dogs is they don't rely on seeing what they are searching for; instead they smell the trail she'll leave. So even if she hides, we'll find her," Gurka reassured him.

Richard and Kathy did a quick test on the walkie-talkies as the pajamas were handed to the trooper, Eric Chaffin, who had the bloodhound, Fingall. Kate's searchers air scented and didn't need them. Then everyone looked at the big screen above their heads showing the parking lot and the trails leading into the woods.

Gurka spoke. "We'll run a pincer search. The troopers will cover the park trails, beginning with the parking lot. Kate, your team will come toward the same area from the opposite direction starting at the far end of your A trail. This way we'll cover the most ground in the shortest amount of time."

"You've got it," Kate said and handed a key to Kathy. They each got into an ATVs parked in the back of the barn. Cora jumped into the first one beside Kate. Hugo, her Bernese Mountain Dog, settled in the back next to Dillon while Kathy and Alice followed with Tenney and Lucky.

Kate wasted no time as she drove quickly down the main trail behind the barn which would connect at the far end with the park trails. Luckily they'd just cleared the trail for the test practice. When they arrived at a point where this trail met the park trails, they parked the ATVs, and then went on foot to their official start point.

This late in the year, there would be less than an hour of daylight left. Sticking her hand behind the seat, she grabbed a couple of small but powerful flashlights, a jackknife, and two water bottles. She handed a flashlight and water bottle to Cora while stowing her own in her pockets, then they walked over to where the others had parked. Even though the troopers began at the spot where the girl was last seen, the wind was blowing toward Kate's team which meant the girl's scent could easily drift their way.

The trail down to the park was like the yellow brick road. The golden Maple leaves mixed with the browns from the oaks and occasional maroons from the sumac. In another week everything would be brown, or white, if the warning of an early snowstorm came true. The breeze in her face felt crisp, putting a spring in her step. She breathed in the clean air, happy that the humidity of summer was gone.

They no sooner reached the level ground when Dillon stopped and lifted his head. Kate had only just spotted his signal indicating he'd caught the scent when Hugo did the same thing. She let the 15-foot lead extend to give him his head and began moving forward at a trot, though, at the same time, watching her step. The dogs stuck to the trail, thank goodness, rather than pulling them toward the brambles on her left. Kathy called in their probability of area with their position and all four dogs headed forward at a good clip.

***

Harry reached the driveway but as he turned in, he spotted police cruisers in front of Kate's barn. He screeched to a stop by Kate's house, slammed the car door, and only just remembering to click the lock as he ran toward the barn at full speed. Yanking open the side door, he spotted Richard whose dog Spike was on a table covered in maps.

"Where's Kate!"

"Harry great to see you. Kate is on a search. A child is missing."

Harry felt himself breathe again. Kate was safe. "Where is she? Can I get to her?"

"They've just called in their position."

Richard leaned over the map in front of him and pointed to a pin marking the spot where Kate's woods connected with the state park. "If you go down the main trail and turn right where it meets up with with the purple trail, you should find her."

"I'm on it. I know that trail." Harry sped out of the barn and ran behind the kennel. After waving at the barking dogs, he dashed up to the main trail. It felt good to run after all the time he'd been stuck in the hotel room. He wouldn't be able to relax, though, until he saw Kate. Until he held Kate. The longer he was away from her, the more he realized he couldn't be without her. She was his world.

The tree with the blaze for the purple trail came up quickly and he turned right. He'd gone only about 200 feet, when the ground began to slope down. Reaching the park trail, he had sped up and turned right when he heard Kate call a warning, "Careful, everyone, the ground here is crap. It's slate, shale and some sandstone and it drops off steeply." Dillon suddenly veered toward the ravine. Harry watched Kate tighten the lead as he increased his speed. The dog was focused on the scent and he still moved forward. She'd tightened up even more on the long lead, shortening it to about eight feet when suddenly there was the sound of cascading rock which broke the quiet. Dillon let out an anguished cry as the ground beneath his feet gave way and he disappeared from sight.

***

Kate screamed, throwing herself backwards onto the ground and digging in her heels as she tightened her grip on the lead. Rocks and gravel ripped through her clothes, scraping her skin, as she was dragged nearer to the edge then a shooting pain shot through her body. A sudden stop came as a jolt. Her body had hit a boulder, which shook her from teeth to toes. The part of the rock which extended about eight inches above the ground and was a foot across, Kate could also attest was solid. Struggling to think, as pain took over her mind, she rolled further onto the boulder, then worked to twist into a sitting position.

The lead burned her hands, but she refused to ease her grip while she struggled to keep from following her dog off the newly formed cliff. Her walkie-talkie, now lying on the ground squawked.

"Kate, you've got to pull him up at least four feet before he can get a purchase. That harness is not made to hold his weight. You've got to get him up fast and not let him swing."

She didn't have the energy to answer. Instead she worked to still her arms in hopes of stabilizing the lead. She heard rather than saw movement to her right. Kathy King, approached carefully, slithering forward with her weight distributed evenly over the ground. Her Newfoundland bitch crawled behind her.

Harry ran full out the last fifty feet of trail, then sliding on the shale and rubble rock, he slid his body in behind her and reached to grab the lead at a point beyond her grip, he pulled back as much as he could. Kate squeaked out a yell. "Dillon, stay. I'll get you."

Kathy, now level with the lead, attached a carabiner with a strap to the line about a foot below their hold and hitched the other end of the strap to Tenney's harness. The massive black and white bitch slowly turned around. Checking the connection was secure, Kathy eased herself slowly back onto solid ground and then, moving one step at a time, she led the Landseer up

Peggy Gaffney

the slope. As the Newf moved forward, the lead pulled up and soon Dillon's paws scratched and scrambled at the ground in front of them. When he found enough purchase, he pulled himself over the edge onto solid ground. Once clear, he stood for a moment, then shook himself all over and slowly looked around for Kate.

Harry reeled in the lead as he called Dillon over to where he and Kate sat. The dog's studied movement showed the effect of hanging midair with only a harness to keep him from falling. By the time he reached the two of them Harry had Kate held tight against him as she cried. Dillon inched forward and began licking the tears from her face. She reached out and hugged his white head, the lead still tight in her grip.

Harry saw her clenched fists, took her hands, and showing gentle care, eased each finger up, so he could free the lead. Her hands refused to flatten. He pushed himself from behind her, stood, and lifting, gently freed her from her rock prison.

No sooner had they stood than Dillon lifted his head and began moving down the trail following the scent. A cheer went up from her friends for Dillon's rescue, only to have it be drowned out by a child's scream.

Chapter Six

"Kate, are you okay?" Harry slid his hands gently down her body as she took an awkward step forward.

"I'll live, let's go," Kate said as she followed her seemingly unhurt dog as he pulled her toward the place where they'd heard the scream. Just beyond a giant hemlock, they spotted the girl. Unlike the wide gravel area where Kate had been positioned to hold Dillon, the land where the girl was sitting showed recent cracks in the ground. This was a landslide waiting to happen. The edge of the cliff to the left of her still had chunks of shale and gravel sliding over the edge and falling into the gully about twenty-feet below.

"Nobody moves!" Kate said. Pulling up her walkie-talkie, she called, "Gurka, where are you and your searchers?"

Peggy Gaffney

"We're moving down the gully trying to position ourselves below her. We have eyes on her from below. If she moves, she's going to be badly hurt. It looks as though there was a recent rock fall and most of the rubble is sharp."

"Got it. We'll try to figure a way to get her into a harness from up here."

"How?"

"I'm thinking. Give me a minute."

Kate stared at the girl then raised her voice. "Jennifer, we need you to stay very, very still. Pretend you're playing statues. Absolutely no moving, okay."

"Okay. Don't let the doggies bite me."

"We won't, though these are all sweet doggies who love little girls. But if you can stay still and not move, the doggies will stay back."

"Okay."

Alice leaned into her and whispered, "This is a mess. You put weight on that land and it will go. What we need is a small miracle."

Kate froze, gawked at her, and then smiled. "That's exactly what we need."

Kate pulled her phone from her pocket and dialed. "Richard, we need you and Spike at the site now. Bring Mr. Windom with you but warn him not to call out to his daughter because if she's startled she could fall. Before you leave, go into the closet to the left of the barn's back window and you'll find climbing harnesses. Bring the smallest one you can locate as well as a couple of hanks of parachute cord. And, hurry please."

"How are you doing, Jennifer?" Kate called to the girl.

"Okay."

"Help is coming and you'll be going home soon but I still need you not to move, honey."

"Okay."

Kate listened and for a few minutes, all she could hear were the footsteps of men moving in the gully below her. Dillon lay beside her pressed hard against her body. Her hand slid under the straps of the harness to check if it had cut him but his skin was fine, and she thanked God for the amount of coat he carried.

She wrapped her arm around him and leaned back against Harry. Searching for calm she took a few slow breaths, and then turned her attention back to the girl sitting at the edge of the cliff.

"Jennifer, my name is Kate. they said that you were in second grade. Do you like school?"

"Yeah."

"I heard you were gathering leaves to make fancy Thanksgiving displays for your table. Did you find a lot of leaves."

"Yeah, but I dropped my bag when the ground went away."

"Well, don't worry. On the way back, we'll help you gather some really beautiful ones, and I know where there are pine cones that you can use as well."

"You do? The pine cones near the parking lot were all squished from cars."

"Ah, but I grew up here so I have the inside track on where there are good sized pine cones that are perfect. They're on the trail back. When we head home, we'll get you some."

"I'd like that. Nobody else got pine cones."

Kate stopped talking when the whine from the high-pitched motor of the ATV filled the air. She listened to the sounds of running feet behind her moving down the green trail which ran parallel to the gully.

"Jennifer. This is important. I need you to stay very still. Your father is coming and I want to show him how grown-up you are and how good you are at not moving. So when he talks to you, remember, you can't move."

"Kate, we're here. I told Windom that he can't call out to Jennifer for fear she'd fall. He promised to wait." Richard whispered. Kate turned toward the men and quietly thanked the father. Then turning to Richard, she quietly laid out her plan.

Spike moved forward gently setting one paw down, checking the ground, and then the other. The added weight strapped to his back was making him walk slowly, but Richard's voice, quiet but firm kept him heading toward the girl.

"Okay, hold," Kate murmured. "Jennifer, your dad says that you don't like dogs."

"I don't. They're scary."

"Sometimes big dogs can be scary. But have you ever seen a tiny dog so small he could sit in your cereal bowl?"

"No."

"Well, I've got a teeny tiny dog for you to see if you slowly turn your head toward me."

Search

Slowly the girl's head turned until she spotted Spike sitting about six feet from her. He tilted his head and wagged his tail, pouring on the charm in gallons.

"That's a tiny dog. He's cute. Does he bite?"

Richard huffed and Kate put a hand on his arm to mollify the insult. "No, Spike doesn't bite. He loves everybody. He's bringing you a present."

"A present for me?"

"Yup. See the harness he's wearing? It has a long lead attached to it so that if anything happens, he'll be safe. He's bringing you a harness so you'll be safe too. Do you want Spike to bring you a harness?"

"Okay."

"Go," she whispered to Richard and slowly fed out the line that was attached to the harness on Spike's back. When he got to within a foot of the girl, Jennifer suddenly reached for him.

"Eeeeeeeeek!" she screamed as the ground shifted. Another foot of the land to the child's left fell into the gully. Her father jumped up and stepped forward when Kate yelled, "FREEZE!"

"Jennifer, quiet," Kate's sharp tone startled the girl into silence. "Don't move. Let Spike come to you. When he is sitting next to you, I will tell you what to do." She nodded to Richard who gave Spike his command. The tiny dog inched forward and finally sat next to the girl's knees.

"Jennifer, look at Spike's back. Do you see the two big bows?"

"Yes."

"Good. Moving your arm and hand, and only them, slowly untie the bows and pull the harness into your lap."

As soon as the harness was off his back, Spike turned and picked his way carefully back to Richard. Jennifer looked upset to see him leave.

"You can play with Spike after you put on your harness. Now, the padded part is going behind you with the green dot facing up. See that?"

"Yeah."

"Good. Now you're going to put your right arm through the hole made by the red strap and your left arm through the hole made by the purple strap. Got it?"

"I did it."

"Now comes the fun part. You've got two funny buckles. The top one has funny looking teeth on one side and a black part with a slot on the other side. The trick is to push the teeth into the slot until it goes click. You've got to push hard."

Kate eyed her struggle but finally, the clasp clicked home. "Good, one down and one to go. Do the same thing to the bottom straps." This one went faster and clicked home as a collective sigh went through the group.

"Okay. Now I'm going to have you pretend to be Spike. Remember how he tiptoed lightly across the ground? I want you to crawl carefully across the same way that Spike went trying to copy his footsteps. Ready?"

"Yup."

No one was breathing as the girl inched forward. She'd gotten about fifteen inches from the edge when the ground behind her let go. Kate had a tight hold on the wooden peg holding the parachute cord so when the ground beneath her shifted and she could have gone over, she instead got pulled

Search

forward. It took ten minutes of her inching forward before she was on solid enough ground for Kate to let her father go scoop her up into a hug.

Kate dropped her head onto Harry's shoulder, letting the tension in her neck and shoulders go. She groaned as his hands massaged the pain that the move brought on. Richard leaned in. "I'd recommend a long hot soak in the tub as soon as you get back. Kathy told me you already held onto Dillon up after he fell. A hot bath, pain pills and a cup of tea and you'll be a new Kate. You take care of her, Harry."

"You know me too well," Kate said.

"I've known you forever. And now, It's time to head home. Luckily Brandon is cooking tonight, so I can just kick back and relax with my hero dog. Spike was a true hero today. Thanks for giving him a chance to prove his chops with the team. It means a lot."

"Every dog has his day. Each one of the team has a special talent. We've just seen Spike's specialty demonstrated spectacularly."

"What a shame we didn't take pictures," he chuckled.

"We did," Alice said, coming up behind them and pulled up the gallery app on her phone. There it was. The entire rescue displayed in glorious color. "I'll send it to the team and then post it on Facebook. Two-to-one, it will go viral."

Kate, Harry, and Dillon began heading up the slope toward the ATV feeling as though she'd aged fifty years in the last few hours. She was too tired to walk, talk or think. She climbed in, happy to see Dillon able to jump up behind her and Kathy.

Harry slid in next to Dillon and Tenney, and they all headed back.

"Thanks to you and Tenney for your help. Nothing like having a one-hundred and forty-pound bitch who likes to pull, lending a paw. I wasn't sure I would have been able to hold him, but I would have died trying."

"That's what friends are for, Kate. We can't let you be hurt. We've got a wedding to attend. You go home and let Harry take care of you."

"Excellent plan," he answered, resting his hand on Kate's shoulder

Search 59

Chapter Seven

The front door of the kennel slammed open and Sal rushed in. "Kate, why are cars leaving? Gurka said something about the rescue of a child. Dammit, the one time I forget my phone, everything happens. Are you okay? You look terrible."

"Thanks, I got a little banged up but that's my new style. The search turned out fine, Sal, so that was no problem. My team and Gurka's troopers worked together. It was a little hairy for a while, but in the end, the girl was safely returned to her father. We got her back unharmed thanks to Spike, though I almost lost Dillon out there." She reached down to pet the Sam and winced as pain shot up her side and her hand refused to open even to scratch Dillon. "If you'll excuse me, I'm heading to the house. Roger was with Gurka, so he'll tell you about it on the trip, speaking of which, you all take care and be safe. It sounds as though there will be lots of snow. If you've got to stay an extra night, do it and be safe. Oh, and you can see reruns of the search online. Alice apparently got the whole thing on video and is putting it on the website. A bath and a cup of tea are next on my agenda, so take care. I'll see you tomorrow evening."

"Of course, you go take care of yourself."

Kate used her arm to push open the door and limped, feeling pain with every step, down the walkway toward her house.

"Wait a minute. What about Harry? Someone said he's back," Sal said, holding the door open.

"His timing was perfect. Actually, he made it back just in time to help Kathy and Tenney save Dillon. I was just hanging on for dear life. Ask him. He'll tell you all about it. He's just putting the ATV away." She caught the sound of the door to the kennel runs shut. "There he is now. You two can have a chat before you leave and if you want to do me a big favor, you could feed the few boarders we have left."

She limped a few more steps and raised her arm without turning. "Have a good conference. I hope everyone does well on the test."

Kate continued inching slowly down the walkway without Dillon pushing her to go faster. Both of them moved stiffly. As they went by the fence, Dillon traded sniffs with Quinn, and Liam. She studied his gait as he moved slightly ahead of her. He wasn't limping but instead moved with the same caution as she. A breath of relief whooshed out as she reached the kitchen door. Any idea of letting the other dogs in got shoved aside, as she leaned against the edge of the table for stability. The pain increasing with each step. The distance from the supporting table to the bedroom door grew longer as she waited. So she took a deep breath, shoved herself forward and into the bedroom. Without stopping, she grabbed fresh underwear and moved into the bathroom before losing momentum. Once in, she leaned against the sink, turned the hot water on full blast and with extreme care, stripped.

Hot water started easing her muscles as inch by inch she lowered herself into the tub. As it filled, she savored the heat. Through half open eyes, she noticed that the Technicolor display of each bruise rose as the pain level dropped. When her body began changing from a rosy glow to lobster red, she added some cold water. With a sigh, she finally turned off the tap, lay back and closed her eyes. She lifted her arm and let it dangle over the side of the tub with her still fisted hand resting on Dillon's head. He'd settled on the bathmat and fell sound asleep.

Her body had begun to relax but not her brain. The events of the day raced round in her head. She marveled at the fact that her recently peaceful life had, in the span of a few hours, disappeared. Her thoughts bounced from the killer to her wedding gown, to the terror of almost losing Dillon's life and her own, to the thrill of rescuing Jennifer. She tapped her phone resting on the stool next to the tub. It was only six-fifteen. Was that too early for bed? The only thing she wanted was to crawl between her sheets, pull the covers over her head and sleep for a week.

Sal was finishing feeding the boarding dogs when Harry entered the kennel. "Hey there, Sal, where's Kate?"

"She said something about a bath. She said you'd tell me about the rescue I missed."

Harry leaned against the check-in desk and gave him the fifty-cent version of the afternoon's adventure. "I was so terrified when I spotted her holding Dillon's lead as he dangled above that rocky gully as that huge Newf worked to pull him out. I slid in to take to weight off her arms, but I'll tell you, I had to pry back her fingers to make her let go. But no sooner was Dillon up and safe than they were back on the trail to save the kid. Sal, she humbles me."

"I understand you. I've had that feeling often since I started working for her. You're a lucky man. But we've got to keep her safe from that killer or there won't be a wedding."

"Killer? What killer?"

"She didn't tell you about the man who tried to murder her this morning?"

"No. All I have been able to find out is that Agnes called Des and told him that Kate was in danger and for me to hurry home."

Sal reached in his pocket, then dropped a fist full of spent cartridges onto to desk. "If she weren't so smart, she'd be dead. What sounds like the hired muscle was sent after your girl. He found where she'd be this morning, snuck in from the logging road behind Connelly's place, and came armed with an automatic with an extended magazine. She managed to outsmart him and get rid of the gun before the troopers and their search dogs went after him. He escaped but dropped this."

The paper he spread on the table showed what looked like a Google map of the woods showing the logging road and the trails on Kate's land and the state park. But it was the words written in marker at the bottom that knocked the air from his lungs, and he gasped. He lifted his eyes to Sal whose expression was furious.

"Kate never hurt anyone in her life. Nobody would want to kill her, except maybe to hurt you. Why were you away for three weeks? What was so important that you'd stay away from your bride before the wedding? Could it be behind this?"

"I was searching for my father's killer. However, the trip turned into something much bigger. I don't have all the answers yet but I'm close. Could it lead to someone going after Kate? I don't know. But I feel certain these people use murder as the tool of choice to achieve their goals. I've got to move her somewhere safe."

"She won't leave. She's got her responsibilities here and the wedding's in a week. Don't even bother suggesting canceling the wedding. If Kate doesn't kill you, Agnes will. No, now is the time for you to take that mega-brain of yours and figure out how to stop this guy. I've got to head out. I want to beat the snow to New York, in time to give my speech. The tests are in the morning, so we should be back by late afternoon, supper time at the latest if the storm doesn't close the roads. Your job is to keep her safe. I'm counting on you."

Harry went in search of Kate.

Peggy Gaffney

Quinn and the others raced to the fence which ran along the walkway between the kennel and the house. Quinn bounced against the fence, trying for all of Harry's attention. He stuck his arms over the fence and rubbed ears and muzzles as he walked by. He noticed that Dillon wasn't with them, but he was probably with Kate.

The door to the kitchen opened and resisting the urge to let all the dogs in, he just looked around trying to spot his bride-to-be. "Kate?" There was no answer. Worry gripped him. He stuck his head into the living room. Nothing. Then he noticed her bedroom door was partly open and there was a light coming from somewhere inside.

Gently pushing the door further open, he let himself see his fiancée. She was sprawled half on, half off the bed. It looked as though she'd just fallen to the side. A finger was hooked around the waistband of sweatpants, and she had one leg half inside. The sports bra and panties didn't cover much for which he thanked all the saints. He called her name again as he stepped into the room. Nothing. Not even a blink. As he moved behind her, he felt he'd been punched, as all the air left his lungs. Her back was a garden of colorful bruises and nasty cuts. He realized her panties were stained with spots of blood across her bottom from hip to hip. Several of the cuts on her lower back were still bleeding and her white bedspread would need work to return it to its pristine state. He stepped into the bathroom and found a large first aid kit under the sink.

Dillon slept on the bath mat, as exhausted as Kate. Harry laid a hand on the dog who woke enough to wag his tail, then stretching, sank back into sleep.

Search

Returning to the bedroom, he put the kit on the bed then rolled her gently so that her back was facing up. The ointment luckily came in a large tube. He would probably need almost all to treat her cuts. Her upper back was untouched but beginning about five inches above her waist, were between twenty and thirty scratches and gouges. He checked her breathing to be sure she still slept and set to work. When he reached the waistband of her panties, he lifted the fabric gently, easing it free of where the dried blood had glued it to her skin. Squeezing a glob of the ointment, he rubbed it gently all over. Ignoring his body's response, he focused on Kate. *How had she been able to stand up and continue the search when her body must have been screaming in agony?*

As he moved to roll her higher onto the mattress, he spotted that her hands were still clenched as they had been around the lead while holding Dillon. He lifted her hand and moved to flatten the fingers. They barely moved, but the movement brought a whimper from her, luckily not waking her. He turned the hand he held so that the light is shown on the palm. "Dammit!" The palms looked like hamburger torn raw with rope burns running across them. The surface of the skin was a dark crimson, but he didn't see any active, bleeding wounds. Flipping open the cover of the first aid kit, he found packets of two-inch sterile gauze. He also found rolls of bandages. Squirting the ointment onto each fisted palm, he used his fingertips and delicate strokes to spread it over the surface. Then, he covered each two-inch square with the medicine and placed them face down on each palm. Finally, he wrapped each hand with sterile roll bandaging and then added a layer of self-adhering bandage to keep the hands protected.

Though he knew he wasn't responsible for these wounds, he still felt guilty that he hadn't been there to help sooner. He knew what he did for a living could put her in danger but giving her up would kill him. Even being away from her the last few weeks brought on an ache as bad as any physical pain he'd ever endured.

He reached down to pull the sweat pants free of her leg and found bruising in shades from yellow to deep purple covering the insides of her thighs. There were no cuts, but the bruising had to make any movement almost crippling, and yet she had stood, hiked, though she'd been slower than usual, and finished the rescue. She was incredible.

Tossing the sweatpants aside, he stepped around the bed, folded back the covers, then gently, avoiding contact with any bruises, lifted her and placed her on the bed rolling her body so that she wasn't lying on her wounds. He pulled the sheets and blankets over her shoulder and tucked them around her.

Back in the kitchen, he grabbed the dogs' bowls and put together their dinners. He didn't bother calling Dillon. Sleep was more important than food to him now. Once they were fed, they returned to the yard, and he went out to the rental car to retrieve his suitcase and briefcase.

As he'd reached for the car keys, his hands felt the bullet casings he'd put into his pocket when Sal left. *He had to keep her safe.* The deadbolt slid firmly home as he locked the front door. Not wanting to leave her, he called Seamus to ask if he and his

Search 67

brother could take care of the boarding dogs tonight and tomorrow morning.

His bedroom was filled with boxes. Kate had said something about his mom sending his father's things because they were building the house. This meant sharing his sleeping quarters with what looked like more than fifty UPS boxes.

He returned to the kitchen, let in the now snow-covered dogs, and turned off the lights. Bolting the back door, he returned to Kate's room, shed most of his clothes and climbed in next to her. Careful not to touch her cuts or bruises, he let go of the lonely ache and allowed himself to sleep.

Chapter Eight

"Arggg. Ouch. Damn, I've got to pee."

"Kate, don't move. Let me help you." The other side of the bed shifted as he got out.

"Wha..., Harry? I hurt, everywhere. I can't move without knives cutting into me. Why are my hands bandaged? Why are you in my room without your clothes, not that I'm complaining, mind you? Oh, God. I remember. Dillon!"

"Dillon's fine, see." The Sam jumped up on the bed next to her which set off new cries of pain.

"Dillon, off. Okay, dogs out." He opened the slider and the dogs in her bedroom bounded out into the snow. Harry dashed to the kitchen door and released the rest. Then he came back in bearing water, two Tylenol tablets and the promise of a cup of tea. Once she had gotten the pills down, he gripped her undamaged shoulders, helping her to a standing position. With one arm around her shoulders, and a hand steadying her, he walked her into the bathroom.

"I'm going to lower you slowly onto the toilet after I remove your panties. Oh, good, the ointment stopped the bleeding and kept your panties from sticking."

Kate, realizing that pain trumped embarrassment, let him lower her onto the toilet.

"If this embarrasses you, love, wait until next Saturday night when we will take a shower together." Her head jerked up in surprise. "Oh, I didn't tell you about that?" he said. "Well, lady, get used to me seeing all of your beautiful body because I intend to spend a lot of time getting up close and personal with my wife. Now I'll give you a minute of privacy while I fetch you something to wear."

Once she was done, he returned from the bedroom with fresh underwear and her sweats. It only took a few minutes, and he had her dressed and seated on a cushioned chair in the kitchen with a pillow behind her back. He ducked into his

Peggy Gaffney

room and was back dressed in similar sweats a minute later. As he walked back in, she was staring at her hands.

"When did all this happen? I was taking a bath and I remember managing to lever myself out of the tub. I think I was getting dressed but I don't remember anything after that."

"I found you asleep, half dressed and bleeding onto your bedspread. I took care of your wounds and put you to bed. The dogs were fed. The kennel dogs are being taken care of by your brothers. Everything is fine. You just need to heal from the damage your body sustained while saving Dillon. Now, what do you want for breakfast?"

"Pancakes. But you're going to have to cut them up for me. I feel as though I'm wearing boxing gloves or mittens." She wrapped her bandaged hands around her mug of tea and sipped it.

"Before things become too wild around here, would you like to tell me about these?" He dropped the cartridges next to her plate.

"They recovered the bullets but did they find the gun? I don't want some kid wandering down in the gully, finding an automatic and shooting himself accidentally. I hope they found it. If I went back out there, I might be able to spot where it went over the edge. It arched when it flew out of his hands."

"Whose hands?"

"Oh, I guess I forgot to tell you about the shooter. Things got so wild, all I could think about was getting back and into the bathtub. Um... yesterday morning, when I was running the final practice search, a man came walking down the trail below where I was hiding and pulled out a gun. He was probably as frightened as I was because when I threw a stone to distract him, he shot at it. Then when he was getting ready to shoot the troopers who were searching for me, I had to stop him, so I knocked the gun out of his hand with a rock. He spotted me, but then he became aware of the dogs coming and took off. I wasn't hurt, just scared because I didn't have Dillon with me."

"Sal said you described the guy as a well-dressed thug who had a map and instructions to kill Kate Killoy."

"Yeah. That sort of threw me. Who have I pissed off so much as to send a hired gun after me?"

"I thought about it last night. You are not the one who pissed them off. I did and they've figured out we're connected. They want to stop me by going after you."

" Come on Harry, you're not any more responsible for someone trying to shoot me than Agnes was when I got shot at last winter."

"Actually..."

"Don't say it. She's my maid-of-honor and has worked her tail off to make this wedding happen. In each case, it was evil people who decided that they had a right to murder whomever they wanted. They didn't want us to stop them and that was the problem. So, how do we stop this character?"

"I'm not sure. I suspect that this might be connected to the information I discovered in Washington and if so, we're up against the mob. I went looking for answers about my father's murder but found much more."

They finished breakfast. After he put the dishes into the dishwasher, fed the house dogs, all getting gentle pats from Kate, put them back out and ducked into his room, returning with his laptop and backpack then setting them on the table. "This information is what I found in Washington. The files on my computer are the research I did for the three weeks I was there and is based on the information Des had about what happened following my dad's death. The rest is on this thumb-drive. Des was loading it with the final data to give to me when he got the call from Agnes. He gave it to me as I headed home. I haven't had time to look at it yet."

Kate stared at him open-mouthed. "Agnes called Des? I didn't think she knew him. Why did she call Des?"

"From what he said, she called him based on Sadie's information that he'd be the person in D.C. who might have information on my whereabouts. I am sure you didn't tell her, so how did she figure out where I was?"

"Damn it, I must have blinked. What a rat. I'm sorry for all the good things I said about her earlier. She's a sneaky, underhanded stinker. She came over yesterday morning for the first look at my wedding dress and arrived right after the shooting. Agnes went ballistic. Then she found you weren't here. Apparently having the groom not in residence a week before the wedding is a crime."

"In her book, it probably is."

"She grabbed my face, and stared into my eyes, then named every city you've been in over the last year. I must have blinked when she said Washington. That's a trick she used when we were kids. She calls it her lie detector. I can't believe she tracked you down based on a blink. It is so Agnes. Considering when she questioned me though, you got here fast."

"Des' friend owns his own plane. He flew me into Oxford Airport. Des had it all arranged by the time he got to my hotel room, and I was in the air fifteen minutes later. He'd also discovered I'd be outed. I knew the hotel was under surveillance. He made sure I got out unnoticed, and we weren't followed to the airport but the attack on you might have been connected to this investigation. They may have tried to use your death to stop me. God, I'm so sorry, Love. I was stupid to believe you'd be safe when these criminals are everywhere."

"So, Agnes calls, and Des has you in the air that quick. Amazing."

"Considering how often Tom goes to D.C., I may talk to him about our buying a small plane together to keep at that airport. The airport is only fifteen minutes from here. It would be much quicker than flying out of Windsor Locks, and we'd avoid all the traffic going through Hartford."

"Let's stay on topic, Lindbergh. Don't start the flying lessons yet. Is all this data just about your dad's murder or is it something else? There are a lot of files on this thumb drive for one murder."

"As it turns out, his death is connected to something bigger, much bigger. After going through all this, I think my dad discovered the beginnings of a massive criminal operation and that's what got him killed. I've been checking hundreds of cases and following countless leads through the system. What's going on is huge. But, searching for answers in all these facts is like working a jigsaw with no picture on the cover of the box. I feel in my bones, *something* is happening. Too many people are dying, and their crimes all remain unsolved. I'm close, but I haven't fitted in all the pieces."

She smiled. "Then you can count this as your lucky day, my good sir, because you are marrying a puzzle wizard. Set up my laptop and I'll load the evidence from the thumb drive Des gave you onto my laptop, and you can pull up what's on yours. This way we can both work and compare notes." She smiled as she opened her laptop, but the smile morphed into a yawn.

"Kate, no. You need to rest. You've had a day from hell and the last thing you need is to face is mind-numbing research. Your bruises must hurt considering their color."

"Harry, I'm fine. I find jigsaw puzzles very relaxing."

"This isn't 2,000 pieces waiting to become a picture of Sammy puppies romping in the snow. What we will be working on is a record of ugliness, death, and destruction."

"One hour. Then I'll go rest, I promise, though I think I would heal faster if I worked those muscles. I wouldn't sleep now anyway. As you pointed out, yesterday was a rough day and I still have to take care of the kennel dogs."

He grabbed his phone and typed. It buzzed two seconds later. "Seamus and Tim are doing the kennel dogs this morning."

Search

They'd worked sided by side with Kate losing herself in the sorting and filing, and began humming. Harry grinned. She really did love puzzles and solving problems. He studied her fighting her pain as the hour became two. Finally, she stretched and said, "I think I'm ready to rest now."

A heavy knocking sounded at the front door. "Kate!" They knew that voice, and he reluctantly moved to unlock and open the door.

"Since when do you lock your door?" Agnes marched into the kitchen followed by Cathy. Kate smiled at her bridesmaid twisting in her chair to hug her. "My God, your hands. What happened. You can't be a bride in bandages."

"When Dillon fell into the gully, I got a bit banged up trying to save him. I'm recovering. Harry treated my wounds and I should be back to normal by tomorrow."

Cathy looked at him. "When did you last treat her?"

"Last night. Then she slept for nine hours."

"Let's move you into your bedroom, Kate, and let the only nurse in the room check you out."

Kate glanced at him and their work. He gave a slight shake of his head, so she went with Cathy.

Fifteen minutes later, they were back. "You did a good job on her, Dr. Foyle. She's healing up nicely and I don't think she needs her hands covered now. Exposure to the air will aid in the healing. Just keep her from getting them exposed to caustic soaps or any irritants."

Cathy walked to the kitchen door to watch the pups romp in the deepening snow. "I assume that Lily's coming to the wedding. She'll be pleased with the way Quinn is turning out. His angulation is excellent and I love the head carriage on him. Dillon, of course, is magnificent and Shelagh is lovely. Is that her mother with her?"

"Yes, that's Kelly."

"You can see the resemblance, though Liam's influence is obvious in the thickness and quality of her coat. They're having a ball in the snow."

Harry had made tea and coffee for them and warmed up some scones in the microwave.

Agnes sighed. "I don't understand how you did it. You got dragged all that way and cut up, but none of it will show due to the cut of the dress. It must be the luck of the Irish. You'll still be a beautiful bride."

"No matter how banged up she is from saving Dillon, she'll still be the most beautiful bride ever," he said, kissing the top of Kate's head.

Both her laptop and her phone dinged. Kate reached forward and clicked to open an app and the end of the driveway appeared with a sedan she'd seen before turning around. She ignored the soreness of her fingers as she typed in a code. The program asked if she would like to save the photo and information she had gotten. She clicked yes, adding a print command.

He stepped over to the printer which rested on a small table by her bedroom door. It didn't take long to finish. Pulling out the sheet of paper, he handed it to Kate. She froze, silent as she stared.

"Kate, what is it?"

Search

"That's him."

"Who?"

"The shooter from yesterday morning. The man who tried to kill me."

Chapter Nine

Harry was around the table and pulling her into his arms before she could say anything else. He reached down and took the papers from her hand. When he held them up, he noticed they were a printout from the security system showing a car's license plate number and a photo of a burly man looking into the camera as he prepared to pull back out of the driveway. The face was vaguely familiar, but he couldn't say who he was. He looked at Agnes. "Call Sean, now."

The next few minutes passed in a blur as Harry, still holding her, explained to Cathy, with Agnes filling in details, about what happened yesterday morning. He had just finished telling her as well about Dillon's fall and the child's rescue, when a sharp knock came at the front door. He let her go. "Hang in their, Sweetheart, I'll be right back."

Kate watched him go the door to look through the peep-hole and then saw him smile. "It's Sean." She let out her breath in a whoosh.

Sean rushed into the kitchen. "Where is this picture of the shooter?"

"On the table, along with his license plate." She pushed a copy of the printout towards him. "He was here right before Agnes called. He pulled into the driveway, stopped, then pulled back onto the highway. The security system was able to capture his license plate, and I managed to take a photo of his face as he turned to look down the highway. This is definitely the man who was trying to kill me yesterday morning."

Sean pulled out his phone and began his call only to stop and ask, "Is there any way you can send me that file?"

Kate leaned in and hit a few buttons and then nodded, "Done."

Sean continued his call for a few minutes and then disconnected and turned back to them. She felt Harry's arms tighten around her as Sean asked, "Do either of you have any idea why this guy is trying to kill Kate? She's hardly the average victim. I can't think of anything that would cause someone to come after her."

Harry let her go and began pacing. Kate studied him and then said, "We need all the help we can find. Sean can be trusted to protect me. If he didn't, Agnes would kill him."

"Absolutely." Agnes agreed.

Peggy Gaffney

"Okay, Connelly, what you're going to hear is highly classified. This information is not even available to ninety-nine percent of the FBI nor the Department of Justice. You cannot repeat it to anyone. Lives are at stake, starting it seems, with Kate's and mine. Agnes? Cathy?" They nodded.

It took the better part of an hour to fill them in on Harry's investigation. They all listened silently until it came out that they were dealing with the mob. Then all hell broke loose. "The guy in the photo looks vaguely familiar. I've spent the last three weeks following up on crimes tied to most of the crime families up and down the east coast. I may remember him from a mug shot. Perhaps that is the reason he's here. From Kate's description of him in action, my guess is that he's a hit man who is more familiar with the streets of Boston, Philly or New York than her fifteen acres of nature."

"Kate smiled, "He'll also be itching up a storm. He plowed through multiple patches of poison ivy."

Cathy laughed. "Serves him right."

Sean's phone rang. After listening for a minute, h e grabbed his hat from the table and told them he had to leave. He promised to have cars patrol the area as best they could. "The snow is piling up and businesses are closing early. Luckily, since today is Saturday, we don't have to worry about the school kids. We're short-staffed at the moment with the six troopers in the canine unit off for their test. Hopefully, they'll make it back later today. Agnes, you and Cathy had better head back to your place. I'll follow to make sure you arrive there safely, then head back to headquarters." He looked at Harry. "I won't mention what you're into now, but if this is going to bring mob hit men into my jurisdiction, you're going to have to deal with my bosses."

After Sean left, Kate stood by the back door watching her dogs who were either sleeping or, in the case of Quinn and Shelagh, racing as fast as they could around the yard. The racers whizzed by and then circled back to jump at the door. Dillon walked to the door looking for access, but when that didn't happen, he returned to his spot under the overhang of the massive electric cable spool. It provided both shade and a playground to those pups who loved to jump and play king of the mountain. Kate smiled as he pushed in next to his mother. She had stolen his spot when he came to the door. Kate moved to look out the window over the sink. The snow was still falling hard but her brothers had kept the driveway and sidewalks relatively clear.

Harry made tea for Kate and himself before settling at the kitchen table and going point by point through the research he did on his case. He went into much more detail with her than he had with Sean. After two hours, they'd covered all the major points, and began to form a plan. Harry told her that he had made some phone calls. Des was expected either tomorrow or Monday, and Maeve would be coming as well. Kate laughed. "This guy doesn't have a chance now that you're bringing in the big guns like Maeve. I assume Sadie will be in the middle of it as well."

They kept working on the information from the thumb drive. There was s definite pattern forming, but they still needed more. They needed to understand not just what these mobsters had done in the past, but what they were up to now.

Peggy Gaffney

"What could be so important that we have to be killed now?
Why won't next month or next year do? Why do it at all.
Something must be about to happen which could be stopped
by your information. What is hiding in all this data? But I can't
seem to find any pattern that might give us an answer." Kate
said.

Harry looked out the window. The snow was still coming
down at a good clip.

"We missed lunch. I'll throw some sandwiches together.
You just sit and relax."

Kate stood. "Actually, I feel pretty good. Cathy found
some stuff in Gramp's old first aid kit he used on the dogs. She
said it was just what I needed and to tell the truth, I'd say eighty
percent of the pain is gone. You can see, even my palms are
skin color again. All the redness is gone and I can flex my
fingers."

"Wow. I'm impressed."

"Cathy told me a friend of hers uses it on her horses as
well."

"Well you may not be a mare or a bitch, but it worked
beautifully on you."

As he made lunch, Kate put the cushion and pillow away
and then began packing up the stuff from the table. "We've
been slogging away on this too long. I don't know about you,
but I need to give my brain a rest. Your room is filled with all
the boxes of your dad's stuff, so I'll put this in my closet. I
don't want Quinn or the others to grab any of it when they
come in. Plus this way there be less chance for someone
walking in to accidentally pick up the wrong piece of paper.

Search

Kate looked out the window and realized the snow was still coming down and in spite of the fact that the dogs had been playing in the exercise yard all day, the packed snow was now at least eight inches high. The snow, that which hadn't been beaten down by dogs all day, was well over a foot deep. Kate decided to check on the boarding dogs. Her brothers had fed them this morning, but she'd check to see if they'd had enough time to play outside. So she told him that she'd go feed them a little early and settle them for the night. He argued that she shouldn't go alone if this shooter could be lurking around. They reached for their coats when her brother Seamus came in and asked if she needed any help with the dogs. Harry said, "If you want to help your sister, I'd like to make some inroads on all those boxes my mother sent. They've stacked up against the point where they're giving me claustrophobia."

Kate and Seamus got to work quickly with Seamus cleaning the dog runs and Kate mixing the food. Soon all the dogs were fed, and the outside runs were clean. Seamus told Kate that he and Tim would do the final session with the boarding dogs later tonight. Kate gave him a hug and thanked him.

Tim, Seamus' twin, banged at the window. "I'm going to take another pass at clearing the driveways now. By the way, Hotshot, your girlfriend is getting ahead of you. Satu just drove past me on the sidewalk plow. She's a third of the way done, so you'd better go and help her. It will make it more manageable later on. They're saying it will at least be two feet deep before it stops tomorrow, maybe closer to three. Pardon my shouting but these dogs are barking as much as yours are. Your Sams, Kate, are all lined up against the far fence going bat-shit. There must be something by the woods that has them stirred up. Anyway, I need you to have Harry to move his car, so I can plow the drive and not plow him in. He can put it in the barn with yours. There may be some deer or coyotes is out there? I tried calling to them but not even Quinn would stop long enough to come to say hello. Something is up for sure."

"I better go check and make sure nothing dangerous is going on." She went back through the kennel and pushed open the door to the exercise yard. For once, she didn't have to brace the door to keep dogs from pushing through. All of them were lined up as Tim had said, along the fence that faced out toward the woods. Kate called to the dogs but not even Dillon or Quinn came to her. She walked over to where they were all lined up against the fence. As she put her hands on Shelagh and Liam's backs she felt the tension in their muscles. Something had them really upset. The angle of their sight line seemed to follow out along the trail that led into the woods. Though the dogs were indicating that someone or something had passed that way recently, the snow was coming so heavily, that no tracks showed. Whatever it was, it still held their attention and was causing them to bark up a storm.

Kate reached down and took Quinn's collar moving him towards the house. Calling the others to follow, she told them it was supper time. Reluctantly, they slowly moved to follow behind her and the puppy. When she reached the door to the kitchen, she looked back and caught sight of both Dillon and Liam still at the fence staring into the woods. She opened the door and urged all the other dogs to go into the kitchen and then called the last two. They came reluctantly, stopping often to gaze back in the direction of the woods.

The door between the kitchen and the living room had been shut. Harry must have closed it, so he could use space in the living room to sort the contents of the boxes. Whatever he was doing, the distraction level was high. She decided just to feed the dogs and let them back out rather than letting them lose all over the house. They were so jazzed, that if he were sorting stuff, they'd create chaos. She suspected, since he didn't appear, that he had gotten involved unpacking boxes. Going through his dad's stuff had to be hard. Once the dogs were done eating, she'd go check on him.

As she started making the food, she realized Dillon and Liam were still both at the door to the living room, pushing and scratching to be let in. Kate told them to stop and move their butts into line. As soon as they sat with the others, she began setting down the bowls of food.

The dogs ate with their usual piranha style, except for Liam and Dillon who still seemed distracted. They constantly looked over at the door and finally wandered away from their bowls. They probably knew that Harry was on the other side and were eager to be with him. Quinn, never one to let an opportunity to steal food escape him, cleaned his father's bowl while he was distracted. Kate was surprised that Dillon allowed this breach of etiquette in puppy behavior. She recognized that Quinn wasn't the only one. Shelagh had swiped the last of her father, Liam's, food.

Grabbing biscuits, she elbowed open the door and doled them out as each dog raced back into the yard not stopping until they reached the fence. Dillon and Liam had stayed at the door to the living room, more interested in her fiancé.

Dillon began to whine and Liam scratched at the door. Kate sighed and walked over to pull the door open. Both dogs were through the opening in a flash, and their whining changing into panicked howling.

Kate raced into the room behind them and stopped. Chaos was everywhere. The furniture was trashed. Two chairs and the coffee table had been knocked over and one of the couch cushions was lying on the floor. The end table had been shoved to one side with books and magazines scattered everywhere. Even trophies, which had been on the mantelpiece, now lay on the floor. The dogs began clawing at the front door.

"Harry?" she called, panicked. "Harry, where are you?"

Chapter Ten

Her screams got no answer. She yanked open his bedroom door and spotted his go-bag lying open on the bed, half unpacked. His wallet, keys, and phone lay on the nightstand. Kate stopped. His gun lay on the nightstand as well. He never left his gun lying in plain sight. Kate slammed open the door to the bathroom—empty. She yelled, "Harry!"

Dillon continued to claw at the front door and whine. Back in the living room, she yanked open the closet door but Harry's coat was on the hook. She looked out the window by the door. His car was parked right in front. Still shouting his name she spun about to run back toward the kitchen and slipped. Looking down, her stomach roiled. A wet dark stain covered the rug by the coffee table. She reached down to touch it then raised her hand. It came away wet and sticky. Lifting it to her nose she sniffed — blood.

She stood frozen, staring at her bloody hand until Dillon's sharp bark jerked her mind back from the blood to the knowledge that he was gone — and from the devastation of the room, he left against his will and injured.

Her phone dinged. Kate pulled it out and at the same time looking out the window saw Sal's car pull into the driveway. She ran through the kitchen, down the hall to the back door, and up the covered walkway toward the kennel. She moved faster as his car door slammed. Slipping as she ran on the snowy surface, she stopped at the edge of the parking lot, sliding into the snow which had built up on the newly cleared surface.

"Sal, Harry's missing and the floor is covered with blood!" she yelled.

"What's this about blood?"

"Wet blood is on the living room floor."

Tom approached. "Hey, Sal. I spotted you drive in and caught sight of a rental car. Is it Harry's. If so, I'm glad he's back. Kate, did he say anything about where he was?"

"He's gone. I found blood. He's hurt."

"Blood? What blood? Where?"

"In the house." She turned and ran back, slipping until she reached the covered walkway. The two men followed closely behind. When they reached the living room, Dillon and Liam were still pawing at the door.

Sal pushed past her into the living room and switched into cop mode. He knelt to check the blood with Tom bending over his shoulder to see better. "It hasn't been here very long, This is still relatively fresh."

Kate looked away from the two dogs at the door and stepped back into the kitchen to stare out the window at the rest of her dogs looking out into the woods. Harry was gone, and she was pretty sure in what direction he went and who took him. She took a deep breath and paused to think. Now was NOT the time to panic.

Search

Damn it, she was getting married in a week and this bastard wasn't going to stop her by taking her fiancé. She had to go after him. Standing still, she calmed herself and formulated a plan. Then she ran out to the kennel and pulled two tracking harnesses and leads from the closet. Dashing back into the house, she knelt to put the harnesses on the dogs.

"Where do you think you're going?" Sal asked.

"To find Harry."

"No, you're not. As you pointed out, there was blood. This could be dangerous. I've called the Bethany barracks and the troopers are on their way."

"Good. Tell Sean this might be the guy in the photo. Seamus and Satu are in the main house, so call them for help. Tom, there is a head shot of a stalker along with his license plate number on the kitchen table. Grab it please and check with your sources. It's the low life who shot at me and I'm sure has Harry."

Tom and Sal opened their mouths to ask questions, but she had already left and headed into the whelping room. Along the far wall were closets. She pulled the center door open revealing a line of backpacks owned by various members of the family. They were all basically stocked. She grabbed her pack and pulled open the top. Then, she opened the closet to the right and took equipment off the shelves as she continued to stuff her pack.

Tom stepped into the room to see what she was doing. He pulled out his phone and called Seamus. "Kate needs help now," he said. "We need you over here." He then grabbed another pack and copied what Kate was doing. She kicked off her sneakers and socks, pulled on two pairs of heavy wool socks, then slid her feet into tall, heavy winter boots. Her pack was now half full. At the next closet, she grabbed what had been her grandfather's pack and began transferring extra clothing from it into hers. She added a second sleeping bag, bivvy pack, an extra fleece vest, and waterproof parka and pants, long underwear, and socks. Finally, she pulled a pair of short lightweight snowshoes from the top shelf and clipped them to the pack strap. She knew she would need them once she got away from the pavement.

Seamus dashed into the room followed by Satu.

"Kate, what's going on?" he asked.

"Fill these canteens." she said as she pulled them off the shelf. "Harry's been kidnapped and I'm pretty sure he was taken into my woods. He's not wearing his warm clothes and the temperature is nearing freezing and dropping by the minute. Dillon, Liam and I are going after him. Contact Sadie."

Tom interrupted and handed his brother his phone. "I have some info and a photo of a guy who has been lurking at the end of the driveway. Send it to Sadie and see if she can ID him. Ask Tim to take over Kate's kennel duties. I'll be with Kate."

Kate stopped and looked at her big brother. "When was the last time you were on snowshoes? Were they still the wooden ones? The trail shoes with the long tail?"

"It's been a while."

"Tom, I love that you care but you have to rethink this. I appreciate your help, and I acknowledge that you're brilliant at catching criminals using your computer skills, but you don't have the experience to do this. You haven't been on snowshoes since you were ten-years-old. These new short composite shoes are entirely different from what you've experienced. We'll be moving quickly if the dogs are tracking. The snow is coming down fast and is already over a foot on the ground. Harry has been hurt. I don't know how bad he is. I agree you're in good shape and you downhill ski every winter but you lack the experience snowshoeing. We're talking apples and oranges here."

"Kate, I can do this. I promise, if I'm hurt, I'll call Sal and let you keep going. Grab your pack and let's go."

Satu came in and handed Kate two filled canteens and then gave one to Tom. She shoved her hand in her pocket and pulled out a small brass disk. She placed it in Kate's hand. "This is for good luck. Keep it safe and it will keep you safe."

Search

Kate tucked it into her pocket. She slipped on her down parka, pulled a ski hat over her curls and picked up her pack, and winced as she fitted it against her still tender back. Turning her face turn away so as not to show pain, she hitched the hip strap snugly about her. Her younger brother's girlfriend was becoming a good friend to all of them. "Thank you, Satu. I think I'll need all the luck I can find."

Sal stuck his head into the room to tell them the troopers were on the way, almost here. "Good," Kate said. "Notify the search team, but tell them to wait. Whoever took him, is probably armed. We don't want to scare him into shooting Harry."

She adjusted her pack making sure the most weight was on her shoulders and upper back, then headed for the living room. Slipping into Harry's room, she used her body to keep anyone from seeing what she was doing and picked up Harry's gun. Making sure it was loaded, she slipped it into the pocket of her pack and returned to the living room.

Sal crossed to the living room door, pushed the dogs aside, and stood with arms crossed blocking it. "Kate, you're going off half-cocked. Wait for the troopers."

"I'm going after Harry, now. Don't try to stop me, Sal. I know what I'm doing. I've done winter tracking every year since I was eight. Dad and Gramps taught me how. I'm prepared. I'll stay in contact with you. Just understand, the troopers are on their way but it's a case of sneaking up on this man and it will be more effective with one person rather than a charging army. I'd rather try to rescue him without letting his captor be aware of what is happening. A crowd could get him killed."

"How do you know where he is?"

"They went along the fence line and into the woods. That's why the dogs were barking. Harry's warm clothes are still here and his sweats and slippers are missing. He's out in freezing temperatures not dressed for warmth. He'll freeze to death if I wait."

Tom stepped up next to her, pulling on a ski hat. "Don't worry Sal, she's not going alone. Seamus, text me if you or Sadie get any information. I'll stay in touch."

Kate stared at her older brother, then deciding not to waste time arguing. She made the last adjustment to her pack, trying for a contact point with the least damage. Then, she pulled on her mittens, grabbed her cross-country poles from the closet and passed a set to her brother. When she felt ready, she handed him Liam's tracking lead as she picked up Dillon's, and they left.

The dogs took off at a fast pace circling around the house and moving quickly along the kennel yard fence. Kate stopped before they got more than ten feet. Shoving her poles into the ground, she pulled her snowshoes off the pack and put them on the ground. The snow was between ten and twelve inches deep and slow going for humans. Her dogs were all lined up on the other side of the fence watching, and Quinn jumped up to let her know that he resented being left on his side of the fence. Kate looked at him and saw blood on the fence by his paw. Harry had been here. Taking a breath, she stepped carefully into each shoe and fastened the bindings. Tom did the same but wasn't able to get the bindings hitched.

Kate reached over and pushed his hands aside then quickly set his bindings. As she handed him his poles, she said, "Let me give you a quick lesson about these new shoes. You don't have to lift your whole foot. The bindings flex like skis so the rear of the shoe is in contact with the ground most of the time. They're faster on the flat but can be really tricky on slopes or if you have to back up. Remember, if you fall, just relax and let yourself go. If you fight it, you'll probably break something."

Straightening, they continued toward the woods, with Kate in the lead. They moved more swiftly on top of the snow along the fence line. The dogs who were still in the yard barked. They were very unhappy to be missing out on a walk with mom. Kate ran her hand quickly over each head as she passed and told them she'd be back and to be good. Soon she, Tom, Dillon, and

Search

Liam were past end of the fencing and into the woods. As they hit the trail, Kate slowed the dogs' pace, taking no chance she'd trip and fall in the deepening fresh powder snow. As they pressed on into the trees, the snow level got lower, but it was still deep. Tom walked quietly behind her for a few minutes and then said, "Do you have any idea where you're going?"

"Yup. I'm just following the signs that Harry is leaving for me."

"Signs, what signs? How can he be sure you'll come after him?"

Kate held up the branch at the edge of the trail showing her brother the fresh break. "He knows I'll come because he knows I love him and will move heaven and earth to save his life, just as he has done for me since we met. He'll be praying I stay safe at home, but he knows better, so he's leaving me a trail."

Chapter Eleven

When they moved deeper into the woods, Kate spoke quietly.
"This trail leads either to the park or the Connelly property. I'm
banking on the latter. When I played criminal, my shooter
approached down the back trail which goes by the cabin Sean
Connelly's uncle owns.

"Since I saw the man yesterday, I know what he looks like.
Since he ventured into the driveway, you do as well and we now
have the photo. Of course, that doesn't matter, because Dillon
and Quinn have Harry's scent. Their noses are the equivalent to
GPS. They'll tell us which way he goes. We have a good chance
of catching up with them since we'll be moving more quickly
with the snowshoes. They're on foot, I can tell from their faint
tracks. We will keep our speed controlled. I don't want to move
so fast we run smack into an armed killer."

Search

Kate spotted a couple more of freshly broken twigs hanging from a small maple sapling. She stopped and showed them to Tom. "It seems as though Harry and his captor are sticking to the main trail, which is what I suspected they'd take. If they veer right in five hundred yards, they'll head, more-or-less directly, into the state park. However, since that area was crawling with troopers and search dogs yesterday, I doubt his captor had a chance to leave a car there for a getaway. Even the school bus which brought the kids had to stay outside the parking lot. The park officially closes to vehicles from the end of October and Jersey barriers are moved in to block the entrance specifically to keep all cars out. With this snow, the state plow people won't be letting anyone even pause at the side of the road. I suspect he drove in a back way, parking on the old logging road, so he could approach my property from the rear, to capture Harry." Kate chuckled. "That might have been a good idea if not for the weather. They're in for a big surprise if they plan to leave that way any time soon. With more than ten inches of snow on the ground now and still coming down at more than an inch an hour, I can guarantee that road is already snowed in won't be plowed out until every other road in the county is done."

"How did you figure all that out?"

"I teach this stuff, remember."

"Right. You do the training classes but it is different when we're tracking someone who is probably armed and has taken Harry in a bloody battle."

"I can't think about that now. I have a job to do and will need all my wits about me when we catch up with them."

Kate kept seeing broken branches and trampled underbrush. With this much breakage, he was probably still able to walk and plan. She felt relieved that no more blood had shown up since the hand-print on the fence.

Methodically, they covered the trail until they reached the spot where her security camera covered the trail, she paused to look up. If Harry and his attacker had passed this way, her phone warning should have gone off. The camera should have warned her when his attacker entered. Why not? Tom watched her pick up a fallen branch and reaching up, push aside a broken branch which kept her from seeing the camera. When she found it, a knife had lodged high in the tree by the hookup, and the camera dangled from it by a sliced wire.

"Damn!" Kate spat out angrily. "He wouldn't have spotted it if the leaves had been on the trees. We didn't plan on a threat from bad actors in winter."

"Well, that explains how he got into the house without you knowing. You might want to start locking your front door."

"I only lock my door at night and when I go away. People are in and out of there all the time."

"Including someone wanting to kidnap Harry."

Kate grimaced and signaled the dogs to resume tracking. Twenty feet further along, Dillon veered to the left, scrambling up a path partially hidden by brambles which sloped up at an angle. She swiftly followed Dillon and then stopped at the top. Liam climbed right behind her, towing Tom.

"Liam hold, Tom stop."

He paused, lowering his snowshoe from where he was about to begin climbing.

Search

"Tom, let go of Liam's lead." He did and the dog scrambled up the slope and stood next to Dillon.

"Okay, what I want you to do next is take off your snowshoes. There is no way you can make it up here wearing those. Take them off and toss them to me."

Tom opened his mouth to argue, but stopped, bent over and removed the snowshoes. He quickly tossed each to her with an accuracy reflective of his years as a star baseball pitcher in both high school and at MIT.

"Okay, scramble up here but be careful not to let your pack throw off your balance."

Tom's height came in handy as he reached for handholds to help him climb. His long arms and legs covered the ground, and soon he stood beside her. He slipped on his snowshoes as Kate flipped closed his bindings.

"Thanks," Kate said giving him a hug.

"For what?"

"For not going all 'big brother' on me. You actually listened to what I said."

Tom stared at her for a minute and opened his mouth to argue then closed it. "Do I really do that?"

"Well, yeah, you do. You and Sal to a certain extent. Harry and I have already battled that out. Dad and Gramps understood me and trusted my judgment. I really miss them."

"I miss them too. They were... wise, would probably be the best word."

"They made me feel that whatever I did was right."

"Me too."

Tom reached out to hug her, and she buried her head in his chest before gathering their leads and heading up the trail. Kate knew this side trail. She and Gramps used to take it to go fishing. It led to Innis Connelly's cabin, which was about a mile further on.

She thought aloud as they walked. "Since only family and close friends know about the cabin, the guy who took Harry must have come across it when he hiked in from the old logging road. His GPS must have clued him about the old road."

Her family and Connellys had been friends since her grandfather first came to Connecticut and built his house and business on the land he'd bought. The closeness continued between the families down through the generations. Sean Connelly, who was the town's resident state trooper was engaged to Agnes. Her property ran beside Connellys for about half a mile. Innis and her grandfather used to fish in the stream which ran across both properties to catch trout and relax. As kids, they'd all been taught to catch, clean and cook the fish. Her grandfather's rule was if you wanted to eat, cleaning the fish was part of the job.

They finally reached a part of the trail wide enough for them to walk side by side for a while. They were moving at a rapid clip when the trail turned a bend and narrowed so that they had to return to single file. Liam and Dillon had almost disappeared around the bend, and Tom had stepped in front of her when Kate saw the dogs each leap as though going over a jump. It took a second for that to register to terrify her.

"Look out!"

Search

It was too late. Tom's leg was caught pitching him forward, screaming in pain. A wire, which was stretched across the trail, broke and curled as it whipped back and forth, wrapping around him. Razor like barbs along the wire slashed him with every move. She screamed, "Don't move a muscle, don't even breathe That's razor wire." Quickly dropping her pack, she tore off her mittens and dug into one of the pack's side pockets. Her hands searched until she finally pulled out a pair of heavy leather gloves and her multi-functional tool. The dogs began to move back toward her. Instantly her arm shot up signaling both of them to drop into down position.

"Stay," She cried, focusing back onto her brother.

In seconds, she had sorted the various blades, found the wire cutter and begun cutting the razor wire. She studied each cut before making it to be sure it wouldn't cause the wire to curl or dig more deeply into Tom. Tears streamed down her face as she realized only a sadist would have stretched this across the trail. Thank God the dogs spotted it was there and jumped it. If the monster was capable of doing this, what is he doing to Harry?

She was lucky they hadn't both been caught. Tom's fall made the wire break and just around him. Every barb was cutting into his legs and hips. The end still waved its vicious razors. Kate cut it into pieces about six inches long so that they wouldn't have any curl allowing it to lash out. Each piece she placed next to a pair of logs at the edge of the trail. She had to make sure there was nothing about to cut the feet of dogs or forest creatures.

Tom's eyes were shut and his breathing shaky. How much pain he was in, she couldn't imagine. She finished cutting away the wire, gently pulled lose those pieces which had sliced into his skin until he was almost free. When she lifted his left leg to pull the final piece free, Tom's scream almost made her drop it. The snow which had been covering the leg fell away showing his snowshoe tilting at an odd angle.

"Oh, God. I think your ankle is broken," she whispered while gently easing lose the snowshoe binding. She set the snowshoe on the ground and carefully lowered his foot, setting it on top of the snowshoe. Next, she took off the other snowshoe. Then she reached into her pack, pulled out some short bungee cords and cautiously hitched both snowshoes together, completely immobilizing the ankle.

Next, she pulled a first aid kit from Tom's pack, Tom grabbed her hand. Without even opening his eyes more than a slit, he stared at her and spat out, "Phone Sal."

Kate dug into her pocket for the phone and hit speed dial number three and speaker then set it on the snow. She eased up the zipper on his snow pants leg as it rang. Next, using the scissors tool, she sliced the leg of his jeans and did the same for his long-johns. Finally, she went to work disinfecting what seemed like a hundred bleeding cuts on his legs. She was grateful for some layers of clothing had blocked more cuts. The wire also might have cut deeper if he hadn't been wearing so many heavy layers. Even with that, she was dealing with rows and rows of small slashes which were bleeding heavily.

"Kate, what's happening?" Sal's voice came from the phone, sounding anxious.

"We ran into trouble. The guy who took Harry set up a snare on the trail. He stretched razor wire across it. It caught Tom. His legs are badly slashed with probably fifty small cuts, and he's got what appears to be a broken ankle. He's going to need transport and a doctor. Tell Tim to bring his snowmobile with the sled he uses for giving kids rides. You'll also need a stretcher to lower him down the sloping path to the trail."

"Tim is here with me now. We're on our way out. Hang in there."

Kate pulled a solar blanket from Tom's pack. She bandaged his legs where the wire had sliced into them, and then wrapped the blanket around him. His hat had fallen off, but Kate found it lying in the snow. After shaking the snow from the warm wool fibers, she pulled it onto his head, and raised his hood to cover it.

While she worked, she found herself unconsciously looking down the trail. Time was passing and Harry was still out there. She didn't realize that she was crying until Tom reached up to wipe her tears.

"Kate, go."

"I can't leave you. You're my brother and you're hurt."

"And Harry will be your husband, and he's hurt. Go. Sal is coming for me. I'll be okay. Go find him and bring Harry back. I know you can do it."

"But Tom…"

"Take the dogs and go, now. But Kate, be very careful. If this bastard set up one trap, he may have done others."

Kate leaned in, gently hugged him, and whispered, "Thank you. You are the best brother ever."

Pulling herself up by using her pole and putting her pack back on, she picked up the leads and told the dogs, "Find Harry."

The Sams occasionally would shift left or right which seemed to indicate that Harry was not walking straight or normally but was probably stumbling.

They had covered about a quarter mile when Dillon whined and dove off the trail. She held Liam back as Dillon sniffed in the snow and sat. Kate put Liam on a down and stepped forward. A half-dozen steps in, she spotted it. Blood. The smear was covered with a light sprinkling of snow, like powdered sugar. The bushes surrounding it had been crushed and the snow stirred up. Someone had fallen leaving a crooked snow angel imprint on the ground. She fell to her knees, her stomach heaving at the amount of blood. Drag marks led at an angle back toward the trail. Her mind fought against the obvious. So much blood. Harry's blood. The clear fact pushed into her head yelling—Harry is dead.

Chapter Twelve

Kate fought to find a breath as she collapsed face down in the snow. Sobs choked her. Tears froze on her cheeks. Harry gone, No, No. Absolutely not. It can't be.

Numbness rendered immobile, but then pain forced awareness as paws scratched at her sore back and legs. If she hadn't had the pack on, they'd have torn all her healing cuts open. The brutal cold plus the persistent shoving of two dogs into her lap finally roused her. Her head lifted, and she reached for an ounce of control and stuffed the agony deep inside. With a hand on Dillon, she pushed herself up to kneel, the red ground was all she could see. The blood. Harry's blood where he had fallen and was dragged away. She reached out a finger and touched the liquid.

Liquid? It was liquid. It was fresh. Fresh could mean a heart still beating, still alive? Again she burst into tears.

Peggy Gaffney

The blow came hard and fast, knocking her into the deep snow. She looked up but could only see white. Finally, focusing, she realized this white wasn't snow but hair. The land beneath her was wet deep snow. Dillon stood over her body whining, poking and licking her face. She grabbed him, realizing he needed comfort and wrapped her arms around her dog while gasping to gain her own control. Her voice broke the stillness, shouting, "Jesus, Mary, and Joseph, please let him not be gone. Let him live."

Dillon licked her face and pawed her chest, trying to stop her pain. Liam pushed his muzzle against her, shoving her. His shove knocked her into Dillon's chest. The older dog was trying to make her stand by tunneling under her body and lifting. Kate pushed both Liam and Dillon aside, and changing her mind, she pulled both dogs into her lap and buried her head in their coats.

"Sorry for the meltdown, guys. You two are so good." She drew a shaky breath. These two needed her to be okay and in charge. Suddenly she felt a hand resting on her shoulder, squeezing and heard words fill her head, *"Never give up Katie, keep going…"* She gasped. Her shoulder still experienced the warm grip which was so familiar. This was the same grip which held her shoulder at ringside all her life when she stood ready to go compete. Gramps. He had always grabbed her shoulder to tell her those words, *'Never give up.'* Her face lifted from Dillon's coat to look behind her. She knew she would see nobody, but at the same time, knew her grandfather and father were here, urging her on. The fact that she couldn't see them didn't matter. They were here, with her, as they had been whenever she needed them. Death hadn't stopped that bond of reassurance. She took a long shuttering breath and grabbed the nearest pole. It took two tries, but she stood.

Kate began to study the area. The ground, now that she really looked at it, appeared as though there had been a fight with only one man standing in the end. Someone had been dragged away. Why? If Harry were dead, why not just leave him here? At the rate the snow was falling, he'd soon be covered. But, what if, by some miracle, Harry wasn't dead? If he wasn't dead, his assailant couldn't leave him.

She was a tracker. She needed to follow the drag marks. If he were still alive, his assailant needed to take him. She leaned on her poles to study the marks. The boot prints were facing backward and were mostly smeared by the drag marks. With the leads in hand, she followed the drag marks back to the path.

"Find Harry," she commanded. The dogs had only taken a few steps forward when Dillon stopped. He lifted his head, turned to look back toward where they'd been and dove off the trail into bushes about ten feet from the blood. His tracks broke through pristine snow which displayed not even a rabbit track.

She opened her mouth to call him back to the search when he sat and stared at her, signaling a find. Kate told Liam to wait and moved to see what Dillon found. The dog's hairy head and ruff blocked her view as she approached. His nose pointed straight down. Something shiny was sticking up half-buried in the snow. She urged him aside, and spotted a hypodermic lying in the snow. At first, it looked empty, but when she reached out with her mitten to lift it, she saw it was half filled with a clear liquid. But that wasn't all. The needle tip was red with blood and--from Dillon's reaction—it was Harry's.

She took two calming breaths, and pulling off her pack began to do what was needed. The small baggie she removed from a side pocket was perfect for keeping this evidence safe until she could pass it on to Sean. But before she sealed the bag, she pulled out her multi-tool. With the pliers, she bent the needle to make it safe and finally zipped the bag shut. In her pack, she found a pair of socks which she wrapped around the bag to ensure the hypodermic wouldn't break. Finally, storing it in one of the side pockets, she slipped her arms back into the straps of her pack relieved that her injuries from yesterday now barely hurt. Maybe her doctor could figure out what is in the hypodermic. As she walked back to the trail, she reached down and hugged Dillon and Liam, saying, "Good boys. Seek. Find Harry."

Both dogs moved off at a fast pace forcing Kate to tighten her grip on their leads so as not to be pulled over. They were moving toward the Connelly cabin but the trail was becoming harder for her to see. Darkness was settling in as the hour became later and what little light there was came from the white of the snow. Their pace slowed further as the last light disappeared. Her eyes adjusted quickly, but she was thankful to follow the beacons of the white hairy tails in front of her.

As the force of the storm increased, the dogs picked their way more carefully as they moved forward. The wind had picked up and big heavy flakes swirled, attacking from both above and sideways. Kate stopped and pulled her goggles from a pocket of her pack and put them on. She relaxed somewhat when they let her see without the snow flying directly into her eyes. Liam hated it when the snow flew sideways into his eyes and ears, so he was constantly shaking his head. He moved with his ears turned backward and flattened onto his head to keep the flakes out. The storm didn't slow Dillon at all.

The weather was throwing off her sense of distance and direction. Kate looked for landmarks, but in the dark, there was no way to tell how far they were from the cabin. Her smallest mag light threw a very narrow beam. They were still following the drag marks. The increase in the intensity of the storm may have slowed the man who'd taken Harry. If he was trying to make it to the logging road, he'd soon find that to be next to impossible. Liam whined as he sniffed the marks looking back at her as if to say let's go. She sped up slightly. She shoved to the back of her mind, the fact that Harry was so injured he couldn't walk. Self-pity was a luxury she couldn't afford. She tucked the flashlight back into her pocket and let her eyes readjust to the darkness as she moved forward.

Search

Barely twenty more steps on, she smelled smoke. Somewhere up ahead there was a fire going, at, she'd guess, the Connelly cabin. Their pace slowed, even more, and she'd gathered the leads until the dogs were beside her. Kate crept up to the edge of the clearing which opened in front of the cabin. Cautioning the dogs to silence, she eased off the trail and crept behind the bushes and trees until she could see into the cabin's side window.

The man from the surveillance video who had shot at her stood in front of the window, his cell phone to his ear. He broke off his call, shoved the phone into his pocket and moved to stare out the window at the snow. The light from inside kept him from spotting her. After a minute, he turned to pick up a bag from a table and pull out a sandwich and a can of beer and settled in to eat.

Her attention moved from the window when Dillon pulled his lead and it slipped from her relaxed fingers. Her dog was crawling forward in prey mode, not making a sound. She saw him slip around the corner of the porch and inch his way toward a pile of what looked like blankets. He sat and signaled a find. Kate saw him nose the pile and as the wind let up for a second, she heard a tiny whine.

Kate shed her pack, hiding it out of sight behind a bush and staying low, moved toward Dillon, with Liam in the lead. She inched along the cabin wall, and reeled Liam's lead in until she could slide her hand under his collar. Holding her breath, she stopped and listened. Nothing. Dropping to her knees, she crawled to where Dillon lay. The bundle was snow covered. Her arm brushed the snow clear, and she froze. Harry! He was lying motionless, in an awkward position and his eyes were open. She started to lift his head but it dropped back limp. Kate touched her lips to his and noticed a faint breath but there was no movement in the muscles of his body. He was freezing but not shivering. She lifted his arm and it fell like rag doll. Her gaze turned back to his face as his eyes moved. They were tracking her everything she did. She

Peggy Gaffney

whispered in his ear, "Hang in there, Love. I'm going to get you out of here." Both dogs now lay across him. Kate was trying to think of how she could move him when she heard steps. A door opened.

The man walked slowly across the porch and stopped. The railing creaked as he leaned on it. "Well, looks as though you're getting a nice blanket of snow, Foyle. That should warm you up — not. If it's deep enough, nobody will find you until after Christmas. I take that back. The animals have already found you. Hell, there may not be anything left to find after the animals finish with you," he said chuckling. He aimed a flashlight down on Harry and grinned as Harry's eyes stared back at him. "I don't know what you did to piss people off but I'm not complaining, in fact, you're the sweetest whack I've had in years, weird but sweet. The contract on you was worth leaving the city and coming out into this frozen world. I'm not used to all this fresh air. But two-hundred and fifty large is not to be sneezed at in this economy. The party who asked that you die this way tells me you crossed the wrong man. He sure wants you to suffer. Oh," he said pulling out his phone. "Smile for the camera. Ah, but you can't smile. I'll send these portraits of your icy state and my client will be very happy.

"I'm not to complaining. I'm warm as toast in this cabin. And that sandwich, let me tell you, it was to die for if you pardon the expression. It's from this deli in Bridgeport my cousin told me about. Fantastic. They bake their own rolls fresh and just load them. And the pickles are amazing. It was almost worth driving out to this godforsaken forest, fifty miles from the ends of the earth, in the snow. You know, the food and the quarter mil payout they placed on your head make this a really nice day. Too bad you can't enjoy it." His laughter followed him back into the cabin.

The lattice which covered the crawl space under porch was eased aside as Kate and the dogs crawled out. Using her hands, she felt around for something she remembered was once stored under the porch and prayed it was still there. Where was it? She fumbled in the dark reaching further under the deck. Her hand made contact with a baseball bat, a croquette set, and some fishing poles, as she became more frustrated. There wasn't time to waste. When she began to back out, she banged her elbow against a curved piece of wood and grinned. Her hand stroked the smooth familiar surface of a toboggan. Kate eased the panel in the lattice further aside and whispered for Liam and Dillon to guard Harry.

The dogs crept forward and lay across his body as she slid the toboggan out from under the porch. When she went to pull the lattice back in place, her knee struck some fabric. The old canvas tent they'd slept in during camp-outs was still there. An idea struck her and she pulled it from under the porch.

The toboggan moved easily as she slid it up against his inert body. The blowing wind covered the sled's shushing sound. Harry's dead weight wasn't easy to move since she had to fight the sled slipping away every time she tried to slide him on. She finally reached across the sled and rolled him to the edge of the toboggan, using her mitten to cover his face, so he wouldn't be injured and stopping after each turn to listen. Hand over hand, she slowly moved him to the point where she had his upper body in position. Her breath came in short huffs and her chest heaved from the exertion. He was heavy. His dead weight and limp body made him into a hundred-ninety pound jellyfish.

When she got his top half centered, Dillon, who had been watching grabbed the pants on the nearest leg and pulled. Together they dragged the second leg on, making sure both were aligned to give the sled balance. Their only handholds for lifting had been his sweats which were stiff with ice.

Sweat trickled down her back. He was on the toboggan, but he wasn't secure. She didn't have time to anchor him now. Every few seconds, she paused and held her breath to listen for the man's return. The rope on the front of the sled was old, but she hoped still strong enough, as she grabbed it and eased the sled around the corner of the cabin. They glided smoothly around the corner of the cabin, and her breathing had almost returned to normal when she heard voices.

Chapter Thirteen

The words were rapid though not clear, and she began to wonder if the kidnapper was talking on his cell phone in speaker mode when a familiar jingle from a local commercial began. Then the voices began again. Her breath, when she released it, sounded as loud as the radio.

With her hand on Liam's back, she leaned over him and whispered to Dillon, "Guard Harry," and signaled him to stay. With Liam beside her, she worked her way back to where Harry had been lying. The tent was where she left it just by the lattice. She pulled it out. The canvas was heavy but when she spread the rolled up tent out, she was able to arrange it into roughly the shape of Harry's body. Next, she told Liam to dig, and they both covered the canvas with snow. She eased closed the panel under the porch, noticing that the hard snowfall was already adding a layer of fresh snow on top of what they had thrown over the tent.

With a hand signal to Liam that he should walk around in a circle and up to the pseudo-body, she watched as he left a pattern of tracks that might fool Harry's captor enough to give them time to escape. Back at the sled, she whispered what she was doing to Harry, grabbed the rope and pulled it down the side of the cabin and across the clearing to a side trail that ran parallel to their fishing stream.

Kate stopped after going deep enough along the trail to be out of sight of the cabin. She bent over, hands on her knees, puffing as she tried to breathe. Exhaustion overwhelmed her, but she didn't have time to rest. The tree where she had hidden her pack had kept most of the snow off. She brought it back to the sled and pulled a space blanket from its front pocket. Gently, she lay the blanket over him from head to toe and attached it with bungees. At least it would keep more snow off him though she didn't think he had much body heat to reflect back off its surface.

She needed to raise his body temperature, and fast, so stuffing her pack under Harry's head at the front of the sled she pulled hard on the rope. They moved off as quickly as her exhausted body would let her. She offered up a few *Hail Marys* of thanks for the deep snow. Her snowshoes allowed her to cover ground faster than her boots would have and the toboggan slid smoothly behind her in spite of her fiancé's weight.

Search

She hadn't been to the cabin in several years, but she knew this small path. As kids, they had run back and forth along it to get fishing poles or to carry their catch back to be cleaned and cooked. It ran beside the stream but circled around about a mile further on, and eventually, met up with her main trail. She looked back at the sled. Harry wouldn't make it that long. He was certainly in the first stages of frostbite if not farther along. She had to get him warm, and she had to do it now now. She didn't have the luxury of going all the way home.

Kate studied the bank of the stream. There had been a lean-to along this path at one time which they used for camp-outs. Gramps would take advantage of it when he taught them some winter survival skills. He had learned the skills while a member of an intercollegiate outing club when he was in college. He had, for a number of years, attended Winter Mountaineering School in the Adirondacks on Mount Marcy near Lake Placid. When she and her siblings were little, he managed to make the outings a challenge for them. Even though they were only going out on a cold and snowy night, into the surrounding woods near home. He'd set up challenges to test their skills which sounded almost as exciting as camping out on the side of a mountain in sub-freezing temperatures had been for him. They learned what it was like to sleep overnight with just a lean-to as protection from cold and snow as well as other survival techniques to toughen them up.

Kate began to study the path and follow the indentations where they appeared in the stream bank. She tried to remember which tiny cove was in front of the lean-to. Closing her eyes she pictured the trail at that spot and remembered it was right after the spot where the trail turned sharply left. Dillon, who had been about a dozen feet in front of her suddenly disappeared. Kate reached into her pack for her tiny flashlight. Her steps slowed, then she stopped pulling as she looked at the bushes. She cupped the light to illuminate only the ground. The stream curved here. She stepped off the trail moving to the left, pushing through wild blackberry brambles and wild roses. The thorns scratched as she reached up and forward. Her hand made hit something solid making contact with a log running horizontally. She slid her mitten to the right, and it caught on the edge of a tarp which had been stretched across the opening. Her head rested against the log as she offered prayers of thanks.

This was the lean-to and her thumb now found the rope holding the tarp in place. Her hand fumbled along with the tarp until she found the knot. Luckily, it was a slip knot. The rope was stiff from the cold, but wrapping it around a twig, she got enough purchase to free the knot. With a hard yank, the tarp fell back enough for an opening to form. Kate shone her light inside as Liam pushed past her. She held her breath hoping that no wild animal had taken residence. A few seconds later, Liam's head reappeared smiling with a 'what are you waiting for' expression on his face. Peering inside she saw it was clean and dry with no resident animals larger than a mouse, and she could live with a mouse as a neighbor.

She tugged loose the rope holding the lower corner of the tarp, then pushed back through the brambles and turned the toboggan to line up with the entrance. With the rope gripped tightly in her hand, she eased past the sled and backed into the lean-to. Then, bracing her feet against the bottom log, and using every ounce of strength she had left, she pulled the sled up onto the log at the entrance.

She was getting ready for a final pull when the sled came flying in, and just missed flattening her. Dillon had shoved the toboggan, in his struggle to get to her, as he followed her inside. With the tarp open, the snow flew in. She slid her body over Harry and tightened the rope which was holding the tarp. Once done, it closed the entrance tight enough to keep out the weather. With snow falling this hard, any trace of their hiding place would soon disappear. Once the slip-knot was tied, she collapsed against the side wall, took off her gloves, pulled out her phone to text Seamus.

In Connelly lean-to w/ H. K.

The lack of snow and Harry's weight made moving the toboggan akin to juggling an elephant in a pup-tent. She pushed and shoved and let out a string of her non-curse curses. Using her shoulder, she finally managed to move the loaded and very heavy toboggan so it rested parallel to the front of the lean-to but away from the opening. After the last shove, she collapsed on top of Harry, exhausted. Her hand reached up, and undid the bungee and peeled away the solar tarp from his face. Green eyes stared back at her.

"One blink for yes, two for no. Are you alive?" she gasped.

She saw the first sign of humor in his eyes as he blinked once. "Good," she growled. "Because I've just figured out where the phrase dead weight comes from."

Her hand reached out to touch his face, and she squeaked, "Hell, Harry, you're colder than a witch's tit. We've got to get you warm and fast."

She pushed herself up on her elbows, rolled off him telling the dogs to go snuggle Harry. Next, she eased her pack off, ignoring the stabs of pain which were as familiar as old friends. She unhitched the top and pulled out one of her father's waffle-weave tops, and a heavy sweater she'd knit for her dad two years ago. Her father's scent rose, and she held the sweater up to her face closing her eyes. The scent of aftershave, peppermint, and dog filled her. There was even a slight smell of the pipe he smoked when he relaxed. Memories swamped her as silent tears fell. Liam's whine pulled her back to the present. A piece of flannel toweling was the last thing she grabbed as she turned to help her fiancé.

First, she released him from the space blanket. Then bracing herself, she slipped her arms under Harry's shoulders and lifted him enough to wedge her knee into the middle of his back. With him propped up part way up, she shifted her position to get more leverage. She opened her mouth to take a deep breath only to spit out a mouthful of dog hair.

"Dillon, get your tail out of my face."

Again, her hands, shoulders, and head braced him from behind when she pushed, which finally levered him up enough to sit. Her head dropped on his shoulder, while her panting slowed. After a few seconds to rest, she began tugging the hem of his sweatshirt up his body.

The fabric was frozen and had to be snapped like sheet ice, which wanted to cling. This meant she had to roll it to make it pliable and then ease it off inch by inch. Each arm had to be held up as it was pulled from a wet sleeve and then the whole heavy, sodden mess had to be eased over his head. His glasses were long gone, hopefully somewhere back in the living room.

Reaching for the flannel, Kate rubbed him down from head to waist, including his arms, hands and each frozen finger. Then once he was dry, she slid the waffle weave shirt over him. To do the sleeves, she had to reach in backward, from the cuff, and pull his hands through as though dressing a baby. She repeated the process with her dad's soft warm Merino wool sweater. Next, she added a down vest, zipping it closed. And last, she threaded each arm into a sleeve of a GORE-TEX jacket, pulling it around him and zipping it up. After a final yank to make all layers lie flat at the back waist, she pulled a thermal ski hat over his head which she tucked inside the jacket's hood. Exhausted, Kate eased Harry back to lie flat on the sled and let herself collapse against him, panting from the exertion.

Dillon licked her face and nuzzled her neck trying to see if she were okay. She forced her hand to reach up and wrap around his neck. Using him for leverage, she pulled herself into a sitting position. "Thanks, Dillon. I'm okay—just pooped."

The lean-to seemed to feel warmer now that they were out of the snow and wind. She unzipped her parka, took a breath, and looked at Harry's sweatpants, also soaked and also plastered against him. Kate hesitated. Then, mentally yelled at herself, for her naivete, she muttered, "So you've never seen him completely naked. You're marrying the man in a week. Get over yourself, Killoy, and stop being a virginal dimwit. If you don't get the freezing pants off him and warm dry pants on, you're not going to be able to have kids, so move it."

She pulled out the thermal bottoms and GORE-TEX pants and put them next to her. She moved to the flat end of the toboggan. As she reached for the waistband of the sweatpants, the dogs jumped up and barked. She froze, listened, then thought she heard the noise. It sounded again. Someone was moving along the path. Barely daring to breathe, she reached behind her into the front pocket of her pack and pulled out Harry's gun.

Chapter Fourteen

The gun felt heavy in her tired hands, so she moved to brace her arms atop the pack, flipped off the safety, and waited with her every nerve on edge. She'd only fired a gun at targets, but if the bastard who did this to Harry tried to get at him, she'd shoot. She didn't know which frightened her more, the threat outside, or the gun in her hand.

After what happened at the Samoyed National, Harry insisted that she learn to use a gun. He told her dogs were all well and good, but when the other guy had a gun, having one yourself tended to even the playing field. Sal had given her three lessons in marksmanship since they'd gotten back home. She hadn't wanted to do it, but to everyone's surprise, it turned out she was a good shot. Now, her hands shook as she ordered the dogs back beside her. The steps moved closer and stopped just the other side of the tarp. She held her breath. Then Liam started wiggling, his tail slapping against her head. Dillon shot forward his tail going a mile-a-minute. "Kate?" Sal's soft voice came from outside.

A wave of dizziness hit her, and she lowered her head to the pack, panting. Her arms sank toward her lap as she put back on the gun's safety. She slipped it back into the pocket of the pack and took a deep breath while moving forward. The tarp was tied up tight, but though her energy was non-existent, managed to craw forward and pull the rope holding it closed.

Sal crawled inside and pulled the tarp tightly shut again. "Is this a private party or can anyone join?" he whispered.

"Thank God you're here. I ran out of energy about an hour ago. The dogs and I managed to find Harry, but he's freezing and I think he's in the early stages of frostbite. His skin is so cold. I managed to get dry clothes on his upper body, but I haven't been able to pull off the sweatpants and put him into these." She pushed the thermal and GORE-TEX pants forward.

"It turned out that the man who was stalking me, the one we caught on camera, is the same guy who took Harry. He drugged him with something that makes him literally unable to move even a finger. Oh, and he's working for someone who wanted photos of Harry freezing to death in the snow. Whoever these guys are, they really hate him."

Sal slid off his pack and set it to the side. He reached in and pulled out heavy wool socks. "He'll need these too."

Kate moved to Harry's shoulders and as Sal stripped his lower body, Kate rolled him first one way then the other. Her cheeks flamed as she got her first look at Harry's lower body. She'd assumed that would have happened on the honeymoon. Embarrassed she felt herself blush, then she shook her head to get her mind back on track, and tossed Sal a piece of flannel for him to rub him dry. Quickly he pulled the added layers of both pants and socks onto his inert body. She took a bivvy sack out of her pack and unzipped it. They rolled Harry off the toboggan, slid the bag into position on the sled, then rolling him first one way and then the other, to insert him into the one-man tent. Sal zipped it up and with a final heft, they slid him, so he was again in the center of the toboggan. Kate told both dogs to guard Harry, and they settled with their warm bodies pressed tight on either side of him.

Finally, she turned to look at Sal. "Is Tom…"

"He'll be fine. The cuts were nasty but not deep, so he'll heal fast. His ankle is broken. When I left, the doctor had set it and was on putting a cast. He'll be hobbling you down the aisle next week I'm afraid. I offered to take his place but he was adamant. He said, 'Since your dad and granddad can't be there, it's his privilege to give you away, and he is going to do it.'"

Kate smiled as Sal added, "But he threatened to whip the hell out of Harry for making you worry so much."

"In Harry's present condition," she said looking at his immobile body, "even cut up and on crutches, it wouldn't be a fair fight."

Peggy Gaffney

She sat back and closed her eyes as relief slammed into her, sapping any trace of strength she had. Knowing the danger to both Harry and Tom was over, at least temporarily, relief set in and then she found herself completely immobile, staring at nothing. This was when a familiar feeling washed over her and her body started to shake. It was as though, once her battle was done, her body knew it would be safe for her to fall apart. Kate knew what was happening but still felt out of control. Sal reached his arm around her shoulders to still her, opened a canteen and pressed it to her lips, carefully so it wouldn't break her teeth while she drank. After about five minutes, the tremors eventually lessened. He managed to have her she sip more water and they finally stopped.

Laying her exhausted body down, he called Liam to move to his side. Then he pulled another bivvy from Kate's pack and nudging Harry to one side of the toboggan, laid it out next to him. Next, he lowered her bone-weary body onto the bivvy, pulled off her boots, tucked her inside, zipped it up, and repositioned Liam, so he could warm them both.

The lean-to was not made for someone his size, but he shifted his body, so he sat next to the sled, bracing himself against both packs.

"Tell me what happened," he whispered.

Speaking slowly and with effort, she told Sal about finding the blood, the drag marks, the hypodermic needle, and then tracking them to the cabin. She said Dillon recognized what to her looked to be a bump under the snow was Harry. The shooter was staying warm in Connelly's cabin and talking to someone on his phone while Harry froze outside, not even able to shiver in the cold. She told him about hiding when the shooter came out, onto the porch to heckle Harry, and take a photo to send to the man behind the kidnapping. It was when she was in the crawl space underneath the porch that she found the toboggan.

"With the skill of a fisherman landing a whale, I got him on the sled," she described managed to load Harry and bring him here. She even chuckled telling him about using the tent covered in snow so the man wouldn't realize he was gone. Then she told Sal what he'd said about being promised a quarter million dollars for this hit on Harry.

"That's a chunk of change in any man's world. Don't worry," He told her. "We won't let that happen, Kate. Now you rest." Sal smiled noticing that before he'd finished speaking, she'd already fallen asleep.

He reached across to check on Harry and saw his eyes open. Sal slid closer to him, so he could see his face. "It's a good thing I don't hit a man when he's down, son, because right now I'm at the front of a long line of people who'd like to take a piece of your hide for leaving Kate to deal with everything for the wedding while you went off on a case.

"Sadie and I only found out about your leaving yesterday because Kate has been protecting you. She just smiled and let everyone think that everything was fine, while all the time she worried about you. I don't know who you've pissed off so badly that they're willing to pay to have that big a contract placed on your head, but they've also put a hit out on Kate. Sean filled me in. This is serious. We've got to stop them fast before your two hundred wedding guests arrive."

Peggy Gaffney

He looked down at Kate and then back at Harry. "This girl loves you more than life itself. As soon as she found you were gone, she packed her gear and was after you with the dogs in under ten minutes. Tom went with her but got taken out by a gift of razor wire from your buddy. If Tom hadn't been in front of her, your bride would be cut to ribbons now. I'm not sure what this guy gave you — though I have my suspicions." He looked at Harry and chuckled. "You better get well quickly, because I can just picture her dragging your sorry butt down the aisle if you are still out of it."

Harry's gaze moved to Kate as Sal pulled out his phone and began texting an update. It hadn't been hard to find Kate. Satu's tech talents included some neat toys, and without Kate's knowledge, she'd passed off a tracking device as a good luck coin which she innocently handed her before she left. The teenager had linked it to a tracking program, and they'd all been able to follow Kate's every step on her computer.

Sal watched as Harry gave in to sleep. Liam had managed to get himself wedged between Kate and Harry and was spread out with his head on Kate and paws and tail on Harry. As Sal stretched, he leaned back against Kate's pack. A lump dug into his back. He reached into the pack's front pocket, and found a gun which he recognized as Harry's. Their own Annie Oakley wasn't just relying on the dogs after all.

The quiet hiss of falling snow told him that the accumulation would probably keep Harry's captor from following them in the dark, but it would also keep the troopers, whom he'd texted, from being able to move in and surround the cabin. This potential murderer might escape. If he suspected Harry was alive, he'd probably come after him again, but for sure, he would try to come after Kate.

The snow was still falling in the gray light of morning when Sal received a text telling him that troopers were advancing up the trail from the kennel on cross-country skis and should arrive in ten minutes. He reached over and touched Kate, at the same time whispering for her not to cry out. He told her that help was coming. Kate crawled out of the bivvy sack, tucked her feet in her boots and slid on her parka which was warm from Sal using it to cushion his back. She tucked away her bivvy then crawled over to Harry. His eyes caught hers and seemed more alert. All at once she felt a slight shift in the fabric of his bivvy. She touched the spot where his finger moved against hers. "Welcome back," she whispered grinning and kissed his still unresponsive lips. "I love you."

Both dogs began growling at the same time as Kate and Sal got the same text message.

Hey guy, we are outside the lean-to. Tell Dillon we're the good guys and here to help. Sean C.

Kate reached out to calm both dogs as Sal opened the tarp. Dillon pushed past him, but finding a friend, just wagged his tail then moved back in to tell his people they had company. Sal crawled out bringing both packs with him. The toboggan with Harry still encased in the bivvy came next and last to emerge was Kate, back to wearing her snowshoes. Nobody spoke. Directions were given using hand signals. Kate reached for her pack but Sean already had it slung over his back. Silently, with Harry on the toboggan and Kate following, they moved down the trail, surrounded by state troopers. The trip home went quickly with all the help and soon, the line of dogs at the fence was greeting Dillon and Liam who were leading the convoy.

Dr. Walters, who had been the Killoy family doctor since before Kate was born, lived a half mile down the highway from them. He was waiting when they arrived. With the sled used as a stretcher, he had Harry carried right into his bedroom. Kate was ordered to wait in the living room, but the doctor let Sal stay. As he examined Harry, Satu, who it seemed was running a computer communication center at Kate's kitchen table, informed her that everyone had been notified that she was fine, but on Sal's instructions, nothing was said about Harry. Seamus handed Kate a cup of cocoa and one of Will's blueberry muffins that had been warmed.

Satu pushed her into her bedroom and helped her get her shoes and heavy clothes off and get into the shower. After she laid out clean clothes, she left. Kate, still capable of her usual speed, reappeared in the kitchen five minutes later, warmly dressed and still sipping the cocoa which was warming her all over.

She went into the living room and noticed the furniture had been restored to order and the blood cleaned up. The door to Harry's was still shut, so she leaned against the wall next to the door and waited patiently. Dillon settled beside her, half asleep stretched out against her leg. Liam lay against the wall on her other side of the door, head down but eyes open. She could hear the murmur of voices but not what was being said. Kate slid down until she sat on the floor and Liam moved to lie at her feet. The adrenalin which had kept her going was wearing off. What replaced it was a kaleidoscopic of feelings.

The door opened. Doctor Walters. was still talking to Sal over his shoulder. "If there is any change, call me. Keep him confined to bed. His system will slowly process the drug, and he'll regain his feeling. Hopefully, his body will have warmed by then to the point where pain will not be extreme."

He walked into the living room. "Oh Kate, how are you feeling? You look exhausted. Your fiancé will slowly regain control of his body as the drug wears off. His vitals are surprisingly normal considering what happened. He should be ready to get married next week so you needn't worry. I've been told that I'm not to speak of what happened to Harry and I agreed. I will see you at the wedding. Take care of that young man." Without waiting for an answer, he patted her on the head as he had all her life, and was out the door and soon driving off.

Relief was the first thing she felt as the doctor left followed by love. But soon other feelings pushed their way in: fear, exhaustion, dejection, and anger. Someone was targeting her and Harry. Whoever it was, had painted a target on their backs.

As she sat on the floor, with her hand on Dillon, her mind went to the plans for the next week. She thought about the invitations which had been sent to two hundred of their relatives and friends and all the effort that had been put into making this wedding wonderful.

Now she realized that they had a massive job to do and practically no time to do it. They had to find out who was behind their murder attempts and stop them. Kate sighed. She was exhausted and frightened, but she had no time for that. She eased Dillon aside, as she pushed herself up from the floor.

"Enough!"

She had to go see her fiancé and work out a plan because nobody was going to interfere with their wedding. She hoped that Harry was ready to see a new side to the woman he was about to marry because Harry Foyle was about to meet —Pissed Off Kate.

Chapter Fifteen

Kate slipped into the room. Harry lay on the bed dressed in crisp new navy blue pajamas. Harry hated wearing pajamas. His eyes were closed as she approached, so she dragged an overstuffed chair from the corner of the room to the bed, moving piles of boxes as she did so. She sat and leaned forward, gently placing her hands on the bed as she stared at his face. After a few minutes, she felt him move and take her hand, his eyes opening. "If I never mentioned it, you are very heavy when you're dead weight."

Harry let out a chuckle, a slight smile forming on his face. His hand moved forward, sliding over hers. "Thank you," he whispered, "for coming after me. I kept wanting you to stay safe, but at the same time, hoping that you'd be my Kate." He lightly squeezed her hand while staring into her eyes.

"I will always come for you. You are my love." She smiled at him and chuckled to herself. "Plus, Agnes would kill us if anything interfered with her plans for this wedding." They were both smiling as she leaned in to kiss him and was delighted to find that the drug had worn off as far as his sexy mouth was concerned.

Sal opened the door and said, "Sorry to interrupt you two, but there's a guy here who says he has to see to you. He looks like a Fed, says his name is Des."

Kate stood and said. "You should talk to Des and fill him in on all that's happened then figure out how we can stop these attacks and capture this guy. Whoever's behind these attempts is cramping my style and throwing the pre-wedding schedule off completely."

Harry whispered, "Come back soon, you need to be part of this planning." He reached for her hand as she stood and held her back until she nodded.

Sal saw the move. "Harry! You can move your hand. How do you feel? Do you hurt anywhere? Can you move anything else?"

The pain Harry felt wasn't physical. He focused on the door as he moved his other hand a few inches and bent the fingers and then both feet, but his mind was on Kate. She was the best part of his life, and he'd exposed her to danger. He felt impotent, just lying in this bed rather than working to flush out this killer.

The door opened while Sal was talking and a voice said, "Lying down on the job, Harry?" Des, dressed in his usual dark suit, white shirt, and striped tie, smiled. "Kate looks as though she's been chewed up and spit out. What's happened to you two since I saw you yesterday morning?"

Sal scowled. "Okay, Mr. Fed, tell me what's going on? This idiot was kidnapped as soon as he got home from his three-week vacation by a man who tried to kill him saying there is a quarter-million price on his head. It's the same goon who shot at Kate yesterday."

Sean Connelly pushed into the room behind Des. Sal's anger shifted to him. "Have they caught the bastard? Is he still in the cabin? What's going on? More than two hundred people are about to descend on this place for the wedding next week and a murderous monster is hiding in Kate's woods."

Des turned to Sean, noted his uniform and asked. "Are you the one who rescued Harry?"

"No, Kate is. Where is she now? I thought she'd be glued to your side, Harry, after all the hell she went through to get you to safety. "Kate is wonderful. How did she do it?" Des asked turning his attention to Sean.

"Went out on snowshoes with two dogs and snuck up on the spot where he was held, then managed to steal Harry away from under the guy's nose without him even having a clue. It wasn't easy since this guy," he said pointing at Harry, "was so drugged up he literally couldn't lift a finger."

"Bet one of the dogs was Dillon," Des said.

"Dillon and Liam."

"I know Liam. He's majestic."

"Not to interrupt this family reunion," Sal growled, "but who the hell are you?"

"Agent Des Xiang, FBI and you must be Sal Modigliani. You used to head up the Police Chief's Association. I've heard about you and the great training program you do with Kate. Even Quinn is turning into a threat to the criminal masses."

"You can save the soft soap for someone who cares. Tell me, are you part of the problem or the solution for what's going on?"

"Both. Harry has been working with me on some fallout from a case. We thought we had everything under wraps, with information on a need to know basis but it seems somehow word of the investigation got leaked. Nobody outside a very few people at the Bureau supposedly had a clue that we had almost finished the search. It tells me we have a spy in house."

Harry moved his head and looked hard at him. Then he whispered, "Or this actor is part of what Kate calls the 'long arm of the law club'." The room went silent as the three men stared at each other. It was one thing to track down a killer when he was outside the law, but quite another if he was on the inside holding the keys to all relevant information. They needed to find the man behind the attacks, the man pulling the strings, paying the money to guarantee that he and Kate would die as well as the hired gun who came after them. This could be someone who sat in on meetings with them and read all their reports. They needed to be very careful who they asked for help, or they might be inviting the fox into the hen house.

Kate had barely walked into the kitchen when she heard the front door slam open and raised voices in the living room. Agnes had arrived, and now stormed into the kitchen followed more slowly followed by Tom on crutches. Kate went straight to her brother.

"Tom, are you okay? You got carved up so badly, I've been worried." Kate searched his face for signs of pain and then looked down at his ankle.

"I'm going to be fine. The crutches will just get me sympathy at the wedding."

"Crutches," Agnes screamed. "You're going to walk her down the aisle on crutches? That's going to look horrible. Maybe Will can walk her down the aisle."

"No." Kate and Tom said at the same time. Kate looped her arm through her brother's. "Tom is standing in for my dad and granddad and I think he'll look quite handsome on crutches."

The door to Harry's room flew open and Sean strode across to Agnes. "What are you doing here?"

"Me doing here? I came over to talk to Kate about last minute details with the wedding and I find the brother-of-the-bride limping on crutches, Kate looks like she's been run over, you're in Harry's room and," she stepped to the right and walked into the bedroom, "Harry is finally back and sacked out in bed. We've got hundreds of people coming in a week and I'm the only one taking this wedding seriously."

"And doing a wonderful job at it under stressful circumstances as we all know." He replied, kissing her lightly on the nose.

"Don't try to butter me up. What are you doing here?"

"Kate got lost in the woods last night during the storm and the troopers had to be called in to bring her back."

"Hogwash! That's insane! You don't expect me to believe that. It's a perfect load of cow shit, Sean Patrick Connelly.

You're going to have to come up with a better story if you think I'm buying that fiction. Kate never ever gets lost. She's got a built-in GPS in her brain. And who the hell is this guy? He looks like a Fed. Is anyone in this room going to tell me the truth?"

Kate took a breath. "Agnes, I'll have time to discuss dresses tomorrow. This is Des Xiang, a friend of Harry's from DC who will be coming to the wedding. Des, this is my cousin, Agnes Forester. We ran into Des at the National and showing good taste, he fell in love with Quinn. As to why Sean is here, I went out last night since I hadn't done a snow track in two years. You are right. I didn't get lost. However, those who don't know me as well as you do think that something had happened when I didn't return. I was just testing my bivvy to be sure it was warm enough to sleep in. I was snug in the old lean-to by the stream when the ski patrol found me early this morning. They couldn't believe a woman who is going to be married in a week would do a solo trek to test her dogs and equipment."

"A normal woman wouldn't but it sounds just like you. These guys are just a bunch of old women. Why is Harry in bed?"

"He just got back from working a case where he picked up a bug. Hopefully, it's not contagious. I've ordered him to stay in bed since I don't want him coughing up a storm during the wedding or on our honeymoon. He needs sleep. Des, you can stay and visit a little before checking into your hotel. The rest of you out. Sean, I've got your uncle's toboggan outside. I borrowed it to bring some stuff home. I'll help you put it in your car. Des, don't let Harry talk too much. I don't want him to aggravate his sore throat."

Kate quickly herded everyone but Des from the room. She grabbed her parka and followed Sean and Agnes out. Still grumbling, Agnes got into her car and drove off. Kate went to help Sean put the toboggan in his SUV. As Kate helped Sean settle the unwieldy sled into the car she asked, "Did they get him?"

"No. When we got there, the fire was still going in the fireplace and a half-empty bowl of soup was still warm on the table, but he wasn't there. We checked the cabin and towed his car, but I think he's hiding in the woods." Sean looked away for a minute and then said, "Kate, he'd uncovered the old canvas tent by the porch. He knows that Harry is alive and since he's not under arrest, he's probably figured that you and Sal helped him get away. According to what Seamus shared with me, he's been stalking this place for days. Thanks to you, we have a photo and license plate to I.D. him. I talked to the troopers who trained with you yesterday and it turns out they were chatting all about the search while having coffee and donuts at Dunkin' Donuts yesterday morning. Two to one all he had to do was talk to any of the locals, and he'd know how to find the woods and the talented Kate Killoy who trains cops and is getting married in a week."

"I suspected as much. So both the bride and groom will be wearing targets this year."

"No, Kate. That's not going to happen. We're going to find him. From what we've gotten so far, this setting isn't what this guy is used to. He's more a 'streets of New York' type. Dealing with nature, including two feet of snow, without a vehicle to get him back to civilization is going to put him at a disadvantage."

"So the bottom line is a street-smart killer is out wandering my woods. He's armed in spite of losing his automatic yesterday. This snow is supposed to keep up through this evening. You're sure he's not in the cabin?"

"No, the guys told me they went through it with a fine-toothed comb. There had been no tracks near the vehicle, so we towed it. The bottom line is that he's now up against both us and Mother Nature."

"Well, we all know you don't mess with Mother Nature," Kate chuckled.

"You stay safe and please think of some way to get your fiancé away from here. The last thing I need is for Agnes to get grabbed by this guy."

"Oh my God, you're right. I'll see what I can do." Kate went back inside her brain trying to fight exhaustion and to come up with ideas to keep them safe. She had to think but right now she was so tired she could barely walk. She needed sleep, and tea—her brain needed a cup of tea.

Chapter Sixteen

Kate closed the door then stood for a minute breathing slowly as she glanced around the living room. It had been cleaned and she only paused for a few seconds, to look at where the blood had been, however the fact that she stopped to look meant that the room had been disturbed along with her life.

Coming in from the kitchen, Tom limped toward her, his crutches adding a thump to each step. He looped his arm through hers and pulled her back the way he'd come. With a gentle push, he lowered her to her chair at the table, and placed a warm scone and a hot cup of tea in front of her.

"Nice story earlier, Kate, but telling people fairy tales doesn't solve the problem. Sean said they hadn't caught the man yet. What really happened after I got hurt in the woods? What's the FBI doing here? Why is Harry in bed? Talk to me or I'm going to beat it out of your fiancé. You are my little sister and I can tell when you're upset and hiding something."

She folded her arms on the table, then lowered her head to them, and sighed. Much as she would like to go hide in her room at this minute, she owed her brother honesty and Tom had been a brick, always there for her in a pinch. When he'd taken over running Killoy and Killoy after her father's death, Kate worried it would be too much work, but he had her grandfather's quiet strength and managed to keep the family business going without a blip. But, whatever was going on here meant that danger was now being unleashed on those she loved and Harry's involvement with this FBI operation was bringing them a savage monster who was now hiding in her backyard putting them all at risk.

She lifted her head and stared up at Tom who looked back using silence, to wait her out. He was becoming more like Gramps every day. With effort, she pulled her thoughts together and told him everything about what happened after they separated on the trail. She finished with the information that Dr. Walters thought Harry must not have received a full dose of what had been in the hypodermic because the drug would have eventually killed him. The doctor suspected it was one of the date rape drugs, but the dosage would have been higher than usual. He was getting the contents analyzed.

Another cup of tea was needed and Tom got up to make it.

Search

"So, the bottom line is, a thug, who wants to kill Harry and maybe you, is lurking in the woods behind your home, while Harry is trying to regain the use of his body."

"That's it. Except for the fact that he's the same guy is in the photo I gave you showing my stalker. If we can I.D. him, this would give us a better shot at capturing him. Oh, and Sean told me they towed his car, so he's out there with no wheels. Since next Saturday there is a wedding here with approximately two hundred guests, provided the couple is still alive to be married, we've got to catch this bastard sooner rather than later. Oh, and I didn't mention that he was a hired gun who is being paid a quarter million just to off Harry. So we also need to find the puppeteer running this show."

A smile began to fill his face. "What you're telling me is this little issue needs to be cleared up quickly, and that is why Agent Xiang is here? Do you need him to stay at my place?"

"An armed Fed nearby can't hurt. And since he was working with Harry on this, he won't need to be brought up to speed."

"Not a problem. So what's the plan?"

"What plan?"

"Little sister, you always come up with a plan. That's what you have done ever since you were eight years old, everyone knows that."

"That sounds like Agnes telling people I have built-in GPS."

"Well, you do."

"Sorry to disappoint you but it looks as though the batteries, in my magic wand, are now dead and there are no replacements that are the right size."

"Hey, I know you, and you will come up with something. When did you last sleep without worry?"

Kate snorted, "Sleep? What's sleep."

"Real rest is what you need if you're going to be able to think of a way out of this mess."

"There is no time to…"

"Now I'm going to go all big brother. Passing out on your feet from exhaustion will just impair your thinking. Go lie down for three hours. Don't worry, I'll wake you, I promise. After that, we can work on a way to stop this bastard."

In classic big brother manner, he helped her to her feet and zombie walked her into her bedroom as her mind pulled at something. A comment Sean made wasn't right or wasn't all there. Sleep threatened to pull her under as her body was lowered onto the bed. She fought to pull to the front of her brain what it was Tom had left out. Shoes. It was something about shoes, she struggled to grasp the thought as her shoes were removed. Yeah, shoes played a part in it, but what? The thought was just out of reach. She vaguely heard Tom call Dillon and Liam to come into the room before the thought, which she almost had, slid away, and she slept.

fff

Harry kept his eyes closed when the door opened, not wanting to talk to anyone but Kate. The pain was keeping his brain from focusing. It had kept him from giving her all the details about Washington. He needed her unique way of

Search

thinking and there wasn't time to do figure it out without her help.

The fingers of his hand tried to make a fist but the burning pain made it feel like the hand was pressed to a griddle. Making any movement was impossible and every attempt brought him close to tears. Both his hands and feet were on fire. The exposure had attacked his extremities more because they had less blood flow, and were harder to keep warm. Even his neck, where he'd been stabbed, throbbed. He needed to pull the sheet they had put over him away but even the air felt hot. Only his face and cheeks were beginning to lose the frying pan feeling. The doctor had left after bandaging his hands and feet and covering every painful inch of his body with ointment.

Des had gone to check out of his hotel since Tom agreed to put him up saying it wouldn't be a problem. Harry felt movement accompanied by a couple of thuds and the chair beside the bed creak as a heavy body settled in. Damn, the last thing he needed was the company.

"You can open your eyes, Foyle, I know you're not asleep." Tom, muttered.

Harry opened his eyes to the sight of his future brother-in-law holding crutches.

"What happened to you?"

"Since I wanted to help, I went out with Kate last night searching for you and the only reason that Kate's not slashed to ribbons with a broken ankle is that I was in front of her when your friend's razor wire booby trap went off."

Harry sucked in a gasp and swore, looking away. Tom continued. "And even after seeing what he did to me and the danger he posed, she went on alone to get you and bring you safely home. So I want to know, how you could be such a stupid idiot?

"First you disappear. Kate wouldn't tell us where you were. Oh, yeah, I know about how she thought she was protecting you from the wrath of the rest of the family which adores you. Even I didn't find out you had left on her own her until a day ago? She didn't want you to be criticized, so she covered up for you. I can't believe you left her to go play with your FBI buddies. Then, when you come home, you bring a killer here."

Tom turned to look out the window at the still falling snow and asked. "Isn't your ability to analyze a situation with your mega brain, supposed to figure all the angles before you rush off? Which was it, the mob or your father's murderer, that sent you racing off?"

Harry stared at him. How did he find out? Kate didn't tell him. "You're right. Everything you say is true. I was a smug, egotistical ass, believing that if I could solve this case, which has been hanging over me for years, and get it out of the way before we married so my wife wouldn't need to worry about being a target."

"Well, you were wrong. Do you know how much danger Kate is in? When I did some research on this piece of scum, I found out he gets off on torturing women? So tell me, Mr. Former FBI, what happens next? And don't say Kate goes into hiding, because we both know that's not going to happen. You're lucky my grandfather isn't here because he'd beat you bloody in spite of his age. Kate has always been beyond precious to Gramps and Dad and it wasn't just because of the dogs."

A door slammed and Tom was instantly on his feet, hurrying to check and see who had come in. With Kate asleep, she could be in danger.

Harry lay there, helpless and wondering if he'd just destroyed the best thing that ever happened to him. Without thinking, he'd put the woman he loved more than life itself in danger. And why? To chase an old nemesis?

Tom was right. He was the biggest bastard on earth. He'd set her up to be a target. Kate wouldn't leave, no matter how he asked. He brought this danger to her and all he could do was lie here and wallow in pain and self-pity over his stupidity unable to keep her safe. Hell, she was the one who saved him.

He was tired of lying here. In anger he shoved his arm out to throw the blankets aside. The blankets fell to the floor. He suddenly realized, that if he had the strength to push off the blankets, he might have enough to sit. Reaching back with arms that now operated though still screamed with pain, he arranged the pillows carefully, moving the bandaged hands as little as possible. Then using every ounce of fortitude he could muster, and ignoring the urge to scream in pain, he began to hoist his body into a sitting position. Conquering Everest must feel like this as he inched himself up to the head of the bed. When the pillows hit his back, he collapsed unable to move.

Tom returned to tell Harry it was just the twins Tim and Seamus who'd finished cleaning the kennel and began to dig paths in the exercise yard so Kate's older dogs wouldn't need to plow through the deep snow. As he turned to shut the door, it slammed open, and a white, snow-covered streak burst through.

"Quinn!" Harry said as the pup leaped onto Harry's bed pushing himself into his arms and soaking his new pajamas. "Quinn. How's my buddy? Damn, you're all covered with snow."

Tom reached into the bathroom and then tossed a towel to Harry who wrapped it around the squirming puppy.

"God, I've missed you." In spite of the wet hair, Harry buried his face in the puppy's coat, tears adding to the dampness.

Tom moved to the side of the bed and laid a hand on his shoulder. "My dad used to say that life isn't perfect and everyone's entitled to make an idiot of himself at least once."

Harry lifted his head, using the damp towel to dry his face. "I wish I'd known your father and grandfather.When I'm with Kate, it's evident that they had a special connection which wasn't just the dogs? She didn't choose math for her career the way everyone else has. Yet I know she has serious skills."

Tom sighed and smiled. "My grandfather had four major focuses in his life: my grandmother, the business, the dogs and Kate. He loved and cared for all of us, but Kate has always been different and he realized early in her life that our mother wouldn't understand anything about her. But Gramps was fascinated by the way her mind worked. I don't know how much you've learned about the way Kate reasons out a problem. You and I are mathematicians. We see math in a relatively linear form, solving each step on a voyage to a solution. Kate is also a mathematician but her approach to reaching the solution to problems doesn't follow a natural progression."

"While at the National, I saw that when she seemed to pull the answer to the puzzle out of thin air."

Tom laughed. "The answer wasn't in thin air I guarantee, though it often seems like that to those of us with logical brains. Let me explain. As kids, Gramps would give us a situational puzzle based in math. We would each take a crack at it but it would be Kate who'd come up with a solution every time. Our egos got thumped when she'd tell us her approach after she got the answer. It would be completely off the wall and a thing of beauty."

"She always had it right?"

"Yup. It later became something we'd all play coming up with harder and harder scenarios for her to solve. She still would nail it."

"It sounds great, but now we've got an armed killer roaming Kate's woods determined on killing us. That's real. It's not a game."

"No, but it is a problem in need of a solution. I have every faith that when she wakes, she'll have found the answer. I told her I'd expect it after her nap."

"You turned this into a game?"

"Yup."

"And she's just going to say 'abracadabra' and a plan appears?"

"She doesn't say 'abracadabra.' She'll just walk in and tell you the solution. Can your ego take that?"

"If it's Kate, then yeah, I can take it."

"Good."

"Tell me about your grandfather and your dad. I only know about the dog aspect of their lives, but how did they come to build Killoy and Killoy?"

"Well, one thing I know, they'd have loved you, except for the part about putting Kate into danger."

Harry leaned back and listened to Tom tell him about these two men who had influenced her so much. Kate's brother Will wandered in to say he'd brought food and stayed to share stories of what it was like growing up Killoy. Sal joined them. Harry filled them in on the details of what had happened at the National Specialty and what they'd done, with Kate's super brain and bravery to keep the country from being thrown into chaos.

Hours passed, and suddenly Kate opened the door to Harry's room. They all looked at but nobody said a word.

She rubbed the sleep from her eyes and looked around the room taking in the gathering. Turning to Harry she asked, "Are you better?"

"Almost back to normal," he said grinning.

"Good, because there is a lot of work to do."

Tom turned to Harry. "She's got the answer." He hobbled over to give her a hug, kissed the top of her head and grinned. "You've got a plan."

"Yes, and we're about to have some company."

Chapter Seventeen

"Ah company, do you mean me?" a voice came from behind her.

Kate whirled and then smiled at the man behind her. "Hey, Des, no, I wasn't talking about you though you will hopefully be part of the solution. I'll tell you guys, my brain has been going ballistic coming up with Wylie Coyote plans to solve this problem and the longer I slept the worse they got, so brace yourselves."

Tom laughed and looked around the room. "And now the fun begins. Okay, Sis, lay it on us"

Kate looked at them, took a breath, and began. "The temperature isn't supposed to moderate until the middle of next week and the snow is just now slowing down, so this is going to require a search in the snow for that bastard. He could be anywhere, either in my woods, on Connelly's land or in the state park. It's all wooded and we will need six to eight officer/dog teams who can track wearing snowshoes and use a gun accurately. At the same time we'll need another group to guard the home front. I doubt even you, Sal, would refer to this as a 'piece o' cake'." Her manager always said this as his go-to answer to any problem.

She put the print out of the photo she'd gotten from the security camera and placed it on the bed. "From what we know, this guy is a hired gun, and from the way he dresses, he's more use to the streets of New York than the woods of Connecticut. There is big money behind him. Someone is willing to pay for us to be killed and who, because he could be recognized if he did it himself, is is happy to shell out big bucks to remain anonymous.

"Everyone will need to know what our target looks like so that he can't just walk up to any of the houses in the neighborhood and start shooting people. Satu can probably send that to the various police stations in surrounding towns and the barracks can put the information on the town's websites, the local TV stations and have the various departments make robo-calls to townspeople. She and Seamus worked well helping to keep us safe at the National Specialty. They're experienced, so they'll know what's expected and are even on Harry's payroll."

Tom raised his eyebrows at that news, but he didn't argue and only said, "Really?"

Search

Kate chuckled. "They're basically sneaky. A characteristic of which I approve wholeheartedly. Apparently, Satu put a tracking device on me before I left yesterday, so she knew exactly where I was every minute I was hunting Harry. That is how Sal found me so easily."

Tom stood. "It's time we talked to the B team."

"I think they'd consider themselves the A team," Kate laughed.

"Probably, but we know differently." Tom threw an arm over her shoulder and ruffled her curls with his hand as they all turned to leave the room so that Harry could get up and dressed.

Harry looked hard at Kate and said, "Des can get you into witness protection in less than an hour and you can take Dillon and Quinn with you. I want you to go. I can't let you be endangered."

Kate walked over to the bed, bent down and kissed him quickly. Standing she said, "Thanks for the thoughtful offer, but it's not going to happen. It would only put off the problem, not solve it and I'd rather not get shot while going down the aisle at my wedding. What we've got to be is proactive. We've only got a week until people arrive for the wedding and I'm not going to allow anyone of them to be put in danger."

Harry opened his mouth to speak but Kate reached out and covered it. "Don't say it. Don't even think of putting off this wedding." She reached into her pocket and hit a key on her phone. "Sal, could you bring the white-board from the kennel and put it in the living room?" As Harry dressed with Des' help, she followed Will into the kitchen and turned on the kettle. She needed a cup of tea and maybe some lunch. She lifted a pot and smelled some of Will's thick chicken-vegetable soup, and saw the loves of crusty bread rising under towels on the back of the stove.

"I picked up an easel as well," Sal said as he pushed the white-board through the doorway and into the kitchen.

"Sal, tell Kate not to be stupid. She's got to go into witness protection." Harry's voice was rough but firm as he appeared in the doorway.

"No can do. You might as well save your breath. She won't go, and to be perfectly frank, I think we need her." He turned to Kate. "Well, Boss, what's the plan?"

Des opened his mouth to say something but Sal silenced him with a raised hand and pointed at Kate. She grabbed her tea and went into the living room. Setting her tea by the white-board and taking a marker, she wrote Problems in the upper left corner of the board and drew a line blocking off a third of the white-board. Under this heading, she numbered one through ten. Turning to the top of the larger area of the board, she wrote Plan and below that using a green marker, she quickly drew a map of the woods, filling in landmarks and access roads. Then using a brown marker, she marked the trails through the forest. Finally, using a red marker, she broke the map up into a grid of six sections.

Setting down her marker, she turned to Sal, placed her hands on her hip and asked, "Doable?"

"Kate," Harry interrupted, "You can't have your friends go after a stone-cold killer."

Search

Sal studied the board for a minute and said, "We'll need to clear it with the troopers, but I can have Satu set it up as a conference call. I think, after doing so well on their tests yesterday, they'll all want in, especially since it will be added to their resumés. They'll need to pick up winter trekking equipment if they don't have it, for both themselves and their dogs. The master list was included in their course manuals and I think most of them stocked up when we got the bulk discount for them."

Des had been watching and now interrupted. "Am I looking at a search grid to be worked by six teams?"

Sal smiled and looked at Kate. "This guy is a smart one. Figured it out first try."

"Before we get this plan underway," Kate said, "we have to outline the problems. The first is snow tracking. Though it will be new for our guys, I suspect that our target will never have dealt with the problem of being tracked without dark alleyways to duck into. Second is that we will need to coordinate everyone. Sean and Satu can do that and set up the kitchen as headquarters." Writing each topic on the board as it was discussed, they had filled the board with problems and suggested solutions quickly.

Sal had pulled out his phone and was soon texting. "Don't worry, Harry, she's not going to try this with amateurs. You forget the business we run here, which has grown to be about a third of our income." His phone buzzed and he checked the text. Then he looked at Kate. "Where's your tablet?"

"On the kitchen table."

Sal was gone less than a minute and was hitting send on his phone when he sat again. Des picked up his chair and moved over where he could watch what was going on. Sal had just opened Skype on the tablet when a series of dings sounded.

Kate had been busy adding details to her map and filling in information on their man. Then she added a list of equipment at the bottom. She pulled out her phone and photographed it, sent it quickly to the tablet so Sal could upload it as he began the conference call.

Kate stood next to Harry holding his bandaged hand. She could tell by the tension in his body, he was upset because she was putting herself in danger. But the truth was; there *was* no safe place for her to hide until the threat was stopped. The puppet master needed to be found.

Questions and answers went back and forth. Finally, there was an agreement and Sal's final count was six teams, those who'd been part of yesterday's test. Sal wrapped things up by telling them the paperwork with all the details would follow. They agreed upon an arrival time of eight o'clock tomorrow. The room fell silent. Everyone seemed to have realized at the same time, the significance of tomorrow being Saturday, though no one said a word. It would be only one week until the wedding. So little time.

Dillon stood and went to the back door and barked. Kate looked at the clock and realized that the dogs needed out and people needed the late lunch Will was cooking. She stood and said, "I'm going to let out these dogs and check the kennel then Will and I can fix lunch for everyone."

Sal stood, "Sorry. Kate, you can fix lunch and I'll handle the dogs and the kennel. I hate to do this to you, Boss, but I agree with Harry that making yourself a target by walking around outside by yourself would be putting too much temptation for our nasty friend. I know it's not your style to let other people handle problems that you usually manage, but you've got to suck it up and follow the rules or the your plan won't work."

Kate looked around the room at concerned faces, all male. With so much testosterone in the room, any urge to argue would be a waste of breath. She nodded. "Okay, I won't fight you. Lunch will be ready in about ten minutes. She went to go help Will, when Harry grabbed her hand, wincing from the pain. He nodded to the others as he pulled her into his room and closed the door. Kate stood in front of him, staring at the door, waiting. Finally, as the pull on her hand got stronger, Kate turned to look at Harry. He pulled her hand to his chest and reached for her cheek, turning her head and forcing her to look at him. His hand slide to her neck holding her face so they were nose to nose.

"Kate, Sweetheart, I love you more than anything. You scared me to death, last night when you rescued me, but at the same time, you were the most beautiful sight in the world. Lying there, I remembered all of the scary times we've had. Now I've pulled this terror down on you by bringing a mob threat into your life. But Kate, I would be lying to myself if I wished you safely hidden from danger. I am slowly coming to realize that you are right. We are a team. You complete me. I can no longer fight alone. You asked me to be your partner, not just your husband." Harry sighed and kissed her gently. "I want to be your partner. I won't ask you again to go into hiding nor will I treat you as a fragile helpless flower. A flower does not rescue the man she loves nor lift someone weighting as much as a whale with the strength of jello onto a toboggan. A flower does not keep him alive. Does not risk her own life to bring him to safety from right under the nose of the enemy. You are not a delicate flower, my Kate. You are my avenging angel. I promise I will shake off this drug and get stronger so that I can fight beside you. If I slip and try to be overprotective—just slug me." Then he kissed her, not so gently this time. "By the way, the plan you've set up is brilliant."

Chapter Eighteen

Kate was smiling when she left the room, passing Des and Tom, and her brother Will who reached out to hug her as she went by. When she reached the kitchen, she lifted the lid on the pot of Will's thick stew, simmering gently on the stove, and opened the oven door to breathed in the smell of bread baking. She opened the refrigerator and pulled the apple pie she'd made for Harry's homecoming and placed it on top of the stove by the vent, and covered it with a dishtowel to help it begin warming.

After setting out the dishes, she set the table, and let her mind wander over the relationship she'd had with Harry since they met. It had been fraught with danger over and over again in those ten months. Their lives had been threatened repeatedly.

Harry had been shot—twice. But yesterday, it hadn't even crossed her mind that going after him might be dangerous. Maybe they really had become a team. She heard the timer go off for the bread and stood, pulling the wonderful smelling crusty loaves from the oven as she heard the men coming.

Kate placed a stack of soup bowls in front of Will's chair, transferred the bread into two baskets and put several butter dishes within easy reach. Then she turned on the kettle for her tea and began pulling beers from the refrigerator. The door to the kennel opened and Sal, surrounded by four dogs, entered the room.

"Ah, exactly what I needed." He said reaching for a beer and accepting a bowl of stew and a hunk of bread as it was handed to him. He sighed. "Perfect."

Kate pulled biscuits out of a tin and stood still. Three dogs sat immediately, but Quinn couldn't resist rushing to greet Des before joining the lineup. "Rory, Liam, Dillon and Quinn, go lie down." Kate told them, handing each their treat and then moved to the chair next to Harry.

Des looked at the dogs, leaned over and asked, "I know the others, Kate, but who is Rory?"

"He's Liam's father, and therefore Dillon's grandfather, and Quinn's great-grandfather. He's fifteen and has begun slowing down, but he likes to think he can keep up with the young guys."

Tom hopped up on his good leg and pulled out her chair before Harry could try. Conversation ranged from what needed doing, to stories of Harry's adventures back when he was with the bureau in Washington.

Search

Kate listened, and relaxed, letting some of her stress abate. She had unwound enough that she was leaning against Harry when her phone went ding at the same time Sal's did. She gazed at the screen and turned pale. Looking around the table she said, "Mom." Their mother had arrived home from work. She was someone they'd failed to add to the problems column. Her mother lived in a world of mathematics and didn't deal with life's challenges. She needed to be removed from the equation as quickly as possible.

Profanity flew from her sons' mouths, filling the room until Kate held up her hand and said, "I've got a plan. Will, I want you to call your favorite professor at MIT and get him to arrange a series of talks to extend through Tuesday. She can do a series of master-classes based on her latest book. Tom, book her into the Hilton and make sure she has all the amenities. Will, make sure there's a welcoming dinner tonight. Explain to the professor that your sister is getting married in a week and is going to commit matricide if her mother isn't away for a few days. Tom, finish up eating, because you've drawn the short straw and get to explain to her that you accepted, on her behalf, a request for her to fill in at the last minute as a speaker for one who'd gotten sick.Tell her that they would love to have her give a the series of talks about her latest book and the insights it brought to the field. If you can think of any other plums to add to the mix feel free. Let's see it's two-thirty so tell her dinner is at seven. That will give her a chance to pack, get there, check into the hotel and still make it to the dinner. Tell her she should take Gram since the hotel has a spa."

"Done."

Kate picked up her spoon and began eating. Sal looked up from his phone. "Grace is on board and is packing."

Harry passed her a slice of warm buttered bread and smiled, mouthing the words "I love you." Des asked if she wouldn't come work for the bureau and everyone laughed. She looked around and smiled. "This does mean that whatever this thing is it must be finished before Wednesday. Des, do you think that you could find an agent/reporter who wants to write an in-depth article on The New Working Woman and plant her in my studio starting tomorrow, and covering Monday and Tuesday. I don't want the women hurt, but there is no way they'll leave with the finishing touches on my wedding dress to be done."

"I'll take care of it."

"Then, I'm going to go take another nap before I fall face-down in my stew, or rather my empty bowl. Thanks, Will." She stood and signaling Liam and Rory to stay with Harry and took Dillon and Quinn into her room. They had the plan. Now all they needed was for it to work.

When Kate opened her eyes she saw that dusk was settling. She started to move but found herself pinned by the weight of an arm holding her tightly. She heard a click and Sal's head peeked around the door.

"I found him."

Des looked in and smiled. "Supper in fifteen minutes. Your brothers will be here as well as a girl named Satu."

The door shut and Kate looked over her shoulder to find a pair of beautiful green eyes watching her. She rolled over so that she was facing Harry, and her hand reached up to stroke his cheek. "How do you feel?"

"Back to normal. If we were married, I would show you," he grinned, wiggling his eyebrows. Kate giggled, happy to see Harry's humor back.

"Soon. I'm looking forward to it. But we're about to have my four brothers on site and they will happily pull you off my bed, and read you the riot act, so I think that we should get up before they begin protecting my honor."

Harry rolled off the bed and stood as Kate threw off the covers, sat up, put on her shoes and grabbed a heavy sweater to slip over her head.

They had just reached the kitchen when the front door opened and everyone walked in. The smell of roasting chicken filled the air. Will carried a basket from which he took a large casserole with mashed sweet potatoes, another with broccoli in a cheese sauce and a basket of rolls. Nobody fought him when he took over the kitchen, taking the chickens from the oven where it had been staying warm and put the casseroles in to warm up. Then he slipped the rolls onto a cookie sheet, and slid them into the warming oven.

Will had helped her choose her stove when she'd moved into her little house. It turned out to be a top of the line commercial appliance, with all the bells and whistles, which Kate was glad to have on days like today. He filled the kettle, then got the coffee going and opened a bottle of white wine.

Soon they were comfortably seated and the food was on the table. Platters of chicken slices were passed around, followed by the casseroles and rolls. Those who wanted wine had it. Kate found a cup of tea at her elbow and looked up to see Harry putting one by his plate. They chatted as though this were a normal dinner. Tim talked about the upcoming basketball season and how they expected to do. Satu mentioned a new piece of software that could be used to identify cell phone owners and location. Will spoke about the conference he'd pulled off for their mother to speak at, beginning tomorrow at MIT. He'd managed to get four speakers including their mother, and it would run through Tuesday. Tom added that both their mother and grandmother should be settled into their hotel in Boston and be getting ready to go out to the dinner that would launch the conference.

Des asked about their training program so Sal filled everyone in on the details. He pointed out that they hadn't really had a chance to run a snow search up to now so this was extra training for which the state troopers weren't being charged. The benefit was that this was a live situation, though he pointed out that their last training session had become a live session when this guy decided to target Kate and start shooting while she was unarmed and playing bad guy. Knowing these teams, they would probably end up competing as they did in practice exercises to see how fast they could make the arrest. It will definitely add to the enthusiasm as they work. The fact that the object of tomorrow's search had already shot at their trainer will add to the reality.

In this last search test, Kate was the 'object'. She was very tough to find because she grew up in these woods and knows every little creek, rock and hidey-hole. Any of the men who had thought that the 'little girl' would be a cinch to find were proven wrong. And when the roles are reversed, she finds them in record time.

"Dillon finds them. I'm just along for the walk." Kate put in.

Chapter Nineteen

"We're not going to have Kate out in the woods with this guy?" Tim asked, concerned.

"No, but she'll be coordinating the search. We'll be running it in a similar way to the time when Jordi was kidnapped. Surprisingly enough, it was Quinn who managed to startle that kidnapper enough to facilitate the capture." Sal added.

"After Kate got the woman's head spinning with enough psychobabble to have her ready to shoot her accomplice." Harry added, laughing.

"All of the teams taking part in the search have graduated from the program and were certified this week. They'll have the advantage of having worked the area, though not with snow. In a way though, the snow may be an advantage. Moving on snow shoes and cross country skis is relatively silent." Kate pointed out. She smiled across at Satu. "It would be handy if he was wearing one of Satu's handy little tracking devices so we could just push a few buttons on a cell phone and have a blinking light saying 'here I am.'"

Conversation became distracted for a few minutes when the now hot apple pie and ice cream appeared on the table. Kate did the honors with her pie and Harry added ice cream for those who wanted it, which turned out to be everyone.

Des groaned, "Foyle, I thought you were marrying Kate for her looks and brains, but now I know it's for her cooking. This is the best pie I've had in forever."

Kate laughed. "Thanks, Des. Actually, Harry's a good cook as well, so you have a standing invitation to dinner. My grandmother made sure that all of us learned to cook well."

"You'll get to sample the family's cooking at Thanksgiving. We all cook. Will does the turkey, Tom the rolls, Gram the vegetables, Kate the desserts, Seamus the salad and I do the appetizers." Tim told him.

"What does your mother make." Des asked.

A chuckle went around the room. Tom finally said, "As a cook, our mother is a fantastic mathematician. She can burn water so we don't let her anywhere near the kitchen. Now that she has an electric tea kettle, she's allowed to make her own tea. My father cooked for the family while we were growing up. That was why it was so important for him and Gramps to work at home. Mom would go off to teach at Yale and we'd come home from school to find snacks and dinner waiting for us no matter when she got home. When both Dad and Gramps had to be away, my grandmother would be there. With Kate and Harry building a home that will become part of this family complex, their kids will grow up surrounded by that kind of support as well."

"The workmen break ground on the house while we're on our honeymoon," Harry added while scraping the last bits from his plate. "We should be able to move in during the last part of February or early March provided that the weather cooperates. We'll live here while they build the main house. After we move, they'll convert this into my business offices. The best part is that Kate designed it so that it doesn't impact the dog yards or the kennel, so these guys' routine," Harry bent to scratch Quinn's head, "will continue undisturbed."

"The foundation and cellar won't take long. The house is being built as we speak and will be brought in section by section on flatbed trucks and put together using a giant crane. Then, once all the sections are hitched together, and the heating, wiring and water connected, they'll come do the final siding on this place to match." Kate told them."

"How many bedrooms?" Des asked.

Kate paused for a minute and then answered, "Five."

"Way to go, Harry." Des teased. Kate just blushed.

Harry grinned and wrapped his arm around Kate's shoulder. " I've told Kate I never back down from a challenge."

Kate noticed that Satu had had her nose buried in her tablet since she finished her pie. Whatever she was working on held her complete attention to the point where she jumped when Kate said her name. "What has you so enthralled, Satu?"

Search

"Oh, I did not wish to be rude but I had an idea that I needed to check before tomorrow morning."

"What is it?"

"Kate said something about wishing this man had a locator so that we could track him. It occurred to me that we were able to track the man in Louisville using his cell phone. Of course, then, we were able to get into his phone number when he called someone. I assume that this terrorist also has a phone."

Silence filled the room. Seamus grinned at Satu, "Brilliant." He 'high-five'd her.

Des whipped out his phone and placed a call to his boss.

Kate walked over to Satu and hugged her. "You go girl." She told her grinning. "Des, when I found Harry last night, this guy was in the cabin on his phone to someone. See if you and Sadie can track any signal from there at that time?"

Satu grinned back at her and then went to work. Seamus began tracking down additional portable charging stations for the use of the searchers as well as sending an email to those attending tomorrow's search to bring phones and any portable chargers they might have.

Sadie called to say that she had checked the numbers called from the GPS coordinates which Satu had sent her during the last 36 hours. After eliminating all of the Killoy's numbers, there were only three. Kate looked at the list Satu handed her. One was Sean's uncle and one was Sean's. The final number was a New York City listing. She circled it and gave it back to Satu to see if she would put it into a program to track it.

Kate began to clear up the dishes and her brothers and Harry helped so it was done in just a few minutes. Seamus and

Satu huddled by their laptops, whispering and typing. Sal and Tim headed out to the kennel to take care of bedding down the dogs.

After half an hour, Satu had the program set up and told Kate the phone was not moving. Checking the clock, Seamus and Satu left promising to be back early tomorrow. Tom took Des to get him settled into his room and what had been a room filled with people, became a room echoing with silence. The silence stretched for several minutes.

Kate came back to the table and sat holding a new cup of tea. Harry looked over at her and noticed that she was simply staring off into a space with silence.

"A penny for your thoughts," Harry said as he pulled out a chair across the table from her.

"With all that's been going on, we never did talk about your search for your father's killer. Did you find out anything?"

"The funny thing is that while I was lying out in the snow, during the few minutes I wasn't thinking about you, I was thinking about what I learned while I was in DC. All I knew about my father's killer was he'd used a knife to do the job and that he wore sneakers, because there was a partial tread in the blood. Bleeding out is a very slow and painful death. Des thought there might be a connection to a killer who had risen in the Boston mob around that time. But then I found a connection to a low level mob boss in Philadelphia who was active several years ago. Unfortunately, after some killings in Philly he seemed to vanish. Des gave me a thumb drive when I left that might hold a further clue, but I've just been too busy to spend much time looking at it."

"Excuses, excuses. Just lying down on the job, I bet." She teased and kissed him. "Look, why don't we go open some of the boxes your mother sent and get them organized. After we label them, we can store each one that doesn't need attention in the bedrooms above the kennel offices."

"Space. You know the way to a man's heart. Let's go."

They had been at it for about half an hour when Kate found a box filled with loose photos. "Let's take a break and look through these. There may be some of you as a little kid. I'd love to see them."

"My mother always said she was going to organize all the family photos into albums but it never happened." They took the box to the kitchen where the light was better. Kate grabbed some empty shoe boxes from the back of her closet so they could sort as they went. "This way we can give Sarah the photos of her growing up."

They worked side by side for a while, sorting out photos of Pete Foyle in his different police uniforms as he rose in the ranks. There were also a bunch of Harry's parents, courting, getting married, and in their first apartment. The ones of Harry and Sarah as kids, they just put into boxes, not taking the time to look at them. They'd go through them later once everything was sorted.

Kate opened another photo envelope and pulled out a batch of photos, leaving the negatives behind. She began looking quickly through them but stopped and then went back to start again at the beginning. It was a collection of shots of Pete Foyle standing with a boy who wasn't Harry. The shots were of them together having fun at the amusement park, at a

Red Sox game, at the beach, and sledding on a hill in Boston Common. The fact that the whole roll was only of him with this boy even though it obviously covered a number of seasons seemed odd. Kate studied the face of the boy. She didn't know if Harry had any cousins, but this kid didn't look anything like him. He didn't look Irish at all. She looked up to see Harry looking at a photo of his father with a young Harry, probably only two or three years old. He was staring at the photo and there were tears in his eyes. Kate set aside the photos she was going through and leaned in to hug him.

"This was when my dad still loved me. I was his little man. He'd take me to the station and brag about his wonderful son. It wasn't too long after that when I started making him uncomfortable with my math ability. But back then, I was his son and he was proud of that."

Kate looked at him and finally said, "If it helps, I can tell you I understand. Your father didn't understand you because you were into math, and my mother didn't understand me because I wasn't."

"Sorry to bring down the mood." He said placing the photo into the box. "What have you got there?"

"I found some photos of your father with a boy but it obviously isn't you. Who is he?"

Harry picked up the stack of photos and flipped through them and then went back to do it again. As he was about to begin again, Kate asked, "Who is the kid with your dad?"

He tore his gaze from the photos and stared at her. "I have absolutely no idea."

Chapter Twenty

Kate moved her chair closer to Harry's and took each photo after he finished with it and placed it on the table. When he studied the final one, they both stared at the spread of pictures. What it showed was a man and boy, very happy, bonding with each other. If she didn't know better, she'd think they were father and son. Reaching out, she flipped the first one over and checked the date when they'd been printed. Pointing to the date, she asked, "Were you still at Caltech then?"

"No. I was at MIT. It was my first year there. My parents had convinced me that Sarah was too upset by my return to have peace in the house, so since I had a full scholarship including room and board, I should live on campus. It was only fifteen minutes from home, but I didn't feel welcome, so I tended to stay on campus."

"Let me get this straight. You had been living apart from your family for years, since you were eight years old going on nine. You finally manage to make it home as a young teenager. You were working on your second PhD locally at MIT just fifteen minutes from where you lived but you were told not to stay there. You were sent away again with your parents not making any effort to assume their parental role. What was wrong with them? I mean, I have had problems with my mom for years, but she never threw me out of the house."

"It wasn't their fault. I was too different for them to be comfortable. My father wanted a normal child, not one who was doing differential equations in kindergarten. He obviously wanted…, he wanted this." Harry's large hands spread across the photos. "And, it looks as though my father got just what he wanted." Harry pushed back his chair and walked through the living room and into his bedroom, closing the door softly. Kate watched him go, aching to reach out and comfort him. However, she realized that nothing she could say or do would wipe out the pain he was feeling. He would have to work his own way through it. She only hoped that he'd come to her when he was ready to accept the love that she offered and realize that his loving his parents could not make them capable of showing their love for him.

She'd recently, after years of assuming that her mother didn't respect her, learned that she was actually quite proud of what she had built. Her mom still didn't understand every choice her daughter made, but she no longer assumed that her choices were wrong just because they weren't choices that her mother would ever consider for herself. Her mother-in-law-to-be had a lot of bridge mending to do as far as Kate was concerned, if she expected to be warmly welcomed into their family.

Kate had only visited Harry's mother once. It had been a somewhat stilted visit. She was taken aback by Kate's career choices, and wasn't a fan of dogs, another reason to keep visits to a minimum. His sister Sarah needed to talk to Harry as well. That childhood friendship had been torn apart by their parent's choices. From what Sarah had revealed when she was here to see the dress, Kate was beginning to feel that at least that relationship wasn't without hope. She gazed out at the dog yard. The pups were all relaxed and collecting icicles on their coats. Kate gathered up the photos and put them back in their envelope. Then she put them in her room. If Harry needed alone time, he'd have it.

She let the pups inside. Since the guys had fed them earlier, she just told them to go lie down, made sure the doors were locked, and then she went into her bedroom leaving the door to the kitchen slightly ajar. She'd sleep better being able to hear any disturbance in another room. Plus, she just felt safer with all her dogs around her. She needed sleep . Tomorrow she was going to need to be working along on all cylinders if they were going to catch this guy. Plus, he was just a pawn, a hired gun.

The one they really needed to stop was the puppet-master who was pulling the strings. Their danger wouldn't end until he was behind bars. Her mind fought sleep as she tried to think of who this puppet-master could be, but eventually, sleep won out.

Kate woke to the shock of a cold nose being shoved down the neck of her pajamas. She yelped. Quinn smiled back at her, as he lay across her, pinning her under the covers. Dillon barked at his son, probably telling him that dogs weren't allowed on furniture, but Quinn just wagged his tail and snuggled closer. Before she could order him off, the bed was suddenly covered with white wriggling bodies. "Off" Her scream of off was muffled by the quilt which she'd pulled over her head to protect herself from so many Sammie feet.

"Out!" Harry shouted, sliding open the door. Suddenly all the weight disappeared. She peaked out from beneath the quilt to see her fiancé grinning at her from the foot of the bed. "Rise and shine, sleepy-head. You've got thirty minutes until all the searchers will be here and Padraig just called to say they'll be here in fifteen minutes.

With a yelp, Kate was on her feet, grabbing clothes and heading for the bathroom. Harry snagged her arm just before she disappeared and kissed her. Then he shoved her into the bathroom with a swat on her bottom. Kate heard the sound of her brother's voices and hoped that meant that breakfast was happening. Now that things were moving forward, she had an appetite.

Five minutes later, she joined her family, plus Harry, Satu, and two minutes later, Maeve and Padraig arrived. Maeve hugged her and said, "My brilliant husband found a shortcut on a back road and we got here quicker. It is so good to see you again." Letting go she moved to hug Tom and was startled by the crutches. "What happened to you?"

"A gift from the guy we're trying to catch. He stretched razor wire across the trail and it caught me. The ankle broke when I fell. I think I'd like five minutes with this monster when he's caught." Tom grumbled but returned her hug and pulled out a chair for her to sit. "Ah, Harry, I'm glad you're feeling better. Agnes said you were sick when we chatted last night."

"You didn't tell..." he said, a look of panic on his face.

"Of course not. Agnes is very talented at decoding, but this type of investigation is not part of her skill set. Ah, Seamus, who is your friend?"

Seamus introduced Satu just as Des walked in. Maeve greeted him like a long lost nephew. The kitchen was now filled to overflowing. The men began heading out to the barn to meet the search teams. Will already had breakfast going out there so the teams would be well fed before they started out. Harry and Padraig took over serving breakfast inside and they all ate quickly. As they finished, the space at the table began being filled up with laptop computers. Then Satu, with Seamus' help connected them. Kate pushed her computer over to Seamus so he could load the program they were using, but he just handed it back telling her, "I loaded it yesterday while you slept. I made your computer the master that can talk to all the teams at once or to individuals. Satu's computer will back yours up as well as connect to the barracks. He pulled up the program on her laptop. Eight small boxes appeared around her screen, in lines of four.

Seamus glanced at Harry several times looking uncomfortable as he set things up. "Umm, Harry? Could I talk to you for a few minutes?" he finally said.

"Sure, what's up?"

"Ah, could we go into the whelping room? I need to show you something." Harry raised an eyebrow at Kate, but she shrugged. Satu kept her eyes firmly on the screen in front of her. So he followed Seamus down the hall to the whelping room beyond the kitchen. Rather than going to the closets where Kate kept all her camping gear, he headed to a long counter covered with scales, stacks of baby blankets, and boxes of items necessary to have on hand when puppies are born. He started opening a cupboard, but then stopped.

Closing the door most of the way to muffle the sound of information Kate was feeding the searchers, Seamus cleared his throat took a breath and began. "You know when you gave me the business credit card to buy the equipment we used to bring down the guys you were after at the National last month? Sadie said I could use my judgment about what was needed. Well, when this came up, I contacted my trainer and used the card to buy what we needed from his stock. I got certified on the same model so it's legal."

"This would be a fascinating discussion if I had a single clue as to what you're talking about."

"I've been taking UAV instruction and have qualified to be part of a SAR/UAV volunteer group. The only problem was I didn't have the equipment. I mentioned to Sadie that I'd finished my training and got my license and she okayed the purchase."

"Question, what is UAV?"

"Oh, sorry, it's an unmanned aerial vehicle. A drone. They've begun using them for Search and Rescue all around the country and in more than forty other countries. They're cheaper than helicopters and can get in close as well as transport equipment or medicine to inaccessible areas. Ours is equipped with two cameras, one with infrared heat sensing. It has GPS, and I added a pair of Lume cubes to light an area at night which could really help the searchers. The battery pack has a flight charge length of half an hour but I have extra batteries if needed. The claw-arms can carry up to forty-four pounds so it can transport medical supplies or a stretcher."

"How come I didn't know about this?"

"Sadie said you had gone dark so for me to just find what we might need and get it. It was pricey but she said not to worry and to go ahead since I had the business credit card. I was going to tell you when you got back but then you got kidnapped. Then you got involved in the search set up, so this was the first chance I had to tell you. Sadie said you wouldn't mind, but if I've done anything wrong…"

"Let me get this straight. You have a drone with a camera which can fly over the woods and search for our man and you're trained and licensed to fly this thing. Can it be linked so that we can get the visual fed to us in real-time?"

"Yea, I was tinkering with that feature last week so it's hitched to my laptop. Satu's running a feed to the closed circuit so it should be visible on all our feeds. She is just finishing it now."

"Where is this drone?"

"I put it in here to keep it away from the dogs, since there are no litters due now."

"Get it out. I have to see this thing. Oh and Seamus," he said laughing, "you just shot to the top of my favorite 'about-to-be-brother-in-law' list."

Seamus grinned and opened the cupboard. "Here it is. It looks like a cross between a helicopter and a raptor. Do you want me to demonstrate how it works?"

"Absolutely, but give me a minute to go settle in the kitchen. I want to watch everyone's face when this newest member of the team arrives." He strolled back into the kitchen and, grabbing his cup from the table, went to make a fresh cup of tea.

Kate looked up. "What was that about or can't you tell me?"

"Your brother is a genius. He's come up with something that is going to make our work here exponentially easier."

"I know he's a genius, they all are. But what's he doing to help in the search?" Suddenly Dillon woke, jumped up and started barking at the ceiling. Quinn began racing around in circles, barking and leaping in the air. "Hey! What the…, what's happening?" Kate stared at the far right screen. Up until a few seconds ago it had shown the satellite image of the woods behind the kennel. Now it showed the kitchen, with her and Satu sitting at the table and Harry making tea. Whipping her head around and up, she spotted a flying robot hovering over their heads. It lowered itself gently until one of its dinosaur like arms reached down, picked up Harry's tea cup, and without spilling a drop, moved it to his place at the table, setting it down carefully. Quinn scrambled up onto Harry's chair and jumped, trying to catch it, and succeeding in tangling his paw in

Kate's headset wires. Kate threw off the headset, and tackled the puppy. The drone sailed up across the table landing gently on the back of Scamus' chair at the same time as he entered the kitchen.

Sal and Des had slammed open the back door at that minute and walked into the sound of chaos.

Kate yelled, "Quiet! Sit!" The dogs stopped barking and sat.

Looking at the large dinosaur-like object perched on the back of a chair with two dogs poised to attack it, Sal yelled, "What the hell is that?"

Des grinned. "When did you guys get a drone? Wow, that's a beauty."

"That's a drone?" Sal grumbled. "I thought they were little things that kids flew. That thing's as big as an eight year old."

"Rex is not a toy," Seamus interrupted with pride in his voice. "He's a viable member of this team. He can scan the area and help direct the search teams. He can transport materials to inaccessible areas. Plus he can see in the dark with infrared thermal scanning to track people by their body heat."

"You seem to know a lot about this thing, Mr. Hotshot Killoy. It's certainly ugly as sin. Do you know how to make this thing fly?"

"I got my pilot's license two weeks ago."

Des had been grinning as he stared at the drone. "How did you get it perch itself on the back of your chair. It's like it your pet." Moving to the table, he spotted the video feed of all of them and asked, "How soon can we get this in the air?"

Chapter Twenty-One

"Satu is working the video feed. Once I discover the GPS coordinates for the start point we're ready." Seamus looked at his sister.

"The best place to start this search is the last place he was seen: the cabin. Sal, the troopers did say they checked the cabin?"

"Absolutely, inside and out even under the porch"

"They looked under the porch? What about root cellar?"

"Root cellar? What root cellar?"

"Dammit!" Came the shout in her the earphone she had dropped on the table when she was wrestling Quinn. Sean's voice came through loud and clear. "There's a trapdoor under one of the throw rugs in the kitchen which leads to a ten by ten cellar. While we were looking for him up above, he was hiding down there, laughing his stupid head off. This also means he had access to winter gear. The heavy-duty gear, skis, snowshoes, packs, supplies, even parkas, and boots are stored there to keep the animals getting at them out of season. If he found the cellar, he is kitted out with everything he needs to go anywhere he wants in the forest, snow or no snow. Damn, damn, damn," Sean's self-recrimination was fierce. "My uncle made me clean the damn thing every summer during high school. How could I forget?"

Kate's heart plummeted. This meant he could move easily anywhere in her woods and the surrounding area. If he knew how to use cross-country skis, he could have used the trails to travel out of the area. If he was good, he could be halfway to Litchfield by now. She pulled on her earphones and tapped a few keys on her computer. "Update on our target," she broadcast. "Because of his finding access to cold weather equipment including skis and snowshoes, he will be able to keep warm and move fast. We are bringing in a drone to do aerial surveillance. Hopefully, we'll spot him so that you can move in. Remember he's armed. He should be wearing a parka and pack and is on either cross-country skis or snowshoes. Oh, and guys, if something that looks like a flying dinosaur appears overhead, you will just be meeting the newest member of the team so please, hold your fire."

Seamus tucked the controller into his parka, grabbed the walkie-talkie Harry shoved into his hand, then lifted the drone off his chair. "Where should I launch from? To get the best view, it pays to be as high as I can so you have the best view of the drone in action because of Rex's ability to send photos of where it is, we obtained a waiver that Rex would have to be within my sight. Also, the snow has picked up. It looks like we've added a couple more inches in the last half hour."

"How about the little cupola on top of the kennel? There is even a widow's walk. Use the pull-down ladder in the closet of the second bedroom to reach it. The elevation is as high as the barn and the windows open." Kate told him as her eyes continued to scan the screens before her.

"Team four, you are approaching a blackberry bramble. Advance with care and keep the dogs close to you. We don't need thorns in paws. You may have to chop your way through them." Kate stretched, glancing up from the monitors, and dropped a hand on Quinn's back to restrain him as he began to follow Seamus.

"I'll go help him," Des said, grabbing his jacket and not to be left out, Padraig was right behind him.

"Boys and their toys. No matter what age they are, they're all the same," Maeve muttered.

Sal moved to the counter to use the coffee machine, and made a cup to go. "I'm going to check the dogs and sweep the perimeter. You two stay put," he said pointing at Kate and Harry. "Satu, warn me if they try to leave."

"Sal." Kate groaned. "We're not kids."

"Yeah, right. You keep believing that. Going after killers with only a pair of dogs for protection." He muttered as he stomped out. Maeve chuckled and moved to sit quietly next to Satu, in order to follow her progress.

Harry slid his chair behind her and reached for Kate's shoulders, his thumbs moved in circles pressing into her tense muscles, until she dropped her chin to her chest and sighed. He leaned in and kissed her gently on the back of her neck and slid his chair back next to hers.

Kate turned in surprise, realizing he was trying to divert her stress, smiled, "Thanks."

"I am so sorry about bringing this whole mess down on you."

"Stop saying that. This isn't your fault. Obviously, someone has a problem with you and that is on them."

"Unfortunately, that problem is causing you pain."

"Harry, remember, what we're doing next week. The vows say, 'for better for worse.' This comes under the heading of worse, but we can handle anything so long as we're together, right?"

Harry stared at her, the sadness in his expression tearing at her heart. She lifted her hands from the keyboard and placed them on his cheeks, repeating, "Right?"

"Right." He murmured, his voice barely audible in the silent room.

"Damn straight it is and you had better remember that fact, or I'll set the dogs on you and Quinn will lick you until you're screaming like a girl."

A shadow of the grin she was looking for flickered across his face. "Scream like a girl?"

"He's relentless."

A chuckle came from the other side of the table and Kate looked over to find Maeve and Satu grinning. The monitor in front of her flickered and the scene changed showing the woods from the air with a view of tiny men and dogs working

Peggy Gaffney

their way through the trees and brush. Kate became fascinated as the view moved over the main trail heading in the direction of the cabin.

Kate heard Gurka's voice. "I'm spotting your raptor overhead, Kate. Connelly, come over to this cabin and tell us what's missing." The men converged on the cabin. They disappeared inside.

Soon Sean's voice came through. "He's got a parka, and long johns, and ski boots, but he didn't take skis. He took the old-fashioned snowshoes, the wooden trail shoes. Two to one, he's never been on them before".

She would guess he might have seen them in a movie once. If he's trying to run wearing them, he's not going to be moving fast and his leg muscles are going to start hurting soon. Plus he's wearing them with ski boots. Idiot! I think the closest this guy has ever been to nature is a walk in Central Park. I found a dress shirt stuffed into one of the packs, so I'll bag it. The dogs can get their scent from that which will help."

"Are you sure it's his?" Kate asked.

"Pink silk?"

"Right."

"Okay everyone, the perp is dressed for the weather and on snowshoes. He doesn't show any experience with hiking, especially in snow, so as you track, check the ravines. If he doesn't know what he's doing, he's a good candidate for a fall. If you spot him, remember he's armed. Sean is bringing an object to use for scent detection for the bloodhounds, so work your way to the main trail and someone will bring it to your dogs."

Search

The drone, which had been hovering over the cabin began to rise up giving a wider view of the area. She spotted Sean leaving the cabin at a fast pace behind his Golden, Patrick. Kate watched as Gurka and his shepherd followed. Patrick quartered the area in front of the cabin and raised his head, signaling that he'd picked up the scent. The rest of the men moved in the same general direction. The dogs were now moving fast, and she warned the teams not to let the dog's enthusiasm pull them off their snowshoes.

Suddenly the drone coverage disappeared from her screen. Kate looked at Satu who told her it was okay. "Seamus is pulling it in to put on the heavy-duty battery. We'll be back in about five minutes."

Kate looked at the screen and realized that a lot more time had passed. Glancing around, she noticed that Harry was missing.

"Where's Harry?" She worried he might have slipped out after this guy.

Maeve looked up. "He went into the front bedroom muttering something about a flash drive."

Kate nodded. The drive needed to be checked to find what Des had given him. Harry's kidnapping delayed him. This search didn't need him, so this was a perfect time to check out all that information. If there is a possible tie to this bozo, all the better.

Gurka's voice came up. "Okay, everybody. I want the teams to move into caution mode. We've got tracks. This guy definitely doesn't know how to move on snowshoes. He fell twice and had to struggle to stand following the falls. He's tiring."

Billy's voice broke through as his screen showed a different angle from those who'd gone to the cabin. "Kate, I'm following the same track that Rosco took to find you the other day. He got a good sniff of the guy and seemed to have picked it up again. If the others have his trail and I'm picking something up here, he's got to be heading northwest."

Kate smiled. "Well, that is some good news."

"Thought you'd enjoy that piece of information. Our perp is about to find that the wilds of Connecticut is not Fifth Avenue."

Satu signaled Kate that Rex was back in the air. Kate gave her a thumb's up. She was studying the trail in front of Sean and Gurka when she noticed a flash. It disappeared immediately, but Kate needed to look at it again. "Satu, do that sweep again closer to the ground. I think there is something on the trail."

The drone swung around and repeated the move down the trail only much lower. After a few minutes, the flash shown again. "Stop. Go in for a closer look." The camera on the drone moved in for a close-up and off to the side was a slight flash. Seamus picked up her request through Satu and began to move the drone to the left. And there it was. Tightly strung across the trail was a piece of razor wire.

"Everybody," Kate said as she shifted her contact to an all call. "There is a piece of razor wire stretched across the trail about a hundred feet in front of Sean. It's what this guy used to slice up Tom and is really nasty stuff. Try taking a couple of branches to weight it down for the first cut and get it to wrap around a branch or log. Whatever you do, keep the dogs away from it. I'm sending everybody the drone broadcast showing it up close. Sean, check the surrounding area and find if there is any trace of this guy or his tracks. He may be lying in wait to shoot whomever he snares."

She hadn't realized how tense she'd gotten until Harry's hands rested on her shoulders. She leaned back into him as he massaged her neck. "Did you find anything in the files Des had on the thumb drive?"

He chuckled. "I was just beginning to go through it when Maeve came in and told me I was sorting it all wrong. She ended up commandeering my laptop and is having a ball. So I went through that box of photos some more and found these." He put two more envelopes of photos in front of her. Keeping one eye on the monitor, she pulled a stack of photos from the first one. It was more of the same with Pete Foyle and the same teenage guy. The first envelope held shots of them on what looked like a camping trip, and the second one showed them at the beach at what looked like the Cape. Still keeping her eyes roughly on the screen, she flipped the photos over, checking for a date. Nothing. She began stuffing the first bunch back into its envelope when she stopped. She gazed at Harry in horror.

He looked back at Kate who was dividing her attention between Harry and the screen. She reached back over her shoulder and grabbed his hand, holding tight. He began to pull away, but she wouldn't let go. Finally, he leaned over and kissed the top of her head.

Peggy Gaffney

"I'm going to go check on Maeve. You and I will talk about this tonight."

"Are you going to be okay?"

"Yeah, I think I am. It isn't the first time he rejected me. I'd just like to know who his substitute son was."

"Maybe Sarah knows. We can't ask her until this is finished, but she may know. Though, if she did, I'm surprised she's never mentioned it when she lashed out at you. She's used everything else." That drew a slight smile from Harry as he turned back toward the bedroom.

Chapter Twenty-Two

Kate had turned her attention back to the screen when Billy called his dog to halt. She studied his screen but couldn't find anything unusual. "Billy, what's up?"

"Not sure, Kate. I thought I heard something moving up ahead and then a yell. I've got Rosco on a short lead and we're moving in slowly. I'm at right angles to where Sean and Gurka are. Randy is behind me off to the left and Eric is moving down the gully. I just passed the area where you pulled in the little girl so I'm staying clear of the drop-off. Everybody knows it isn't the drop which will get you, it's the sudden stop at the bottom. Since I weigh a lot more than your friend Richard's Chihuahua,

I'll leave at least ten feet between me and the edge. Wait. There it goes again. Someone is yelling."

Kate scanned the screen but nobody was having a problem. Sean and Gurka had removed the wire and were moving steadily along the trail. She looked over at Satu. "Can you make Rex pass near Billy?" Clicking onto Billy's screen she asked, "Billy, do you have any idea where the sound is coming from and how far away?"

"West-northwest of my position about a quarter mile, but it's hard to gauge the position exactly with the sound muffled by the snow."

"Thanks. I'll have Rex take a look."

On Billy's screen, everything seemed normal until Rosco jumped up in the air and barked as the drone passed overhead. She now concentrated on the drone's feedback. Flying over the trees it moved quickly, then slowed once past Billy. The trail Billy was on, a little further on, would turn toward the south to connect up with the main trail which ran up to her kennel.

The memory of yesterday and Dillon's fall still fresh, and she told Satu to have Seamus sweep the edge of the gully moving close enough to spot people. For about three minutes all she saw was snow on rocks with the occasional scrub piece of brush. Then there was a flash of red.

"There!" she shouted.

Rex turned around and focused his camera on the red spot below. The camera zoomed in, showing a man, lying amid the snowy rocks. He moved his arm trying to push himself up. Kate signaled Satu to move the drone higher, to give a better picture of the location of where on the trail the man had apparently fallen. She switched the feed so that everyone had that same view. Kate spotted Billy, Sean, Gurka, Danielle, and Randy all heading toward that spot along their trails and Eric approaching from below. Kate signaled for the zoom lens to move in for a close-up of the guy again. His arm was moving, and Kate noticed he had something in his hand and waved to indicate a need to bring UAV even closer. The camera zoomed in and Kate spotted the shape of what he was holding.

"Everyone, this is a warning! The suspect is armed and dangerous. He has a gun and I can tell you from experience that he likes to use it. Eric, stop where you are. When you go around the next outcrop you'll be an easy target." With the connection on all call she said, "Gurka, Sean, you're almost up to the spot where he went over. Move forward slowly. Sean, if you move off the trail to the right, there's that overlook rock we used to climb as kids. You can climb up on that, and view him without him getting a clear shot."

She studied the monitor as he left the trail and circled around until he was on the part of the bolder which gently sloped up and out over the gully. As he dropped to his knees, he brushed off as much of the snow as he could, and worked slowly toward the top. Reaching for the edge, he leaned over so he could see their quarry below. The man's upper body was moving, but one of his legs was lying at an odd angle.

Sean pulled back and spoke quietly. "Do we have an ID on this guy yet?"

Des' voice came from the walkie-talkie beside her laptop. "Kate, I've been listening in and I've just gotten an ID on our friend. The government moves slowly, but eventually, it gets there. Our man is Gaetano Campanelli. He's a hit man for hire. He's associated with the Zuccarello Crime Family in Philadelphia. And you won't be surprised to find, his nickname is Razor. We can pretty much figure how he got that?"

"Sean, did you hear that?"

"Got it. I think I'll go have a chat with Mr. Campanelli."

Kate was holding her breath when she heard the front door open and close and the sound of women's voices. Agnes walked into the kitchen with Cathy right behind her and Maeve bringing up the rear. "Killoy, what the hell is going on here. I'm supposed to be showing Cathy your wedding dress and I walk into what appears to be the control room for a space landing."

Gurka's voice sounded in Kate's ears. "I've got eyes on our man from behind a big hemlock which is leaning over the edge of the gully. He's covered. Any attempt to give us grief and I've got a clear shot."

Sal walked in from the kennel. "Seamus is bringing Rex in to change batteries again. He said to hold off until he's back in place."

Kate clicked her mouse and spoke into her mic. "Hold off for a couple of minutes. Rex is getting a new battery."

"Will do, Kate," Sean answered.

She had switched the incoming to the speakers so that everyone could hear what was going on. Unfortunately, timing, especially bad timing, was what she was dealing with lately as Agnes screeched, "Is that Sean out there? Is he in danger?"

Kate sighed and looked over her shoulder. Harry and Maeve were standing in the living room doorway behind Agnes and Cathy. "Hi, Cathy," she said brightly. "We're doing a winter simulation search to earn extra certification for the teams. I need you to be very quiet. Maeve, perhaps you could take Cathy and Agnes over to the studio to see the dress. You haven't seen it yet either. We should be done here, checking all the equipment and the trooper/dog teams in about three hours.

"Excellent idea," Maeve said quickly picking up her coat. "I'm dying to see it. Agnes, didn't you say it was the best thing Kate ever designed? We don't want to do anything here that will interrupt the simulation. It could hurt their certification. I remember having to do these simulations when I was in MI 5. They were so realistic until you came upon the 'killer' or 'bank robber' and realized that you'd had tea with them after work the day before."

Cathy piped up. "I'd love to hear about your days working for MI 5. Kate says you still like to keep your hand in."

Maeve laughed as she linked arms with the women. "Well, I do have some stories to tell that are both scary and fun."

When they left, Kate looked at Satu and got a thumbs up. She passed on the information that Rex was again in the air and heading toward them. Harry moved into the chair beside Kate so he could see her screen. Kate had Rex's camera zoom in once it was in position over Campanelli. "His leg is twisted and somewhat jammed between two boulders. I can't tell if it's broken, but it might be. To move him out of there with the snow so deep is not going to be fun. It might be easier to drop a harness and bring him up rather than trying to reach him from below and have one of you slip and be out of commission. Sean, why don't you go have a chat with the man?"

While Sean eased up the rock, Kate signaled Satu to pull Rex back so that when the man looked up he wouldn't spot the drone and shoot it. She nodded. The drone's view drew back and now included the whole scene including Sean stretched out on the rock, with his Golden lying next to him and Gurka, holding a rifle pointed at the mobster below him on the landslide.

Sean leaned over the edge and said, "Connecticut State Police, Mr. Campanelli, how are you doing down there?"

The startled man whipped around and fired a burst of about five rounds, completely missing Sean.

Sean rolled over, so he was half on his back, with one arm keeping his dog down. "Now that wasn't very smart. We've got a number of troopers and their dogs up here. They're not too happy that you shot at them the other day. In fact, I think, now that some of the canine officers have your scent, they'd like to be up close and personal with you and give you their opinion of the practice. From what we've been able to see, you seem to have fallen as part of a rock slide and are now wedged halfway down to the bottom of the gully. Is that about it?"

Kate watched Rex's feed which showed the man trying to shift his position in order to pull his leg out from where it was wedged. She also saw that his snowshoe was one of the reasons he couldn't turn it. The snowshoe wasn't one of the small, modern, light-weight ones, but the old-fashioned wooden-framed trail-shoe with a long tail. His right leg was being held aloft, while his left seemed to be crushed beneath him. The snowshoe for that foot lay about five feet below him sticking out of the snow.

Search

"Mr. Campanelli, you never told me how you were doing. I guess you've discovered that the long-tailed snowshoes aren't appropriate for these trails. They're made for walking in cleared areas, like fields and wide groomed trails. It looks as though one of your shoes is wedged between two rocks. You're never going to be able to pull it out. Well, if I were you, I'd release the binding and take your foot out."

"What do you think I've been doing, you stupid cop. It won't let go."

"Ah, so it's wedged. That's probably because your boot is a ski boot. It's not made to be used with snowshoes."

Harry reached for Kate's microphone and said, "Sean, tell him if he uses the knife he's got in the leather case strapped to his leg, he could probably pry up the edge of the boot and make the release work."

Sean chuckled for a second and then raised his voice. "Mr. Campanelli. A suggestion has been made that if you use the knife you're carrying in the leather case strapped to your leg, you can pry up the edge of the boot that's stuck and get the latch to release."

"What knife are you talking about, copper?"

"I'm sorry, did you think that you could come to Connecticut, and we wouldn't know everything about you as soon as you took a shot at police officers, and civilians? Not to mention the blatant murder attempt of Mr. Foyle? I'm sorry, but you're not in the big city now. We do things differently here."

"Yea, well the first cop or his dog who comes after me is a dead man."

Peggy Gaffney

"Okay! That's not a problem. We'll just wait. There are seven of us here, fourteen if you count the four-footed canine officers who work with us. We can just wait. It will be dark soon and be too dangerous to rescue you anyway. We'll just post teams throughout the evening to keep an eye on you. This will allow the rest of us to go back to our base. It's warm and the food is fantastic since we have a five-star chef working with us. Breakfast was excellent. I can only imagine what he'll have waiting for us after we've been tramping around in the snow. Oh, how's your hand feeling? Being hit with a rock the size of a baseball, but a lot harder must have hurt. I hope you didn't break any of the small bones in your hand. It can really affect your grip. Your trigger finger accuracy seems to be off as well. Why don't you go work on your boot? You can let us know later if you decide to be rescued. The snow has stopped so the temperature will be getting down in the single digits tonight. Mr. Foyle can probably tell you that lying out in the snow after dark is not fun."

Sean stopped talking and just settled in to give Campanelli time to stew.

"That went well," Kate said quietly. "He's still pulling on it but since it's a ski boot, it's not going to bend. The unbending sole became stuck under the cross-piece, most likely when he put his weight on it. Wait, there he goes. He's drawing up the leg of his pants and removing the blade. He took off his glove for a better grip. Hmm. That's quite a bruise on the back of his left hand. It's a shame I didn't target his right. Ah, it's working. Okay, he's freed the boot. Now he can turn the foot and the latch should come free." They watched him free the foot and watched it fall. What startled them was the scream that immediately followed.

"What's the matter, Campanelli?" Sean asked.

"My...ankle. It's broken. The pain. You've got to take me to the hospital. I'm hurt. It's your duty as a search and rescue cop. I saw what you guys did at the World Trade Center. You've got to bring me to a hospital."

"I believe you said that the first cop who came after you was a dead man. We are dedicated to rescuing, but not when the person who needs help is armed and threatening us."

"Look, I won't hurt you. I need to get out of here."

"Then, I would suggest you throw your gun and knife into the bottom of the gully. We want to see you do it before we arrange to remove you."

"Okay, I'll toss my gun and my knife." Rex's camera watched as the man first threw the knife. It lodged in a Maple sapling in the gully. This was followed next by the gun which landed in the snow not far from the tree.

Harry leaned over Kate's shoulder and spoke into her microphone. "Tell him he needs to ditch the other gun. The one in the holster at the back of his waist."

Sean spoke up. "That was good, Campanelli, now all that's left is the gun in the holster at the back of your waist. Just dispose of that one please, and then we can proceed."

The close up that Rex's camera got of Campanelli's face was priceless. His head spun around, looking left and right, trying to see who could see him. He moved his leg as he turned and the pain of his ankle had him doubled over. With his good hand, he reached under his coat and pulled out his second gun.

After looking at it for a minute, he threw it. "Okay, you bastards. Get me out of here!"

Chapter Twenty-Three

Sal headed to the barn. "Kate, tell them I'm bringing a harness and the ropes. The only way we're going to get that guy out of that spot is to pull him up. With the slope of the rubble, lowering him is not an option. We will need the basket and the ATV with the trailer on the back. Tim's going to put the plow on the vehicle because both the main and this side trail are under two feet of snow. Tell Gurka we're coming."

Kate passed the word to the searchers in the field. She bowed her head and reached back to work the tension out of her neck. A cup of tea appeared at her elbow and hands took easing out the pain. She sighed. The hands that gently eased those sore muscles began on her shoulders, and she tilted her head to rest on the right hand.

"You know," she said, "not only do we need to get this bozo out of the mess he's gotten himself into, but then we've got to get information from him and find who's behind him pulling the strings. Not to mention, we've got to do this in the next few days."

"I know. Maeve had some ideas that we were discussing before Hurricane Agnes struck. Tonight, after we pull this killer out of the gully, we need to get together with her. One thing we need to make clear to Gurka, before he lawyers-up, is we'd like to chat with him. I think they owe us that." Harry said, watching the screen.

"Sal should question him. Someone put a quarter million hit on you. I wonder what he made for taking me out? Whoever is behind this is not a pauper. He also has good inside connections if he is able to find out I'd be in the woods. Only the troopers knew that."

"I hardly think that they would talk," Harry said.

Billy walked in. "Talk about what?" he asked. "I need to set up the triage for this joker, so Gurka told me to come on ahead."

"Just telling Harry about your conversation in Dunkin' Donuts which this guy used to get at me."

"Yeah, we're sorry about that, Kate. We'll be more careful next time."

"So, we've got a good idea how he found you, though we still don't have any information on who is giving him orders and why. That's what gets me. Why send somebody after you. You aren't hunting for him the way I am."

"Speaking of your search. How did they know where you were? I didn't even know. And, how did they know you left D.C. to come here? They were on you in barely twenty-four hours." Kate turned toward him and waited for an answer.

"I don't have the answer, but someone knew what I was doing which means that there is a mole in the bureau with access to ultra top secret information."

"Well, I can see two reasons for him to send someone after me. The first would be that if he had succeeded, you would stop working on this investigation. Instead, you would be trying to find who was behind my murder. It would not only be a distraction from your work but would mess with your mind by laying on the guilt that you weren't here to protect me. Your work would be the last thing you'd be thinking about."

"Agreed. And what would be the second reason?"

"That killing me would hurt you. This man needs to see you in pain. He needs you to hurt. I listened to what the idiot who grabbed you said when he was complaining to someone on the phone. He wanted to shoot you. But the person who was calling the shots, wanted you to feel anguish. He wanted you to know every kind of hurt. Harry, the man behind this hates you, and it's personal. Somehow or other, you have been involved in with him. Something happened, and he's carried a grudge to the point where he is fixated on causing you an extremely painful demise. If my murder caused you suffering and pain. It would be worth every nickel."

She pulled up Sean's feed. The mobster still sat in the snow halfway down the slope. Danielle, the only female trooper on the search and the lightest, was being helped into a harness by Sal. He had brought the climbing equipment as well as the medical gear and a stretcher on the ATV. The plow on the front had handled the trails well. She was glad that she and her brothers had gone out and cleared them a couple of weeks ago, so they'd be prepared for search practice.

Randy had put his Labrador Retriever on a down and got ready to lower his partner to the injured man below. Gurka told her to stay to the right of their man, so she didn't get into his line of fire. Just in case this idiot tried something. Kate had Danielle do a quick verbal check of her gear and warned her about not trusting any vegetable holds. "Don't depend on any bushes or saplings for support. If they're on that slope, the root systems won't have had time to establish and if you put any weight on them, they'll fall as will you."

"Got it, Kate. I'm ready." She began her descent slowly. Kate switched to Sean's feed because it had a clearer view of the handholds and footholds she'd need to get down and back. She knew the trooper did a lot of rock climbing in her spare time. She was the obvious choice because of her hobby. Randy didn't seem to be having any trouble with her belay. He kept enough slack in the ropes so that she had freedom of movement, but not enough to allow her too much of a fall if she slipped.

She glanced at the drone's feed and saw it had been moved so that it was perched on the handlebar of the ATV. Sal was on the walkie-talkie with someone, probably Seamus. She peeked over at Satu who was speaking softly to someone over her com-line. Suddenly the drone rose, carrying a harness and flew out over the edge of the ravine. Movement in Danielle's feed drew her attention. She had gotten up to Campanelli and was bending over his leg to check his ankle. He moved fast, reaching an arm around her throat and yanking back while he held a piece of razor wire in his gloved hand. She screamed. Grabbing his sleeve. "Get me out of here and let me go or this copper is going to bleed out on this snow."

Everyone froze, except Jake, Danielle's huge, black, Bouvier des Flandres partner. The dog flew over the edge of the gully jumping and sliding until it was almost level with the combatants. "Keep that monster away from me, or he'll get the wire!" Campanelli screamed.

Danielle yelled, "Jake, Platz." The Bouvier immediately dropped to a crouch, not moving.

Both Danielle and Campanelli were focused on him, not noticing Rex as it flew in quickly. The mobster turned at the last second, hearing the sound of the propellers. The drone dumped the harness on his head, grabbed Campanelli, clamping one claw around his arm and using his other one, ripped the wire from his hand which took his glove as well. It then released him, rose and flew out over the gully, dropping it to be caught and tangled in a branch of a maple tree. As it turned to go back toward the now struggling pair, a shot rang out.

Gurka bellowed, "That was a warning. The next will be in your brain if you don't release that officer. I don't care if we bring you in dead or alive, you piece of shit. Raise your hands and put them on your head now, or you won't have to worry about a broken ankle."

Danielle scrambled away from him as soon as she was free. She let out a string of curses that had everyone grinning. She called Jake to her and told Campanelli that if he tried that again, Jake would rip out his throat. Then she set him on hold. "Wache! Gib Laut!" The dog barked, growled, and pawed at the man and goading him to move. The huge Bouvier projected a canine version of Clint Eastwood's 'make my day' attitude — Campanelli froze.

Danielle grabbed the harness and yanked it on him. She attached the rope that would tow him up and signaled them to pull. The man began to rise, yelling as he was scraped by rocks and brush that were hiding beneath the snow.

As he rose past a spot level with Sean, the trooper chuckled. "Be grateful for the pain. We could have not found you until tomorrow in which case you wouldn't be feeling a thing as we dragged you out. If you hadn't been such a dumb-ass, you would have gotten your ankle braced when the officer reached you, but you thought were smarter than mere cops — not. Oh, and I wouldn't pull anything when you get up here. Jake hasn't forgiven you for touching his partner, and I for one would be quite happy to let him go a few rounds with you."

Campanelli growled but kept his mouth shut.

Danielle scrambled easily up the side of the cliff. Jake pawed at the mobster a few more times before following Dani over the edge. Campanelli stayed quiet. Once they got him over the rim of the gully, they shoved the stretcher under him, lifted him onto the trailer and strapped him on. The ATV had been turned around while they were bringing him up and Sal was ready to start the trip home. Sean with Patrick and Danielle with Jake jumped into the vehicle while Gurka made sure the now handcuffed mobster was tied tightly, and then he sat next to Campanelli. His shepherd leaped up next to the immobilized man and panted right in his face.

The rest of the troopers followed on foot enjoying the fact it was still in plow mode, which made the return a mere stroll in a snowy woods. They chuckled, debating if they would all get some credit for this capture. Billy patted Rosco and added, "That drone sure helped. I've got to talk to Seamus about how you get one and how you learn to fly it. I swear if that guy hadn't let go of Dani, I think the drone would have come back and strangled him. Rosco, boy, I couldn't do this without you as my super partner, but it would be fun to have an airborne backup."

Kate smiled as she heard Billy's words in her earphones, and looked around the table. Just then, Seamus walked through the kitchen door carrying Rex on his arm like a falcon and grinning from ear to ear. She and Harry applauded. "Great job, little brother, getting Rex to be a bad-ass. Having him grab the wire was brilliant. I can see you being in demand at searches all over the state."

Harry clapped him on the shoulder and Satu broke with her usual reserve to race around the table and give him a hug. Seamus blushed, but his grin was wide, as they headed to the whelping room to put Rex to bed.

Kate turned back to her bank of monitors to watch the arrival of the ATV at the barn. She noticed that Agnes' car was pulling out of the parking lot and Maeve was being met by Padraig. They both turned as Sal arrived. She watched her great aunt walk over to Gurka as he climbed out of the trailer. Kate didn't hear what she asked, but Gurka shook his head. Then she approached the mobster and spoke to him. The conversation continued as several squad cars and an ambulance drew up. She glanced at the approaching paramedics and said one last thing to the man and then stepped back and joined Padraig heading for her house. They passed Will and Tim strolling into the barn with baskets of food, ready to feed the searchers. Maeve gave each of her great-nephews a kiss on the cheek as she went by them and Padraig patted them on the back.

Satu and Seamus returned from putting Rex away and together with Kate began to take apart the command center. Satu told her that all the feeds from the start of the search were saved as a single file. She then copied the file to Kate's computer and made a copy to send to Sgt. Gurka.

Maeve and Padraig came into the kitchen, and he immediately went to fill the kettle. Maeve signaled for Kate and Harry to follow her and led the way into Harry's room. She glanced at Harry as they followed and once in Maeve shut the door.

"What was going on out there with Campanelli? What did Gurka say?" Kate asked, curious about why her great-aunt needed secrecy.

"Both of you sit." They sat on the bed while Maeve took the overstuffed chair beside it. "I asked Gurka if Campanelli was Mirandized yet. He said no and let me question the man providing I shared anything I learned. I agreed and then went to speak to the mobster. Gurka's shepherd was still on guard duty. Before I asked him anything, I pointed out a few life facts. I mentioned that his two failures had lessened his value as a hit man to zero. Not only was the man who placed the contracts going to be upset that he was out his deposits, but his crime family had lost face by recommending him. I told him, his only chance would be to identify the man who put out the contract as fast as possible if he had any hope of survival. I also recommended that he stay in the custody of the Connecticut State Police as long as possible. They would provide him with the most protection. If they had wanted him dead, he would be. Then I asked for the name. He didn't tell me. But he did mutter something, talking to himself. He said he was already dead. He was trussed up like a Thanksgiving turkey and was being delivered ready for carving directly into the hands of the man he'd failed."

Kate stared at her a minute and then said, "So the man who wants to kill us is one of the 33,533 members of the FBI or the 113,543 members of the Justice Department."

Chapter Twenty-Four

Maeve smiled at Kate. "I think if we work on it, we might be able to narrow those numbers down a little."

"How do you pull numbers out of thin air?" Harry asked her, his mouth open.

Kate looked slightly embarrassed as she raised her shoulders in a shrug.

Maeve placed a hand on Kate. "You should never be uncomfortable with your talents." Kate has been able to do that all her life. She has perfect recall. If she sees something, it's there. Sometimes if she's under stress, she might be slow in making the connection, but the memory is still there,

Search

nonetheless. She probably saw the statistics online when checking out web pages of the FBI or of the Department of Justice.

Harry reached over and hugged her. Kissing the end of her nose as he held her face in his hands, he softly said, "This is one more thing for me to love about you."

Kate looked at him for a minute and smiled. Turning back to Maeve she asked, "How do we find the needle in the haystack?"

"In spite of the fact you two have gained quite a reputation this year for putting away killers and thieves, to say nothing of stopping threats to the country, the people with more than a passing knowledge of you, are very small in number. When you shared your research with me earlier, Harry, I noticed much of the early material was gathered when you were still a teenager."

Harry explained that when his father was murdered, Pete Foyle had been out working on a case involving the mob. He'd only recently risen in the ranks to the level of detective. He'd been a beat cop for a long time, so he was familiar with the streets of Boston and the surrounding area. It was one reason he was proving valuable to the force. He knew most of the runners and fences, the ladies of the evening, their pimps, and the street gang members. He kept a mental list of who had power and who owed whom.

Mob business worked based on power and association. Being connected meant being safe if you stayed in your own territory, so he tended to let other cops do the take-downs of the bad actors he'd spotted. The brass figured he was more valuable as a low key player.

"I was living on campus at MIT. Occasionally, he'd stop by the campus, and we'd go for coffee, but we were really strangers. When he and my mother decided to send me to Caltech, I was in fourth grade. It had seemed a rejection of me. I understood later they saw it as a chance for me to have the best education possible which they couldn't afford.

"The bottom line was, I made my dad uncomfortable. I wasn't a 'normal' kid to him, not the kid you tossed balls with at the end of the day or brought with you when you dropped into the local cop bar. His friends tended to treat me as a freak, a circus performer. They'd sit with him and give me ever harder calculations. As I would give them the answer, I'd see my dad squirm. He stopped taking me places.

"The years we spent apart made it harder when I returned as a teenager. We no longer knew each other. My sister hadn't forgiven me for leaving. She blamed me rather than our parents. So when I returned, and she threw a fit, it was easier for me to move into campus housing. I was on a full scholarship for this PhD.

"Coming by campus to have coffee with me, I think, was his way of trying to repair the breach between us, but neither of us really understood how to go about it.

"The last time I saw him was about two months into the semester. He came by and we went out to have coffee. He told me about a case he was working on. The mob was trying to drag more young kids in, to carry out the grunt work for some of their businesses. They became numbers runners, messengers, small-time thugs to harass business who weren't up to date on protection money. He told me he'd met a kid he was trying to keep from falling into a life of crime. Apparently, the kid's father had been in the mob and had been murdered."

He stopped, and looked reflective for a minute as Kate spoke up. "Harry, is it possible the photos we saw were that kid?"

He looked at her and nodded. "That's what I thought when I saw them. But I think this wasn't a case of trying to save a kid from getting lost in the world of the Boston mob, but rather a case he'd found a kid to be the kind of son he never had. I think the last time we talked, he tried to explain why he'd chosen another son over me. Tried to justify it. I remember the sound of his voice when he talked about this kid. He loved him."

A knock came on the bedroom door. It opened before they could move and Will stuck his head inside. "Kate, your phone is turned off." Kate reached into her pocket and saw she hadn't turned it on after they finished with the capture.

"Sorry about that. Were you trying to get a hold of me for some reason?"

"I wasn't but Fr. Joe was."

"Oh my God, the last Pre-Cana instruction session was supposed to be this morning. I forgot all about it."

"Well, thank goodness you have a fantastic brother," Will chuckled. "I told him you had an emergency search with the troopers this morning. So, I invited him to supper. He accepted, of course, and said he could go over the final session with you to after we eat. Dinner is at seven."

"Thank you, perfect brother of mine. I can imagine going to Mass in the morning if you hadn't saved our bacon."

"You'd probably be reciting Our Fathers and Hail Marys until the day of the wedding. See you later."

"I don't blame you for forgetting, Kate," Maeve said. "With all you've had going on, it's a miracle you're not a basket case. Oh, I never got a chance to tell you how absolutely stunning your wedding dress is. My brother and your father would have been over the moon. Tom mentioned he was going to see if he would be able to get down the aisle using a cane rather than crutches. Ann found him one of Tom's from the old country. It's hand carved with a knob on top shaped like a Samoyed. Your gran knew it would be perfect if he practiced for a few days."

Kate laughed, though it came out as more of a snort. "I seem to go a little overboard with distractions when I'm placed in situations where I'd be expected to panic. In February, I had my first New York fashion show and what distracted me was someone trying to kill me, well both of us," she said looking at Harry. "Now I have my wedding a week away and someone's trying to kill us again. I'm seeing a theme here. A case of 'Kate under stress — let's try to murder her.'"

Harry wrapped his arms around her. "If you hadn't been threatened last February, we wouldn't have met. So I for one, have an entirely different view of the situation. But back to the case at hand. It occurred to me it might be possible to bait a trap for the man we want. I think the Connecticut State Police should hold our friend in custody for as long as possible. If the man pulling the strings has trouble getting his hands on his puppet, he may have to show himself. I think Sal and I need to go have a talk with Gurka. With the weekend now and next

Thursday being Thanksgiving, paperwork efficiency could slow to a crawl. Plus, he's injured. Not as much as he deserved, but enough to add to the paperwork necessary to move him into federal custody."

Harry went in search of Sal, and Maeve said she wanted to spend more time with the files Des had given Harry. So Kate returned to the kitchen as Tim was shutting the back door.

"The last one has left Kate. Mr. Koltin picked up Curtis, the Beagle, and he was the last boarding dog. I thought I'd spring you from your prison and have you help me scrub down the kennel."

"Oh, what a thoughtful brother you are. Actually, it will feel good to do something normal for a change."

They both headed for the kennel, passing Sal heading the other way. He stopped for a minute to let her know he and Harry were heading to the barracks to talk to Gurka. Tom and Des were going too. "Stay out of trouble while they were away."

Kate waved him off, and she and Tim headed for the runs. She stopped when passing her office, noticing the door was half open. Peeking in, she saw three generations of Samoyeds all sprawled in the sunlight from the window, sleeping soundly. Quietly she and Tim continued through the door into the runs.

They blasted all the kennel runs with hot water and the high pressure hose, and scrubbed them down from top to bottom with disinfecting soap. Finally they repeated the rinse.

Kate noticed Tim wasn't as chatty as usual. When they finished, she went to her office and, nudging Quinn to one side and telling him to go back to sleep, sat at her desk, and updated her bookkeeping noting that the last boarding dog was gone until after the wedding. She looked over and saw Dillon, Quinn, and Liam were still asleep. Tim slouched in and sat in the easy chair across from her, his legs sticking out far enough to bang up against her feet under the desk. She added the final entry and put the paperwork into her bottom drawer, leaned back and asked, "Are you going to tell me what's bothering you or do I have to pry it out of you?"

Tim stared at her a minute, "How did you do it?"

"How did I do what?"

"How did you convince the family to let you choose your own college?"

"Where do you want to go?"

"Boston College. They had a scout at my last game. They've offered me a basketball scholarship, but they also might want me to play baseball. I know money isn't a big problem and Dad put away enough for our college years ago, but the honor of being offered a basketball scholarship to B.C. as opposed to going to MIT where sports are thought of as a way to exercise between classes…"

"You want to go to B.C. What would be your major?"

"Political Science." Tim sat there and stared at her then after a minute said, "Mom's going to kill me."

Kate stood and walked around her desk, forcing Tim to stand. She hugged him, grinning. "I think it's great!"

"Which part, the major or Mom killing me?"

"The major. And, Mom isn't going to kill you."

"Dad and Gramps fought for you but they're both gone. I don't know how to fight her. She won't listen. She'll ram it through saying I have to go to MIT and study math and that's all there is to say. I'm not sure I've got your strength to stand up to her. I've always gone along with what she wanted over the years because it was simpler."

"Don't worry, I've got your back and so will Harry and your brothers. Plus I have an ace in the hole."

"What?"

"Fr. Joe is coming to supper tonight."

Tim stared at her for a minute, then scooped her up in a hug, swinging her around in a circle. "You are my best sister ever."

"I'm your only sister, but I am delighted with your choice of majors. If she gets too pushy, tell her you'll minor in math though, Tim, you don't need to pick any course just to appease her. It is your life. Seamus adores math. Having three of her five children continuing in her field and all wanting to work in the family business is enough. I never could picture you as a math major anyway. Would you think about law or politics?" They were both laughing as they headed back to the house with the dogs bouncing at their feet.

"What made you finally decide on Poly Sci?" Kate asked as they entered the kitchen.

"I think the tipping point were the two required introductory courses. There is one mandatory and one you can choose from a list."

"What was the mandatory course?"

"*Fundamental Concepts or How to Rule the World.*"

Chapter Twenty-Five

By the time Harry got back, Kate had fed the dogs, showered and changed her clothes. There wasn't time to talk, so she just turned on the television to check the weather. It looked as though the blast of winter was over for the near future. The snow should be gone by mid-week with temperatures returning to the forties during the day and low thirties at night. She hadn't dressed up but had on clean jeans, a turtleneck, and one of her simple Samoyed sweaters showing a Sam stacked perfectly.

"Do you need help with feeding the dogs?" Harry asked while walking out of his room as he finished pulling on an Irish knit sweater Kate had made him.

"It's all done. We're free to go."

"Absolutely, in just a minute." He reached out and took her in his arms and gently kissed her, holding her head against his heart and resting his on top of hers.

"I just needed to hold you. It seems like forever until the wedding. It's hard to believe it's only a week from today."

"It is hard to wait, and we both know dangerous things can happen, so we have to be on our guard. Did you have any luck with Gurka? Will he and his boss slow walk the processing on this guy?"

"Once we explained the circumstances and what we expected, they bought into it immediately. They both hate rotten apples giving a bad name to law enforcement."

Kate glanced at the clock. "We'd better get going. Fr. Joe may have already arrived."

They got their coats and headed out for the walk up the hill to the house where she'd grown up. They stopped for a minute to look over toward the land beside her tiny house. Her place had been built by her grandfather years ago to be used by a kennel manager if they ever needed one. Following his death and that of her father, Kate had moved out of the main house and into the tiny one. She needed the comfort of being near the dogs and, if she were honest, away from her mother. Though she'd eventually come to a quasi-peace with her mom, it was still easier to be separated physically. "Our house will fit nicely with the main house and Grams. This grassy area will be a great place for our kids to play."

Harry pulled her against him. "Don't plan on getting much sleep next Saturday night, princess."

Kate laughed and swatted him as they climbed the steps of the big wrap-around porch and hurried inside.

"Here they are." The shout came from the living room as they entered. Des came over to Kate and asked if she was doing okay. She gave him a hug and told him she was fine as she approached Fr. Joe. "I am so sorry we missed our counseling session, Father."

"Don't worry about it, Kate. From what I've picked up from the scuttlebutt around town, my biggest worry will not be whether you two are well suited to marry but if you two can stay alive long enough to do it. I only want weddings here, no funerals," the priest said.

Harry shook his hand saying, "I can get on board with that, Father. Any extra prayers in our direction would be gratefully accepted." Kate looked around the room. All four of her brothers were there as well as Satu, Sal, Des, Maeve, Padraig, and Sean.

Sean's presence startled her. "Not with Agnes this evening?"

"Nope. The women are all getting together to plan your surprise shower. All the men have been chased away."

Maeve stood as Will appeared at the doorway to the dining room. Everyone followed her lead, found a chair and settled in. Maeve and Padraig were given the heads of the table and everyone else arranged themselves along the sides with the boys sitting in their normal places. Will had outdone himself with a crown roast, oven-roasted potatoes, asparagus, honey glazed carrots, with fresh herb and cheddar rolls still warm from the oven. For a while, the conversation gave way to the appreciation of a perfectly prepared meal.

Will had two new wines for them to taste. He said he was down to these two trying to decide which to serve along with the champagne at the reception. The discussion went back and forth with Kate just relaxed taking it in. Except for special occasions, she didn't drink, so she happily handed this job off to the experts and leaned over to Tim to ask if he'd spoken to Fr. Joe yet. The priest turned to Tim and asked what he wanted to talk about.

Tim looked at Kate, but at her nod, told him he was interested in attending Boston College next year, explaining he'd been offered a basketball scholarship and they also wanted him to play baseball.

"What will be your major?" the priest asked which Kate thought was insightful of him knowing the family's proclivity toward mathematics. "Political Science."

There was silence at the table for a second, when it exploded with congratulations and support on all sides. Tom explained if he wanted to go on into law school afterward, it would be something really needed by K&K. Maeve told him how proud his grandfather would be of him since he had chosen it as his minor in college.

Everyone had a comment of support and when they all took a breath, Fr. Joe put in his oar.

"Young Timothy, I would like you to know, as a B.C. alumnus, I will be happy to put in a good word for you with the college and more to the point, a strong word with your mother. I am well aware she considers math the only choice for this family. Kate, your father, and grandfather spoke to me when you were fighting to choose your own direction and I interceded with her. Keep the faith, young man, but a few extra prayers wouldn't hurt. Now, not to eat and run, but I've got to be up early tomorrow. He looked around the table. I'll see you all at Mass."

As Tim walked him to the door, coffee, tea and dessert were served. Will, knowing everyone would be full of his delicious dinner, had served a homemade sorbet with lacy, thin, lemon cookies.

Des sighed and relaxed after setting down his spoon. "You do know you could open a five-star restaurant in D.C. or New York and have people lined up around the block."

"I know. But cooking is what I do for fun, to relax. Unlike Tim, I love math and in a few months, I'll finish up at MIT and join Tom at K&K. I'm really looking forward to it, especially since Harry will be setting up next door. There will be plenty of fascinating cases needing my talents."

Maeve looked around the table and told them that now that they were relaxed and well-fed, there was work to be done. She began going over what she'd been discussing with Kate and Harry. She had Harry tell everyone the background on Pete Foyle and what led up to his murder. Then she went over what she'd pulled from the research Des and Harry had been working on the last few weeks.

Sal glanced at Kate as he realized she'd known where he was all the time and had covered for him.

Des went into the research he'd been doing on the mob plus the investigation into the possibility of the mob planting people in law enforcement, specifically in police, FBI, and Justice. Maeve told them she'd seen the start of a pattern in the material she'd gone through, but she needed Kate to go over it since she was much better at finding any flaw in a pattern which might be a clue as to who this person is.

Harry looked at Kate and asked, "Do you have any ideas to share with the group?"

She was quiet for a minute trying to get her thoughts in order. Giving Harry a worried look she began, "I do have a few ideas, but they aren't solid yet. However, if I must share something, I think the person who is behind this influx of mob members into law enforcement was taught a great deal about the subject by someone who knew the workings of this world very well. He knew how it operated all the way from a cop walking the beat to the top brass. He even knew the inner workings of the law on a federal level. And, I think he found a devoted student in a young man who later took all this knowledge and twisted it to his benefit, and also the mob's which had been family to him in his very early years and for whom his father died."

She turned to look at Harry who had turned white as a ghost. He stood and left the room. Though her first instinct was to race after him, Kate sat. She'd known what she had concluded would be adding more pain to his already agonizing battle with his feeling toward his father. He needed time to work through it. Des looked at her and raised an eyebrow. She nodded and he stood and left.

Maeve stood and walked to the sofa where she'd placed a tote. She reached inside and pulled out the photo which Kate had given her earlier after Harry and Des had left for the state police barracks. She returned to her seat and began passing the photo around.

"This is the boy who Pete Foyle befriended. Pete was determined to keep him from being swept up into a life of crime. He took him on, being a pseudo-father to him, taking him to ball games, and amusement parks. Even taking him fishing. Just spending as much time with him as possible. I agree with Kate. Pete was probably thrilled to find a young man who was so interested in possibly having the same career as he. Especially since he was still dealing with the fact his own son had always made him feel insecure and under-educated. Pete was the perfect victim. This boy might have been as smart as Harry but in the ways of an entirely different world--the world of the con, of betrayal, and of crime. I want you all to learn this boy's face. We don't know his name yet. Over the years, I'm sure he's changed it. But the basic facial structure should have remained the same. I have a friend who will have a version of his face, aged to approximate thirty years of age, ready for you by tomorrow and I'll send it to all of you. Any other ideas, Kate?"

"The only other thing I might suggest is whatever name he had might have chosen, I'm pretty sure he'd have kept the same initials. People with egos, I've noticed, tend to mark possessions with their monograms and I suspect this man has an ego the size of Cleveland."

Harry walked back into the room and without a word sat down next to her. Des resumed his seat. Everyone seemed to be watching Harry. Kate finally turned and took his face in her hands and forced him to look at her. When she was sure she had his attention, she began speaking. "I told you many times I understood what you had gone through with your father not understanding you. You've met my mother. You've seen how she openly rejected my life choices completely out of hand without even considering the effect it was having on me. Your father did the exact same thing to you. He rejected the fact you didn't want to become a cop like him. It was what he loved so it had to be what you would love too, if only you understood. I imagine it came as a complete shock when you had to follow your choice as I did mine.

"Now my mother had four other children she could mold in her own image. Luckily, three of them inherited her love for the field. She will not react well to Tim's defection. She will take it as a personal affront, and I am counting on you along with everyone else at this table plus Fr. Joe to bring her around enough to allow Tim to pursue his dream. I also meant what I said when I told you she would love you better than me. You thought I was joking. I wasn't. You will be the replacement for her lost child. She will see you as coming to fulfill her need for another child to carry on her tradition. What I saw in this boy's relationship with your father was similar. A child to replace the lost one. A child to follow in his footsteps so he could feel proud of himself for sharing guidance."

Kate leaned in and kissed him gently and stood. "If everyone can come over for breakfast tomorrow, we've got all the files and can fill you in on what we're up against. Will, I know you have to go back to Boston for your exam and to get

Jordi. You'll bring him here for the wedding. Give him my love and tell him Quinn is looking forward to his visit."

Without another word, she went to the door, put on her coat and left. Her foot had only cleared the bottom step of the porch when she heard the door shut and steps hurrying toward her. Harry's hand reached out and took hers. Talking wasn't necessary. Enough words had been said this evening. They simply walked down the hill, under the stars.

Chapter Twenty-Six

The front two pews of the church held Killoys and their friends when Fr. Joe began Mass the next morning. He looked in their direction and nodded. Kate tried to concentrate on the prayers, but her mind traveled forward six days to when she would walk down the main aisle to marry Harry. If they lived. He reached for her hand and squeezed. The fingers of his other hand reached for her face, and those haunting green eyes held her.

"Six more days," he whispered.

Maeve and Padraig stopped to talk to Fr. Joe as they left the church. The threesome smiled and looked in Tim's direction. Kate felt happy for Tim. She had been right to force the issue last night. Thank goodness, her mother was in Boston for two more days, giving the family time to come up with ideas to convince her Tim should go to the college of his choice, not hers. Kate knew she would fight for him, if it came to a battle.

Years ago she found, unlike her father and grandfather, her mother was not a person to accept any ideas that weren't her own. She was driven and a very successful teacher. As such, she was an asset to the University. However, in her role as a mother, their lives were made difficult. To put it simply, as a mom, she was a great mathematician.

Today might be Sunday, but it was not a day of rest. There was little time to find the man behind these murder attempts. She and Harry made it home first, so while she reheated two of Will's breakfast casseroles, Harry cooked bacon and sausages. By the time she heard cars arriving, she'd managed to set out juice, fruit and two baskets full of blueberry muffins. Hungry bodies and conversation soon filled the room with laughter until Maeve reminded them of what needed doing and took charge.

"I hate to break up this party, but while you finish eating, I'm going to give out assignments. Each of you will take a different section of the research. Seamus and Satu, you two work together and see if you can find any trace information that might still be available in the Boston P.D. records of Pete Foyle's death. Des, you and Harry working on the possible

Washington connections. The rest of you, grab a stack of printouts and get to work.

Kate fed the dogs and chased them back out and then picked up a box full of photos and got to work. Quiet settled over the group. In the living room, in Harry's bedroom, and in the kitchen the only sounds were a quiet swish of papers being shifted and the occasional hum of computers.

Seamus broke the silence. "Harry, were you aware your father had scratched two letters into the pool of blood beside him as he died?"

"No."

"It wasn't in the departmental official record of his death," Satu said. "We searched beyond the information readily available and found it in the notes taken by the patrolman who had found the body. He'd tried to get a photo of the initials, but a young paramedic stepped directly on the spot while trying to revive the victim. Since he didn't have a photo to prove what he'd seen, he hadn't mentioned it, He only came across it recently when he was getting ready to retire and going through his case notes. The notation indicated he'd seen what looked like an 'M' and a 'C'."

Maeve clapped her hands to get everyone's attention. "Add the initials M.C. to the list of possible connections."

Kate stood, stretching. While making a fresh mug of tea, she asked, "Des, would it be possible to get access to photos of the recent hires in both the Bureau and Justice Department as well as the police forces in Boston, New York, and Washington? I was thinking we could run a facial recognition program to search for matches."

Des looked up from his pile of paper, "It sounds like a great idea, but I'd rather not be fired this week. That much hacking of files would be pushing the envelope on what's legal."

Heading back to her chair, Kate stepped outside to visit her dogs. A dozen smiling Samoyeds crowed around her looking for head pats. Dillon claimed for himself one side of Kate and Liam took the other. Quinn bounded up for a snuggle but soon headed back to sleep beside Shelagh, Kelly, and the others who'd already collected their share of attention, When she stepped back inside, with Dillon at her side, all was still quiet. The only measure of progress seemed to be the occasional fist punch in the air when someone found a possible match.

Maeve gathered all possible matches, saying she would work them into a spreadsheet for better analysis. Tom and Harry said that they would run background checks on the possible hires who could be their man. They'd come up with a dozen possibles.

At twelve-thirty, Harry went to the counter and pulled out her breadboard to begin slicing the loaves of fresh bread that Will had left them. Maeve opened the refrigerator finding a platter of cold cuts, some salad and various dressings, pickles, and olives which she passed to waiting hands. Less than five minutes later, everyone was settled with tea or coffee and lunch.

They'd just finished eating when a knock came at the front door. Kate glanced around and with a wave, told people to hold as she and Harry answered the door. When she passed Des, he followed and then moved to a position behind the door pulling out his gun. Harry stepped in front of Kate to check the peephole, relaxed and opened the door to Agnes.

"Hey Harry, I'm here to steal your bride. Maeve, I need you too. It's time to party and no guys are allowed."

"Where are you going?" Harry asked.

"I'm not saying," Agnes smirked at him. "This is a party without guys. "What about Dillon? Can he come?" Kate asked.

"Oh, sure. Dillon's in a class by himself. Come on, girl. Let's get your coat. You too, Maeve."

Agnes headed out after tossing Kate her coat from the closet. Maeve reached over to pick up hers from the back of the couch and handed it to Des instead of Padraig for help in putting it on. Kate saw her whisper to him and as he settled the coat on her shoulders, she watched him slip his gun into her pocket. Maeve saw that Kate had noticed but merely raised an eyebrow. She hooked arms with her as they headed out and whispered, "Better safe than sorry." Harry handed her Dillon's lead, and they headed out to Agnes' car.

"I don't like the idea of Kate being unguarded even if Campanelli is in custody. The puppet master is still in the wind."

Harry watched as the car turned north. When he returned to the kitchen, Satu grabbed his arm saying to wait a minute. Then she asked, "Who do you know who lives at 25 Dogwood Lane?"

Seamus smiled. "You can relax, Harry. She's at my cousin Rory's house. It's only a half mile from here. Sharon must be throwing the bridal shower. They just redid their place into one of those open-plan layouts where the living room, dining room and kitchen all flow into each other. If a lot of women are invited, they would obviously pick that place. She'll be fine. She has Maeve with her and you may have missed it because Des is a sleight of hand artist, but Maeve's packing heat."

Padraig laughed and patted Harry on the shoulder. "I heard that Danielle, the trooper who duked it out with our mobster, will be there as well, along with about fourteen female Killoy cousins, plus your sister and mother."

Tom added, "Mom and Grandma Ann will be missing it, but considering Mom's penchant for bluntness when she's in non-academic situations, that's definitely for the best. I could just picture her duking it out with your mother."

Seamus laughed. "I think we've organized as much as we can of this data on our possible puppet master. Our brains need a rest. Since it's Sunday afternoon, I vote we go watch football, especially since you have installed that massive screen television you brought from your place in Boston, Harry." The men all smiled at each other and headed for the living room.

Kate walked into her cousin Rory's newly remodeled house and looked around. What had been a narrow hall with a small parlor off to the right, and a dining room beyond followed by a kitchen, with a pantry and mud room, had become an open, bright and spacious living room area which flowed into a dining area which was separated from the kitchen by a counter with upholstered bar stools along its length.

Though the windows along the front of the house were the traditional size, sunlight filled the room. She looked up, and saw what looked like bright cam lights.

Rory came up behind her. "You ought to think about these for parts of your new house. They're tubes on the roof which catch the light and reflect it down making the room bright. It's good for keeping the room lit up without having it raise the electric bill." Rory, who was tall like her brothers, put his arm around her shoulders and added, "Have fun. I'm being chased out of this hen party." Sharon came up and shooed him out the door.

The room was filled with women, all talking at the same time. It reminded her of the dogs when she went to clean poop out of the exercise yard and smiled, thinking these women would not appreciate the comparison.

Agnes showed Kate and Maeve where to put their coats and then brought them into the gathering so that she could say hello to everyone. Cathy came forward and hugged Kate. With all that had been going on, Kate hadn't spent much time with her favorite bridesmaid. She needed to get some time alone with her to find how things were going between her and Rufus since no ring graced her finger. At the Samoyed National, they'd given the impression that their wedding would be happening soon. Her last email had mentioned they we're still trying to figure out how to combine two households and two careers in different states. Rufus' son Jordy, an extremely gifted 12-year-old, was part of a special program studying at MIT. He was eager for them to marry so he could live with Cathy's Samoyeds. He'd be coming here with her brother Will when they both finished exams. Kate whispered a promise to Cathy that she'd find time to catch up during the week and find out what was going on with her life and her dogs. Maeve, who had met Cathy at the National, drew her aside to chat while Kate said personal hellos to all the women gathered.

She worked her way across the room, with Agnes at her elbow, herding her through the crowd. Bracing herself, she reached the corner where Harry's mother and sister were sitting. Kate noticed that her mother-in-law-to-be did not look happy.

"Well, it's about time. We finally get to meet the bride. I guess being the mother of the groom puts us at the end of the line." Kate blinked and then forced herself to smile.

"Hello, Mrs. Foyle. I hope you've been introduced to everyone here." Kate glanced at Sarah and asked, "Are you enjoying a break from the little sweetheart this evening?"

"Why would you think that Sarah wishes to be away from her daughter? Don't you like children? Does that mean that you and Harry won't be having any? I suppose I shouldn't be surprised, considering how abnormal he was growing up and apparently you had your own problems socializing like a typical child. I was told you spent all your time with dogs. Very strange. I hope that Harry can afford to support you and your hobbies. Knitting and dogs aren't exactly average ways to catch a man. I'm surprised that you and he ever got together. I'm told this beautiful lady, who we all recognize as one of the country's favorite supermodels, is your cousin. It must have been hard growing up with someone as beautiful as she is around you for comparison."

Dillon, who had been sitting quietly at Kate's side, suddenly stood and pushed himself between her and Harry's mother. He didn't make a sound, but she felt the hackles on his back rise.

Search

Kate reached down and rested her hand on his head to reassure him.

"I assure you that Harry and I are planning a family. I am one of five children so large families are a tradition with the Killoys as you might guess by just the number of female cousins I have here this evening. With only two children, it must have been hard for you to be without Harry when he went to California as a youngster to study at Caltech. I'm sure that you and your husband were reluctant to let him go."

"Well, we could hardly deny him an opportunity to study what he liked. That was all that the boy thought about day and night. He wasn't interested in learning about his father's job like a normal boy. He didn't want to follow in his footsteps. No, he wanted to spend his time with eggheads. That's probably why you two got together. I'm told your mother is a professor at Yale. Harry probably feels right at home with her."

Agnes' hand, which had been resting on Kate's shoulder, tightened. Kate wasn't sure how long she could stand here and be insulted by this woman without the maid-of-honor decking her. A change of topic was needed in the conversation. What popped into her head were the photos.

She smiled at Harry's mom and said, "I hear you will be getting married soon as well. Harry and I were organizing all the boxes of his father's things you sent. Hopefully, we can get a new house built soon, so we'll have more room to store everything.

"We were looking at photos just yesterday because I wanted to know what his father looked like, and we came across one that had someone Harry didn't know. I was wondering if Harry has a cousin he didn't know about." She reached into her pocket and pulled out her phone pulling up the photo she'd copied. "He didn't know the name of the young man with his dad in this photo." She held out her phone and watched Mrs. Foyle's face. It softened and she smiled.

"Ah, Maurio. That is such a good photo of Pete with Maurio. Pete was his mentor. The boy had grown up in the mob, and Pete was working to get him away from those people. Maurio wanted to be a cop like Pete when he grew up. Pete was so proud of him. They bonded. Maurio looked on Pete as his father since his own father had been dead for several years. To Pete, it was like having a new son. He was such a lovely boy but I didn't see him after Pete died. I'm sure he was crushed when he found out. They were so close. I didn't see him at the wake or the funeral, but he may have been uncomfortable since he only knew Pete."

Kate took back the phone and smiled down at Mrs. Foyle. "How nice that Pete found someone like Maurio. What was Maurio's last name?"

"Corsetti. Maurio Corsetti. A lovely boy. I wonder whatever happened to him. I guess I'll never know."

Chapter Twenty-Seven

Agnes raised her voice and suggested everyone get some food before Kate opens her presents. Kate excused herself to use the restroom but said that everybody else should go ahead, and she'd be right there. As they moved toward the tables, she ducked into the powder room taking Dillon with her. Considering the reaction to her future mother-in-law, he might just bite her before the wedding. Locking the door, dialed Harry.

"Maurio Corsetti."

"Kate, what?"

"The name of the boy in the photo of your father. Your mother had a very high opinion of him. Told me that your dad had taken him on because the boy was interested in going into law enforcement. His father had been in the mob and had been killed. Oh, if Agnes murders your mother before the wedding, I want you to know that she is doing it in the role of maid-of-honor, making life good for the bride."

"I'm sorry, Kate. Was she horrible?"

"She doesn't have a high opinion of either one of us. I hope when she marries, she moves to Florida or Tierra del Fuego."

"You sure that's far enough. There's always Tazmania." The warmth in his voice made her smile.

"I like the way you think, Foyle. I've got to go to eat and open presents. Dillon is on guard against your mom. He doesn't like her. Hackles raised and all."

"Smart dog. You go have fun."

Maeve was waiting for her when she got to the buffet. As they filled their plates, Maeve said, "Kate, if that woman says one more thing, she'll be staring down the barrel of a Glock 22."

Sharon eased up on Kate's other side and apologized for inviting Harry's mom. "I always thought that your mom was the rudeness queen, but she's not even in the running against Harry's mom."

"Don't worry about it, something always goes wrong at a family get together. Now nobody has to back into the punch bowl, and Dillon doesn't need to jump on anyone's lap."

Search

The three of them laughed and Agnes herded her across the room to an overstuffed chair in the midst of a mountain of presents.

Conversation in the room had gotten around to the honeymoon and Kate amazed the women by saying, "I haven't a clue where we're going. Harry is making all the arrangements. My clues on what to pack were to bring clothes which are warm and comfortable. Oh, and we won't be honeymooning alone. I can bring up to three dogs with me." Everyone laughed. "After the wedding, we'll spend the night at my house, then come Sunday morning, we are off somewhere and on Monday, they begin the foundation for our home."

Ellen joined the group. "The businesses will keep going without her. All the designs are done for the next fashion show so it's mainly building stock. The smart boutiques have already place tentative pre-orders to hold a place in line for fulfillment. The stores in Aspen, San Francisco and Chicago have all locked in pre-orders and the New York orders are standing and vary only by color and yarns. They tend to market to a more old-money crowd who know exactly what they want. So we can let her leave long enough to have a honeymoon."

Kate laughed. "Well not only does Ellen and the business not need me for weeks, but Sal has made sure the kennel will keep going. My classes are on recess until I return. Plus we just wrapped up a certification class with the troopers, to say nothing of the bonus qualification run in the deep snow…"

"Thank you for that, Kate," Danielle shouted, waving from the other end of the table.

"I keep your life from getting boring, Dani," Kate said.

"So those classes won't begin again until after Christmas. It will seem strange because, unless you count the National, and this year you can't count that, I haven't had a vacation since I was a kid. I suspect Harry is the same way. I told him I would have to learn to relax, but he said he could teach me that, no trouble." Everyone roared except Mrs. Foyle and Sarah whose expressions were disapproving.

Sharon cleared the area in front of Kate and brought in a small table. Then she, Agnes, Cathy, and Ellen all began placing packages in front of Kate. The gifts varied from things for their new house to outfits to wear in the bedroom on her honeymoon, to a couple of books on sex which were given anonymously. Obviously, someone knew of the family tradition of remaining a virgin until the wedding night. Kate felt her face get red, but she had every intention of reading them when she got home.

The afternoon had turned into the early evening by the time people were leaving. All the gifts had been packed into massive totes and loaded into the back of Agnes' car. Kate made the rounds giving hugs and thanks as well as telling everyone she'd see them Saturday. Then, before they knew it, Maeve and Kate had joined Agnes in the car and were heading back down the highway.

They'd only driven a few minutes when Kate noticed a big truck, the kind where its body sits on top of extra large tires, pulling up close behind Agnes' car. Even though there was a dotted line and nobody coming the other way, it didn't pass.

Kate dialed her phone. "We're headed home, but there is a muscle truck on our tail which won't pass and is riding our back bumper. He hasn't hit us, but he's got time and there is a turn with the sharp drop off is coming up in about a mile."

"We're coming. Hang in there," came the shout and Kate heard car doors slamming.

Kate turned to Agnes. "Keep your speed steady. I don't want to reach the drop-off before the guys get to us. This idiot behind us is trying to get us to speed. It could be just a jerk, or it could be someone with an agenda. Two minutes later, they spotted several cars approaching from the opposite direction. The first car, a squad car, shot past them. The other two cars slowed as Agnes slowed down. Kate was still checking the mirror when she saw the squad car do a one-eighty, and was now boxing in the big truck as the first car in the other lane slowly pulled up to cut off any chance to escape.

Agnes pulled to a stop and put her car's flashers on while men got out of the other cars to put flares on the road. Sean approached the truck carefully, his gun drawn, ordering the driver to put his hands out the window. A second later, he had the guy out of his truck, his hands behind his head, leaning against the side of the truck with his legs spread. The door beside Kate opened and Harry stuck his head in.

"You girls have a good time tonight?"

Agnes leaned across the seat until she was nose-to-nose with him. "Foyle, what the hell is going on. You will tell me now or you will need help standing at the wedding." Maeve pushed forward between the seats and laid a hand on Agnes' shoulder. "If you drive us the rest of the way, I'll make tea and explain all. I think that we can leave the cleanup of this mess to the boys." She leaned back and Agnes, checking out her expression in the rear view the mirror, started the car, and they continued the final half mile to Kate's home.

Padraig, Tom, Seamus, Satu, and Tim were all waiting on the front porch when they arrived. Maeve put the men to work transporting the presents into Kate's room. She and Satu started the water for tea and found some scones in the freezer which would thaw in the microwave and Agnes and Kate filed into the kitchen and sat. In two minutes, everyone was seated at the table sipping tea as Maeve took on the task of explaining what was going on to a furious Agnes. When she finished Agnes gazed around the room and then faced Kate.

"Let me understand this. Someone tried to murder you and then the same person tried to kill Harry. You went out by yourself and pulled Harry out from under this guy's nose and that 'search' yesterday with all the troopers and their dogs was them going after this killer and capturing him. Is that it?"

"Essentially, except for the fact that while we were doing the rescue, he tried to kill Dani, which was the inside joke at the shower, and that he is only a puppet and there's a puppet master pulling the strings in a push to make sure we are both dead. I suspect the idiot in the monster truck was trying to reach the drop-off, so he could bump your car and then merrily drive away. He, I assume, was another of this man's puppets. We'll see what the boys say when they return."

"Kate, I'm your maid-of-honor. I should know every problem that might come up with this wedding so that I can fix it."

Maeve leaned in and hugged her.

"Agnes, my girl, you know I respect all the work you've done working with the State Department and the FBI, decoding messages. It's been vital in stopping many crimes. But, this time, it's not in an area where your skill set would solve the problem. This is a fight with the mob and it has to be fought in a whole new way."

"The mob?" Agnes jumped up and began pacing the kitchen. Kate thought she looked like an Irish Valkyrie lacking only a full symphony orchestra for high drama. She was on her fourth trip across the kitchen when the door to the living room opened and Sean pushed through, grabbing his fiancé as she waved her arms and screamed 'mob' again.

"Yeah, but the good part is the score is good guys four, bad guys zero — if you count Dani and the new player tonight." He kissed her nose while giving her a hug. "Let's get you home so you can ask me hundreds of questions you haven't even thought of. If you're good, I'll even answer some. From what Dani told me when she came out to help with traffic tonight, you're going to have more than enough on your hands trying to keep the mothers of the bride and groom from killing each other or being killed by the friends and relatives of the aforementioned bride and groom."

"Aforementioned?"

"I'm broadening my vocabulary. Shoot me." He took her hand, waved to everyone and pulled her out.

Harry and Des passed them as they entered the kitchen and Harry went to Kate. "Are you okay?"

"I'm fine. Thanks for riding to the rescue so. That was a beautiful take-down."

"Yeah, even I was impressed with Sean's 'James Bond' whirl with his cruiser. I've got to have him to teach me that."

Kate turned serious and asked him to tell what he'd found out. Sitting down and accepting the tea and scone Maeve put in front of him, began with Sean getting the guy out of his truck and into cuffs. Sal was handling traffic and I suspect that our puppet master drove by while Sean was questioning the guy because as soon as a bunch of cars went by, the guy's phone beeped with a text. Since he was in cuffs, Sean relieved him of the phone and while at it opened the text. It was short and sweet telling him to keep his mouth shut. He kept saying he wasn't going to hurt the women but only scare them. When it was pointed out that he was less than a quarter mile from a turn where his truck would easily send the car off the road and into a thirty-foot fall leading to their deaths if it got any closer, he shut up.

"I thought the guy was going to faint when Sean told him that attempted murder is taken seriously in Connecticut. He lawyered up after that. This puppet master doesn't seem to care how many others are killed so long as we are." He looked down at his tea and sighed. "Starting tomorrow, we got to find out who is behind this and stop him."

"Was that name any help? Maurio Corsetti?"

Satu sat up straight and pushed her laptop over so Kate could see it.

"Maurio Corsetti disappeared almost immediately following the death of Pete Foyle. He no longer attended his high school. The address listed as his residence said he no longer lived there. The police didn't consider him a suspect since he had met so many of them when he was with Pete. They think that he was so upset by what happened to his mentor that he just left. He apparently didn't have any family, according to the high school.

"However, a person fitting his description turned up eighteen-months later in New Jersey in connection with the death of a lawyer in the District Attorney's office in Trenton. The police came up with an I.D. on him as Marcelo Capurso. Mr. Capurso spent only a few hours in custody before he made bail and promptly disappeared. A year later, a Martino Cericola turned up in connection with the brutal death of a judge who was in the middle of a case in Philadelphia involving the Carlino Crime Family. That case is still in the wind. Mr. Cericola disappeared along with several valuable witnesses. The trial has been postponed for more than ten months."

"If you don't mind my pressing the point that, MC tends to have a penchant for killing those involved with bringing justice," Kate muttered. "From the murder of your father as a teenager, he has aged into being a violent killer with a love of the law. That is a love of killing those involved with the law, a cop, an attorney and a judge. And, I suspect those are only the ones where he was identified. How many others he's gotten away with over the last few years, I don't know, but I suspect that he has been busy. What did he do for a living? Is there any pattern in that?"

"Yes." Seamus added. "He liked to work either in the office or in the building with his victim. This meant that he'd followed through on getting involved in law enforcement but not in a good way. The question is how do we find what branch he works in now. If he is after Harry and Kate, it's got to be one where members are likely to associate freely with them, maybe even be invited to their wedding."

" If I were to guess," Satu said ignoring Seamus' comment that she never guesses, "I would say that he is working tightly with someone on your guest list. Someone who wouldn't raise any red flags if he brought a coworker with him."

"So the bottom line is," Harry said, "that there's a very real possibly we've invited a murderer to our wedding."

Chapter Twenty-Eight

The next morning, Kate woke to the sound of voices in her kitchen. She showered and dressed quickly, realizing that the dogs were gone from her room so Harry or someone else had probably let them out and from the quiet, had fed them. When she opened the door she saw, not a series of laptops with people doing research, but rather, the blueprints of their house, spread across the table as Harry explained them to Maeve, Agnes, Cathy, Padraig, and Des. They looked up when she entered the kitchen."

"Sorry to be so late. I must have slept in. Has everyone had breakfast?" Kate still was slightly sleepy and out of step. Harry pushed her into a chair and Des handed her a cup of tea.

"Oatmeal or eggs?"

She glanced out the kitchen window at the gray skies and opted for oatmeal. This was the kind of day when a stick-to-the-ribs breakfast was needed. Cathy began asking questions about the blueprints in front of her so Kate relaxed and gave both a description and rationale for each room. As she sat drinking her tea, she focused on the blueprints and imagined what it would be like when they actually got to move in.

She explained the schedule. "While we are away on our honeymoon, the basement will be dug, the concrete people will lay the foundation and the electricians, plumbers and septic tank people will install the pipes and lines needed. Once the massive trucks and cranes have lifted the house sections onto the foundation, it will take a several weeks to connect everything and to finish the connection to this house. Then the workmen will convert this place into Harry's business."

The conversation continued on the topic of the house until Harry's phone interrupted. They listened to his side of the conversation.

"Hey, Will, what's up? Oh, that sounds good. It will make my life easier. We'll expect you about seven or eight o'clock depending on the traffic on the Mass Pike at the Sturbridge exit. Hopefully, since you'll be after rush hour, it shouldn't be too bad. See you later."

Harry stared at her. "Your brother and Jordy will be finished with exams by lunchtime. However, Rufus called Jordy telling him that his plane was due to land at Logan Airport around four-thirty. By the time he gets his bags, it will be after five. Will and Jordy will then pick him up and head here, but, with a twelve-year-old's appetite in tow, they'll probably be stopping for food after they pass Framingham. Hopefully, that will thin out the traffic congestion further on. The last time I came back from Boston, it was an extra twenty minutes to travel from Worcester to the Sturbridge exit leading into Connecticut. We are to go ahead and eat and not wait for them."

"Sounds good. I have enough of Will's meals packed in the freezer, we will have a large choice of what to eat." Kate finished her breakfast and headed out to clean the exercise yard. There was something about wandering around the yard, cleaning up after her dogs which freed her mind. Quinn was following her, was looking for hugs as was Shelagh. Both of them were in training for the breed ring but with all that had been going on, they had missed their lessons.

Deciding that a little fun was needed, she reached into a bucket hanging by the kennel door. The bucket must have made a sound because instantly, all the dogs went on alert. Chaos broke out as tennis balls, lots of tennis balls, flew through the air. The fastest, or craftiest to retrieve a ball got it thrown again with another chance to chase it. Balls flew in all directions with the dozen dogs joyfully racing to catch them. Each time one was returned to her, it went flying across the yard again at high speed.

The dogs, except Dillon, had been just hanging out for the week. Now they were using every muscle as they raced around the yard at top speed. What the veteran dogs and bitches lacked in speed, they made up for in craftiness.

Fatigue made her call time out. Kate returned the balls to the bucket.

When the final ball was returned, she hung up the bucket, put her pooper scooper away and headed toward the kitchen door with a dozen Sams following her. Harry met her at the door with a double fistful of biscuits. There was happiness all around. Des and Maeve stood by the door watching the now worn out Sams find their favorite spots to polish off the goodies.

"That was wild," Des said, grinning. "Do they ever not return the balls?"

"Yes. Samoyeds are working dogs, not sporting dogs. It is not instinctual for them to retrieve. But I've found that if you teach one generation, and play with them with the puppies in the yard, the big guys get the word out to the little ones pretty quickly. If one of the puppies doesn't bring a ball back, either Kelly or Dillon will go and swipe it from them and then trot over to me collecting all the pats and praise of returning the prized ball. It doesn't take long for the younger ones, who really crave praise, to understand how the game is played. If you noticed, Quinn was right on the mark returning every ball he got. It makes it easier when they get into retrieving in obedience. Plus, it's fun."

Search

"I think that even my seniors would enjoy that," Maeve added. "Living in Manhattan limits the amount of rough and tumble they can do."

Kate scrubbed up as the others set up laptops around the table. With Seamus, Satu, and Tim at school and Sal meeting with Gurka about classes for the spring, the rest of them were each able to take a section of the research.

They concentrated on the files Harry had brought from D.C. and then went to work doing more research on the leads they found. The highest priority was to find M.C. or not only would the bride and groom be in danger, but the wedding guests could be as well.

Maeve and Cathy began searching online for reports of people who were part of law enforcement in the northeast who had suffered unexpected deaths. After an hour of looking, they had compiled a list of more than thirty names.

Agnes, checked lists of Justice Department hires during the last eight years, with the initials M.C, When the thirty cases came up, she joined them to search each case. She and Maeve both were good at accessing data not easily available to the public.

Cathy worked on the newspaper and online reports of the crimes. Tom, Des, and Harry searched both the FBI files and any information available on the dark web. Harry had even gotten his assistant Sadie scouring the Boston P.D. files and anything to do with his father's death and any cases he might have been working on at his time of death.

Kate set up a separate small table in a corner of the kitchen and pulled out the box of pictures again from among Pete

Foyle's belonging and a box of his case notes that Maeve had found. She began sorting the photos. Maurio was in more photos than those she had found earlier. There were shots of him and Pete at various places which were fun.

But what caught her attention were photos of them visiting the local precinct, police headquarters, and Kate realized from a logo in the background, what was the FBI headquarters. Maurio had chosen well when he targeted Pete. The question was why?

Once the photos were sorted, she focused on those of Maurio visiting law enforcement venues. Each photograph was studied as to who was with Pete and Maurio. One man, in the background, turned up at all three venues, and she'd bet her latest Group One ribbon that he was watching them. He seemed relatively young, so he might still be in law enforcement.

Setting those photographs aside, she began sorting Pete Foyle's cases by who was charged, what was the crime, and what was the outcome. She typed it into a spreadsheet and saw that after the first few years on the force, most of Pete's cases involved the mob. Cases ranged from numbers runners to protection rackets.

Pete's habit of focusing specifically on mob-related crimes continued as he rose through the ranks. As she studied these cases, a pattern began to form which led to only one possibility.

Pete must have had a source in the mob. The source was never named, but the pattern of information he was able to get, pointed in that direction. When she was half-way through the cases, she spotted a possible connection to what was going on today. But she wasn't sure.

She set that case aside and checked the next five.

By the time she finished, she felt that she knew what was behind their puppet master hating Harry and wanting him not only dead but to suffer by watching her die first.

Kate stood and went out into the yard, grabbing her coat on the way. She walked among the dogs drawing strength from them. This calmed her and allowed her mind to sort all the facts she'd found.

Now that she understood this man's motivation, his cunning in building his revenge was impressive. He'd made sure he'd never be connected with these present day crimes and yet would still be able to exact the perfect revenge.

She had no idea how long she'd been walking around the yard, scratching the heads of the dogs and accepting their support when she felt hands gently grip her arms, turn her and pull her into a hug. Harry moved his hands to her back and cushioned her head on his shoulder.

They stood in silence until he said, "You've got it. You know why." Kate's head nodded rubbing against his sweater. He breathed into her hair, fluttering her curls.

"You ready to come inside and tell us all about it?" She glanced up at him, nodded then followed him back inside.

Maeve greeted her with a hug and Tom gave her a cup of tea. She sat and flattened her hands on the piles in front of her, glanced around the room and began.

"What's happening now goes back one generation. The sins of the father, or in this case, fathers has led to the attempts on our lives and the way the attempts have been set up and carried out. I was supposed to die first to cause Harry pain and loss, and then he was to die in the slowest way possible to extend that pain and bring the maximum revenge.

"It all began when Pete Foyle became a Boston cop. He'd grown up in South Boston which was mostly Irish and Italian, though the area was in flux. I don't know who his friends were growing up, but when he became a cop, his focus from the very beginning was on mob crimes.

"When I checked the bottom of the box with the snapshots, I found a high school yearbook. It gave me a possible connection but the cases he worked on and his private notes showed the reason why Harry and I are marked for death. When Pete was in high school, his best friend was Angelo Corsetti. When he graduated, Pete went to the Academy and then became a cop. Angelo seemed to keep in touch but there is no mention of what he did for a living.

Pete got married and had two kids but stayed in touch with his friend. It turns out that Angelo was connected and working for the mob. He got married and had a son. Pete was a beat cop and he ran into his old friend when working a case. Actually, he caught him red-handed, but instead of arresting him, Pete had him become his source.

"Time goes by and Pete rises in the ranks based on his exceptional work fighting the mob. One day, Angelo comes to him and tells him he's got to get into witness protection because he's been made as the snitch feeding dirt to the cops. Pete was working on a case and needed the information. The bottom line is that Angelo didn't get witness protection and he was murdered by the mob.

"So, six months later, when Angelo's son sought him out and saying he wants to become a cop, Pete thinks this is his way of showing penance for not saving Angelo. Maurio treats Pete like a replacement dad and Pete treats Maurio like a replacement son. He teaches him all about the workings of law enforcement. He even guides him through the workings of the FBI and the courts.

"But then something happens. Pete's son is coming home. In his diary, which he kept in code (a very simple one so even I could read it), he mentions telling Maurio about his brainy son who as a teenager but already has a PhD in math will be coming home. Maurio doesn't react well to the news. So Pete decided to talk Harry into living on campus, and he tells Maurio that his son changed his mind and decided to stay in California.

"Maurio may not have believed him but the time for revenge had apparently come. Pete's last entry was he hoped you'd be safe, Harry. He was going to meet Maurio and take him to dinner. That was the day he died."

Kate reached into the box and pulled out a small notebook with notations in a fine, spidery, script which she handed it to Harry. "Your dad made you live on campus to keep you alive. He realized by that time, he was being played by Maurio and when he went to meet him, he lied about where you were. Maurio was walking with him when he knifed him and then just left him to bleed out.

"What Maurio didn't know was that Pete, ever the good cop, had left a clue to his murderer. It just took a long time to find the clue. For many years, all went well because Maurio didn't know you were around and a threat, but when you turned up going after the mob, you acquired a target on your back.

"Angelo raised his son inside the mob which was always his first loyalty. Maurio blamed Pete for his father's death because he 'forced' him to be a snitch and the mob had to kill him. So Pete had to die, and because you now pose a threat, you too must die as well and with his twisted mind for the maximum pain, I must die first. For him, it's personal."

Chapter Twenty-Nine

The room remained silent for several minutes. Then Maeve began gathering up the research and packing it away. Des' phone buzzed. He pulled it out, opened the message, then stared at it in shock.

Kate watched him for a moment then said, "Care to share with the class?"

He quickly clicked several keys of his phone and the screen of her laptop lit up with a text. She clicked and opened the attachment. The screen was filled with a sketch of an attractive man, about thirty years old, with dark curly hair. But it was the hardness in the dark eyes which had her pulling back.

Peggy Gaffney

"This is the aged sketch made from Maurio's photo. The expression in the eyes was in the photo but wasn't noticeable because of the distraction of the scene. My sketch artist noticed it first thing, he says. Actually, he said that they were the eyes of a killer. However, that's not what shocked me. Kate, I've seen him. I've seen him walking in the halls of headquarters in D.C. I'd bet my favorite gun that he's an agent. Though I don't know his name I've seen him, and recently."

Kate saw the boy in the man. The expression, not only in his eyes, and his posture but in how he held his head. She glanced to where Harry sat across from her and was shocked by the bleak menace in his eyes.

"I could have stopped him. I was close enough to touch him. I didn't do more than glance at him in the elevator. He got off on the second floor."

"Des, could you ask your boss on the q.t. to check and see if anyone knows him?"

"Not a good idea, Kate. Someone will talk. He'll know that we know and our chances of stopping him will get smaller."

Maeve studied Harry for a minute and then pulled out her phone and dialed.

"Sadie, yeah hi. No, I'm at Kate's. We came early because someone is trying to kill our kids. Yes, again. I'm texting you a sketch of the man behind the attempts. This man is the one who murdered Harry's father. He's now posing as an agent in the D.C. headquarters. We suspect his initials will be M.C. which they have been for each alias he's used while working for the mob.

Search

"He's made multiple attempts on the kids, so we've got to stop him, yesterday if possible. We're about to be buried under a mass of wedding guests, all of whom could be hurt or killed if he isn't stopped.

"You're coming Friday. Wonderful. That will give you the rest of the week to pull as much information on him as possible. He's holding up as well as can be expected. I'll have Seamus send you our files when he gets home from school in an hour. This will include the entire history, plus everything we've come up with and our conclusions. You get to work on that and let me know what you need. Get back to me as soon as you've got anything."

Kate stood and began carrying all the boxes of files into her room and packing them into her closet. Once done, she loaded her boots on top of the boxes and closed the closet door tightly. Puppies had a way of getting through any door that wasn't firmly latched. Finally, she grabbed her coat and headed toward the back door. Agnes, who had been silent during the upheaval, stood and pulled her coat off the back of the chair. "I'm coming with you."

"I'm just going over to the studio to check on Ellen and my crew."

Maeve stood and grabbed her coat. "Padraig and Harry will be in charge of supper because I know that both of you can cook. Tom, I know you can cook too, but I want you to take Des to K&K and see what your crew can find. We never finished finding all the murders of law enforcement individuals in the area from New Jersey to Virginia. And I don't mean those in the line of duty. This guy goes for fancy and likes to show off. We'll meet back here at six."

"Missing directing operations at MI-5?" Tom asked.

"I haven't lost my touch." She smiled as she followed the women from the room.

The studio was a hive of activity. A stranger was taking photos of the women at their machines, knitting away. The toddlers and young kids were playing in the area that was filled with toys. Two babies were asleep in the soundproof room, visible from the workroom through the large window. Everyone smiled when Kate came in. Agnes went to hug Ellen, whom she had known since Ellen and Kate were small children.

Her studio manager kept everything flowing smoothly as she had done for many years when she had been the office manager at K&K. Maeve moved over to the toddlers and after sitting on the floor, began helping them build a tower. The knitters were all smiled as Kate wandered over to contemplate the wedding dress on the mannequin. She studied the lacework which had begun as cascading shamrocks and evolved into cascading paw prints. After a minute, the photographer approached and spoke softly.

"It's a beautiful dress. You're an amazing designer. You'll be beautiful on Saturday." Kate lifted the train, and the woman pulled up her camera and snapped a few shots from different angles. Then she asked if she could interview her. Ellen must have been listening because she piped up suggesting that they use her office. Once they settled on the sofa in the office, the woman introduced herself. "I'm Agent Louise Marshall. Des said that I would be doing the gig through Saturday. He gave me a tentative schedule."

Kate stood and went to the second desk in the corner of the office. Sitting down, she called up a file labeled 'Wedding' and pulled up the schedule, quickly printing out a copy. Agent Marshall stared at the computer. "You do know that anyone could hack into your computer and steal all your designs to say nothing about this schedule so that they would know where you'd be every moment?"

"They would if they could bypass my file encryption and the various traps and safeguards I have on this computer. It is more secure than those at the bureau. I had to update Harry's system because the security program he was using had a back-door and I managed to get by it in under five minutes. So I installed a program I had developed into his laptop and sent Sadie one for their mainframe"

"Wow, I am impressed. Not only are you marrying Harry Foyle, but you're getting Sadie as a co-worker as well. She's a legend."

"I am lucky."

"Actually, after talking to these women, I think Foyle is the lucky one. You've built and run two businesses, not counting breeding and showing your dogs. I don't think I could keep up with your schedule. Ellen said you developed and market the software you created for your business. According to Agent Xiang, you've been involved in the capture of multiple criminals this year. If I were a real reporter, I could make a great story out of this."

Kate's phone dinged, and she immediately hit a key on her computer as she jumped to her feet to look out the window. A car was turning around in the driveway. Kate dove back to her keyboard and hit the keys to capture the face of the driver. Jumping back across the office, she saw the car pull out onto the highway and pull away. Reaching back to the computer, she clicked a few keys and waited for the images to come up. She'd set it to take five shots. She opened the view option and clicked each one. A familiar face appeared. Kate stared in silence at the man.

Her phone rang as did the office phone. Kate grabbed hers and pushed the answer button as Louise leaned over to pick up the office phone. Before either of them could say anything, a voice came from through the office phone.

"Sorry you won't be able to wear that pretty wedding dress, Miss Killoy, but you'll be dead by Saturday." The line disconnected.

The phone in her hand squawked with a voice shouting. "Kate, Kate, answer me now."

"Sorry, Harry, I got distracted. He was just here. Just at the end of the driveway."

"Don't move, I'm coming."

A minute later, the sounds of many running feet on the stairs was the only warning of an invasion as Harry, Des, and Seamus burst through the door. Harry pushed open the door to the office and after gently taking the phone from her hand, wrapped his arms around his fiancée, and held her. "Where was he?"

Search

"He just turned around in the driveway. But then he called."

Louise turned to Des and said, "We need a trace to find this guy's number. His threat was, 'Sorry you won't be able to wear that pretty wedding dress, Miss Killoy, but you'll be dead by Saturday.'"

Harry reached over to the keyboard without letting go of Kate and pushed a couple of buttons.

"Here is the guy's license number. Call Gurka and see if we can get this guy."

Agnes burst into the room and turned Harry's head toward the door. "Under no circumstances do you turn around, Foyle."

"What the...?"

Maeve called out, "It's okay." Agnes let him go. Harry immediately looked over Kate's shoulder into the main room. What he saw looked like a ghost. A mannequin stood draped in sheets. As he stared, Kate turned and let out a gasp.
Agnes stepped out of the now crowded office.

"There is no way you are bringing bad luck by seeing the dress before the wedding."

"I thought that was 'see the bride in the dress before the wedding'," he argued.

"Whatever. I take my job seriously." Agnes reached in and blocking it from the view of the children behind her, gave him a pointed gesture with her hand.

"You weren't able to get any photos were you?" He asked Kate as he gazed toward the laptop.

She reached out and pressed buttons bringing the photos, the surveillance camera had taken, up on the monitor then clicked through until she stopped at a clear, full face photo. It was the man from the sketch — Maurio all grown up. They all stared at the screen.

"There he is," Kate whispered. "The man who killed your father and who wants us both dead."

Chapter Thirty

Kate looked around the crowded office and suggested they go. As she headed out, Ellen stopped her. "Kate, what was that all about? Weren't you giving an interview with Denise?"

"I was, but then some information that Harry and I have been trying to find came through on my computer and I called him. The whole crew came. Now we need to go to the next step. Sorry to interrupt the work schedule. What had been a relaxing day just got really busy. He's trying to finish up everything before the honeymoon, and I'm helping. We'll get out of your hair. Thanks, everybody. Nice meeting you, Denise."

They walked back through the kennel which was really quiet with all the boarding dogs gone. This had been her grandfather's second business and her father's. When she inherited it, it had been ongoing since the 1960s and was a fixture in Connecticut. The training courses had been started by her grandfather about fifteen years ago with all three of them teaching.

By the time it became Kate's, she already had her design business going, and she knew she'd need help. Luckily Sal Modigliani had just retired from years as a police chief and was ready to take on something new. He took over as kennel manager and together they'd added the police dog training classes to their roster. She was so used to the noise and activity going on that the quiet and the empty runs felt spooky.

Meanwhile, as she reached her office, she stopped to be sure that Hecate, her pure white Maine Coon Cat who ruled that part of the kennel, was well-fed and happy. The twenty-five-pound cat lifted her head for a scratch when Kate entered the room, but when she didn't see dogs who needed to be put in their place, she just curled up on Kate's chair and went back to sleep.

The guys were taking over the kitchen while Quinn bounced from one to another trying to gain attention. Agnes had left. She and Cathy would be spending the day visiting Samoyed breeders in the area.

Maeve grabbed Padraig, and they had moved to the living room to watch the news and weather report, checking when this snow would melt,

Kate took Dillon and Liam and went into her bedroom. Something was bothering her. They'd already found the photo so that they could hopefully identify the man trying to kill them, but it was something else, a clue she'd missed.

Search

Stretching out her legs, she settled on the floor with her back to the bed and pulled the photo boxes over to her. Again, she began going through the photographs of Pete Foyle and Maurio. Nothing stood out, even though she had leafed through them twice. Discouraged, she leaned back resting her head against the quilt, and stared at the ceiling.

She remembered the year she'd covered the ceiling with breed identification posters. During her childhood, she'd lie in bed, studying each dog and the characteristics that made the breed unique. This led to her becoming an expert, of sorts, on the different breeds. People were always impressed when they'd ask about breeds in different rings and Kate would tell them not only the name but all about their purpose and history.

Now as she stared at the white ceiling she thought about the pin holes which had been left when the posters came down. She would have had to stand on a ladder to fill in each hole. Not thinking it was necessary, she'd balked. Gramps however had pointed out that she might not notice the holes because they were in the background, but other people would wonder why she had marks all over her ceiling. Those pin holes would be obvious to them.

"Background!" Kate yelled. "The answer was right in front of me and I didn't see it."

Her bedroom door burst open as Quinn came racing into the room and landed in her lap. The puppy began licking her face and she shoved him off while reaching to save the snapshots she'd been sorting.

Quinn suddenly found himself lifted and placed in the kitchen with Kate's door shut. Harry secured the door, turned and spotted her pawing through the pictures the puppy had scattered.

"Harry, help me find the photo with them at the FBI." He dropped onto the floor beside her and searched all those around where she'd been. After a few minutes, they realized that it had disappeared.

"It was here. Where could it have gone?" Kate felt her voice rise as desperation spread through her. "I've got to find it."

Harry stood and took each box of photos, and placed it on the bed after leafing through it. He finally reached for Kate and pulled her up. In the process of standing, she saw a speck of color peeking out from under the dust ruffle on her bed. Harry reached down and pulled out the photo and stared at it.

"Check the background." She reached into the box nearest them and pulled out the image of their visits to other law enforcement venues. Then pushing the boxes aside, she laid out the prints in a row. "Look at these photos as though your father and Maurio weren't in the shots."

"I'm not sure what I'm looking at."

"Find one thing that is the same in all the shots other than your dad and Maurio."

"Well, this guy in the back is at both the precinct and at headquarters."

"Right, now what about these other shots?" The excitement was growing in her voice. Harry studied them and after a minute was able to find the man lurking in the background in each of the other shots. He gawked at her as Des stuck his head into the room to announce that dinner was served. One look at them had him in the room asking what they'd found.

"Do you know this man?"

Kate pointed to the man in the background as she handed him the second photo, the one with the clearest view of him.

Des stared for a few minutes and then said, "He looks vaguely familiar, but I really can't place a name with the face. Why, is he important?"

"He is important because he is in every single one of the photos of Pete Foyle and Maurio. He's not posing for a photo with them but is semi-hiding in the background. It would be my guess that he is very important not only to Maurio but to our case."

"I don't see how you even noticed him, he disappears into the background so well."

"That's the point. All the time Pete was mentoring Maurio in law enforcement's ins and outs, this shadow was lurking just out of sight. Don't ask me why, but I'm sure he's important." Kate took the photo back and put it with the others.

Her door swung open and Tim called, "Come on, Kate, you're holding up dinner and I'm starving."

"Coming." Harry stood and he pulled her to him. As Des left, Harry whispered, "We'll find them and finish this. Hang in there," Then he gave her a hug.

Dinner was boisterous. They'd made spaghetti plus an absolutely delicious salad and garlic bread. They even found some pies that Kate had made last week in the freezer, so there were both apple and peach pies for dessert.

An unspoken mandate against talking about what had been happening held sway. Seamus talked about his months of training to be certified by the FAA to fly Rex. Tim spoke about the scout from B.C. who'd talked to him after his last game. Padraig spoke about his college reunion and how surprised he was that those who'd survived the war in Korea, were still kicking around and how it was strange that the war had never really ended. The topics bounced back and forth with nary a mention of the killer or the wedding.

They were all sitting around relaxing when Seamus arrived home with Harry's best man, Rufus Blackburn, and his son Jordy in tow.

Rufus had become Harry's best friend when he went to California as a child. Though he was older than Harry, his family had provided a home for the young student. The older boy had helped Harry ease his way into his new life.

After saying hello to Harry and Kate, Rufus looked around the room, his smile fading.

Kate smiled and said, "She's staying with Agnes. She's been visiting Tom and Bev, Sammy breeders near Albany, today. Both she and Agnes will be here in the morning."

Jordy poked his father. "Relax, Dad. You'll be with Cathy soon and then you two can go all mushy." Rufus' face turned red as he clamped a hand over his son's mouth and asked how everyone was.

"Well, other than someone is trying to murder me and Kate before the wedding, everything is fine," Harry told him.

"So, the situation's normal. Who's trying to kill you this time? Drug cartels? Corrupt politicians?"

Search

"The Mob."

"Cool," Jordy said, pulling his father's hand from his mouth and smiled at Harry. "But now to the important stuff: where's Quinn?"

Kate decided not to tempt her puppy's good behavior tonight. "Quinn is out in the yard resting after eating supper. You'll have lots of quality time with him tomorrow, but I'd rather you didn't get him all jazzed at bedtime. If you're hungry, you might want to have some of the desserts that are left from supper. Then, I think, since the clock says it's after nine, and since tomorrow will be a busy day with the barn being converted for the wedding reception, which will really have the dogs all excited, you might want to turn in. Your dad and you will be staying in the rooms over the kennel office. You know the way.

"Why don't you each have a piece of pie with ice cream then head up to your rooms? If you want to say hi to Quinn, you will spot him when you go out the back door and can talk to him through the fence. I would not like either of you wandering around at night on your own."

"Pie and ice cream. Deal!"

Chapter Thirty-One

The sounds of heavy trucks interrupted breakfast. She and Maeve had lingered over tea while the men all disappeared outside at the first sound something happening.

Tom, who was getting along very well on the cane now, seemed to be in charge. But all the guys were like little boys as the massive truck backed up to the barn and began using a crane and forklifts to move all the flooring, tables, and chairs, as well as boxes of decorations into the building.

The company had sent about a dozen men to do the work. They would probably have been much happier to get on with the job, minus the half dozen supervisors.

Search

Kate turned from the window to see Maeve looking serious. She was about to ask her what the problem was when Maeve stopped her. "Kate, have you and your mother discussed the wedding night?"

Kate stopped in her tracks. This was the last question she was expecting.

"Um, no. We don't really talk."

"I was worried about that."

"I, uh, got a couple of books as one of the gifts at my shower. I don't know who gave them to me because there wasn't a card. I haven't had a chance to read them yet."

"I gave them to you. I was afraid of this. I assume you were given Sex-Ed classes in high school."

"Sophomore year. I will admit I didn't pay much attention. I figured I knew all that stuff from breeding dogs."

"Well, though similar, people are a bit more involved. We don't have the instincts that dogs do, though, from the way Quinn was mounting Shelagh's head, they still have to grow up a little. I am aware that you have remained a virgin because your grandma Ann and your mom were virgins when they married. However, they married quickly after meeting the men in their lives. You met Harry in February and have held out until November.

"I realize that Harry cares a lot about you and respects your wish to wait, but I am surprised you made it this long since you love him. However, you might want to do some reading before Saturday."

"I will..." The back door opened and Harry rushed in.

Peggy Gaffney

"Kate, do we still have those six-packs of soda in the fridge?" He froze and looked at both of them. "What's up? What are you two talking about?"

Kate reached in and got the soda and turning to him said, "Sex."

He almost dropped the six-pack and as his eyes darted between them, as his face turning red. Then he focused on Kate, drew a deep breath and smiled. "Good. I will make it as wonderful as you could want, but I don't want you to be afraid to ask me anything. We will talk it all out until you feel comfortable. We've waited this long, so when you are ready, I'll be there for you."

He turned to Maeve and in a quiet voice said, "I will make sure she is happy." Lifting his free hand to cup Kate's cheek, he stared into her eyes, smiled and leaned in to kiss her whispering, "I love you." They were both breathing hard when a shout came from outside and without another word, he turned and was out the door.

"Kate," Maeve said. "The books will make you aware of what is coming so you will feel more relaxed, but I am now sure that everything is going to be perfect. That man would do move heaven and earth to keep you safe and happy. I can read it on his face and in his eyes and hear it in his voice. He loves you very much."

Kate picked up their teacups to rinse and with a smile on her face, whispered, "I know."

She looked out the window to judge how they were coming with the work going on in the barn. A man slowly drove the forklift back toward the big trailer truck after setting his load gently on the ground. Whirling the machine around on a dime, he headed up the hill to pick up another load. He didn't spot her in the window as he drove by. Harry, Des, and Tom walked toward the front of her house, with Tom's cane supported stride setting the pace.

As the driver came abreast of them, he turned to stared at Harry. His eyes didn't leave him until a shift in his load caused him to steer more in her direction. That was when she caught sight of his expression — hate. There was no other word for it. The look on the driver's face had been pure hatred.

Her gaze followed the man until the exercise yard fence caused him to turn around and head back. This time, however, he didn't head toward the barn. She watched as he returned his load to the far side of the truck and disappeared from sight.

She stood, her hands gripping the edge of the sink, her knuckles white and said, "Maeve, call Harry and tell him I need all three of them here, right now."

Maeve had the phone at her ear and was talking as she rounded the table for a better look at what had alarmed Kate. She's barely disconnected when the front door opened and all three men raced through to the kitchen. Kate tore herself from the sink to grab Harry in relief.

"What's the matter?" Tom asked as he lowered himself into a chair.

"The forklift driver. It wasn't until he had to turn that I realized I'd seen that face before. He's older, grayer, and has a scraggly beard, but I'm sure this is the same man, who was in the background of all the photos of Pete and Maurio. And, Harry, the look he gave you was pure hatred."

Maeve had been staring out the window since she'd called the men, turned cursing. They all looked at her.

"He's gone. He just got picked up by someone driving a maroon Chevy Cavalier that's heading up the drive to the highway. The license number is obscured by mud, so I don't have the number," she said holding up her phone, "but I got a few shots of your guy moving from behind the truck to the car."

Des grinned. "You're still the greatest agent ever, Maeve."

Kate's phone dinged and she dove across the table to the laptop keyboard hitting the keys to activate the camera at the end of the driveway.

"I've just sent you all the shots of this guy and I sent them to the laptop as well. Maybe we can enhance some and achieve a better look," Maeve said.

Harry had his phone to his ear. "Will, try to find out the name on the forklift driver who just left, I'll hold. Yeah, I'm here. What did he say? Substitute driver. Does he have any paperwork on him? Snag it if you can. Thanks."

He pulled out a chair and settled at the table. "According to your brother, the company's forklift driver came down with the stomach flu and this guy was a friend of a friend who came on to work for the day.

"Will said he'd press the boss for paperwork, which he has to have for his insurance, but if the guy came on in a hurry and disappeared just a quick, I suspect that anything on paper will be bogus. So, what we've got to work with are Maeve's snapshots and whatever the security camera may have caught."

Search

Kate had opened her favorite graphics program and was working on the first photo. After a few minutes, she loaded the photo with Pete and Maurio and then the one was taken today which had been enhanced and color balanced. The likeness was extraordinary. The enlargements had been sharpened to the point where the fact that their guy had a small scar over his right eye was clear on both.

Will walked in carrying a couple of pieces of paper which he had rolled in a napkin.

"Arni, the job boss, said that the guy filled it out on the spot and then just dumped it in with all the other forms. Nobody else has touched the folder all morning."

"Does anyone want to try to pull a print from the papers. I understand that's not the best surface, but since there is a partial here which is marked by the dirt on the guy's hands, I think we might find something."

She took a notebook marked 'house papers' from the top of the fridge, next to the blueprints, and pulled a couple of empty plastic sleeves from the front pocket, then using the napkin, inserted each sheet into a sleeve. Now they could be touched.

"The man's name, according to the form is Guido Piana, a resident of Worcester, Massachusetts. He's been a forklift driver for more than twenty-five years. There are three companies in his references. Did they check any?"

"The boss said his secretary called two of them and got good recommendations."

Kate Googled for the company names and none of them came up.

"Okay, phony companies. The numbers are burner phones with someone on the other end strictly to give him a recommendation. Short and sweet."

Sal came in and wandered over to look at the screen which held almost everyone's attention.

"So what's the interest in Guido? He seems a nice guy. Used to work in Worcester at Yankee Pipe and something. I don't remember. Why are you guys checking him out?"

"If you look at those two photos, would you say they are the same person about fifteen years older?" Harry asked.

"Now that you mention it, I'd say it was a perfect match. So what's the connection?"

Kate pulled out the photos of Pete and Maurio. "Can you find him in this picture?"

Sal studied it, then said, "Yeah, here he is behind them with the striped tie."

Kate handed him successive photos and in each he found Guido. Never one to hold back, he asked, "Does this guy have anything to do with your father's murder."

"Possibly. Nothing ties him to the actual murder. But he seems to have a tie to Maurio."

"Who's Maurio? God, I babysit my granddaughter for one day and I end up out of the loop."

Kate invited Sal to join her cleaning the dog yard and spent the time going over everything. Sal offered to do the fingerprint testing because he'd done hundreds of them over the years.

Kate looked around the yard and asked "Where's Quinn?"

Sal told her that Jordy had come by with Quinn earlier and asked if he could take him for a walk on the trails in the woods.

Search

They'd been gone about an hour, so they should be back soon looking for food.

"Twelve-year-old boys need to eat constantly."

They had finished the yard and headed inside when Maeve stepped to the door to signal them to hurry. Kate took one look at her face and knew something was wrong.

"Maeve, what...?"

"Kate. When we enlarged the shots of the car pulling out of your driveway we got to the shots of the back of the car and noticed this."

Kate looked at the screen and recognized the rear of the Chevy with the license plate but what horrified her was in the back window were two faces—Jordy and Quinn.

"Call Sean. Launch an Amber Alert, now!" she shouted. They've had enough time to travel halfway to the state border.

"Wait. Jordy's phone has a *Family and Friends* app which is a tracking device on it." she said, slapping her phone on the table and opening the same app.

She clicked on Jordy's name and waited for the tracking to kick in and prayed he had left it installed after he had connected with her last summer. The map appeared on the screen showing his phone was on Route 8 traveling south toward I-95.

"He is approaching Shelton not far from, but heading toward, Bridgeport."

Maeve had Sean on the phone and was relaying the information. Once he had the Amber Alert set, he got the coordinates from her to give the patrol cars already patrolling that area of the highway. Nobody talked, the silence was only broken by the ticking clock. Tension stretched as they all studied Kate's phone. She updated Maeve.

"They are still on Route 8, have gone under the Merritt Parkway but are still heading southwest."

The wait continued. Then Maeve nodded as she heard something from the phone pressed to her ear.

She said, "They got a visual. White dog looking out the back window. Multiple troopers are positioning their cars to surround the vehicle and initializing a takedown. The troopers are going to escort it off onto Old Town Road at the north end of the Beardsley Zoo and pull out Jordy and Quinn."

They watched the little red dot on Kate's phone move down the highway and then move onto the exit, those surrounding her held their breath. When it reached the end of the ramp, the dot stopped moving. A faint voice came from Maeve's phone, and she swayed as she relaxed. Padraig reached out and lowered her into a chair.

She put Sean on speakerphone, so they could all hear him say, "They've got Jordy and Quinn and both are now in one of the trooper's cars. They will head here as soon as Jordy has been questioned. Apparently, there was only one man in the car with them, but he was armed. He has been arrested and will be taken to Bethany barracks. The kidnapper is not talking.

"According to Jordy, the man who had been driving was the one who grabbed him and Quinn and stuffed them in the car. Then he picked up this guy from in front of the massive truck. Once they were on Route 6, they went about a mile and pulled off.

"The driver got out and this guy slid into the driver's seat. The one who got out told his buddy to take the kid to the house in the Bronx and wait for instructions.

When they started up again, Jordy spotted a blue GMC truck parked on the verge of the road about a quarter mile further down, but didn't get the license. Jordy should be back in under an hour, when they finish taking his statement."

Kate reached for Maeve's phone and said, "Thanks, Sean. I'll tell Rufus and Cathy."

Harry blanched. "Rufus! Oh, my God, I didn't tell my best man that his son had been kidnapped."

Sal clapped a hand on his shoulder and said, "I would suggest you wait about an hour. No sense getting them upset now that he's safe. Once Jordy's back, you can have him call and handle it. Otherwise, you may be looking for a new best man."

Chapter Thirty-Two

Kate lay in bed and stared at the ceiling. The dogs were outside even though it was much too early and she had crawled back under the covers to stay warm. Last night had been chaotic. Cathy and Rufus had returned from sightseeing at the same time the trooper had driven up with Jordy and Quinn in the back seat. When Rufus found what happened to his son, he turned on Harry and it took everyone to talk him down from packing Cathy and Jordy up and leaving. Jordy talked about the fact that Kate had known where he was at all time because of the Friend's app, and the troopers had the car surrounded and got them off the highway safely and arrested the goon who was driving.

Search

Rufus was furious that Harry hadn't called him, but Harry pointed out that they were too busy rescuing Jordy and by the time he was safely on his way back, he decided that there was no reason to alarm him.

Cathy finally took over. Turning to Rufus she said, "Have a nice trip home. Jordy and I will be staying. Sal can step in the best man. You take your outrage and have a good trip. Excuse me but Kate and I are going to go chat with Maeve."

The three of them left the room. Harry later told her that Rufus stared after her for several minutes before he turned to Harry and said, "I've got to marry that woman."

Maeve had praised Cathy's chutzpah for the way she handled Rufus and told her that she predicted a long and happy marriage. Cathy blushed but was grinning at the same time. She told them what their plans were. It seemed that Rufus was exploring colleges in Spokane and was thinking about making a move. There was a possibility that he'd be allowed to start his own graduate specialty providing he taught a certain number of undergraduate classes. He was still talking with the school so they had to wait and see.

Maeve had reassured her about Jordy's adventure. By the time Cathy and Maeve left, the kitchen was empty. Her dogs were all bedded down and Harry had left a note that they'd had their biscuits and were down for the night. She'd opened the door to her bedroom and found puddles of white fluff in the form of sleeping Samoyeds. She'd quickly slipped into bed and much to her surprise fell asleep.

Peggy Gaffney

Though it was early the following morning, Kate wasn't sleeping but rather staring at the ceiling when her door opened and Harry walked in. "What are you doing awake at this hour?"

"How did you know I was awake?"

"Dillon came to the back door and looked at me before going off to chase his son."

"They've been so quiet--I didn't notice them playing."

"What is so engaging that you are not watching your dogs act so cute?"

"I was thinking... Why now? What happened to set this guy off. It's been years since your father died. There haven't been any law enforcement murders recently. What is happening to make it vital to go after you now?"

Harry stared at her as silence descended. Then his eyes moved toward the closet. He walked toward it and began pulling out boxes. He looked back at Kate.

"It's this. This is the reason. The fact that I was doing this research. There must be something in here which threatens his plan. This is the reason he will stop at nothing to kill you and me. If he succeeds, nobody will care about what's in here. It will disappear into the back of a closet and he will succeed."

Kate stared at him and at the boxes. Then, she tucked her feet under the covers and said, "Toss me my sweatshirt, and give me a box. We've got to find what it is if we're going to have a wedding."

He carried her sweatshirt to her and kissed her hard, then turned back and handed her a box. Setting a second box on the bottom of the bed, he pulled her chair up close and they both got to work.

Search

It was Sal who found them several hours later.

"You planning on feeding these dogs or just letting them starve?" he asked, pushing the bedroom door open. He stared at the piles of papers and snorted, "Only you two would be ensconced in a bedroom, days before your wedding — doing research. What are you looking for anyway?"

"Motive," Kate told him. "The reason our killer needs to stop us now, not in a month, not in a year, but now. There is a reason somewhere in all this stuff that will tell us why it's vital that he shut us down even if it means murder. And I'm convinced, it's got something to do with timing.

"I originally thought it was connected with a grudge against Harry, but they've had years to kill him if that was the plan. No, this has to do with a piece of information, lurking in one of these boxes, which could stop them from carrying out their goal. Getting me shot was simply to distract Harry from finishing this research. The same with the attempt on his life and everything since. With the attempts getting more frequent, I'd say that whatever is hidden in here, is connected to an event happening soon — very soon."

"I'm going to go feed your mutts and you're going to get dressed. As soon as everybody eats, we'll get to work. With all these Killoys, plus Des and even Rufus, if he's decided he's over being pissed, we'll find what is in here."

When breakfast was done, everyone crowded around the kitchen table as Kate said, "I have a theory that something criminal and very dangerous is about to occur which could be stopped by us. The answer to what it is lies hidden in here. I know that we've been over this data, but we were searching statistically, trying to find how widespread this was. What we need is to find a thread that would tie all those facts to something that is happening soon"

Harry began filling them in on the finer details of his investigation. He began with his search for the man they now knew as Maurio Corsetti and where it had led him so far. His goal had been on solving the murdered his father. and he was pretty sure it was Maurio.

"The relationship between my dad, Pete Foyle, and Maurio was not based on any interest the boy had in becoming part of law enforcement, but rather as part of a plan engineered by the mob. Kate's found a connection. I'll let her explain."

Kate turned her computer so everyone could see it and showed the photos of Maurio and Pete Foyle. She pointed out that by introducing the boy to certain people of power in the world of law enforcement, he'd eliminated the mob's need for him in their plan. In fact, with Pete knowing the connections, he became a danger to their plan so he had to be eliminated.

"I suspected that either Maurio or the man standing in the background, who kidnapped Jordy, was the person who killed Pete. We have been looking at this case, trying to connect people to track down killers. However, the most important question is one nobody has asked — why now. Pete Foyle's death took place years ago and remains unsolved on the books of the Boston Police Department. Not even the threat of Harry looking into that death caused a reaction. However, Des, while helping Harry track down Maurio, found he was someone the mob uses to eliminate problems. Maurio's talent was in being a chameleon, he could become someone else after completing his task. The pattern of mob killings that Harry and Des found is forming that pattern.

"When a cop was murdered in New Jersey who was part of a money laundering task force, another cop is brought in to take his place. The pattern has been occurring over and over again. When the mob is threatened, a member of the team threatening them is eliminated and replaced. But it's not the vicious killing that's their goal. No, it's the careful insertion of their own people.

"What we uncovered this morning though, was a pattern of cases lost and mobsters freed after someone in the prosecutorial chain died.

"Another problem came to light as we found more killings and that was essentially real estate. To use a phrase from that business, 'location, location. location.' This is not just a Boston problem, not just New York, Philadelphia or Miami. The pattern is pervasive from Maine to Florida.

"Someone high up in the mob has come up with the idea to train members of the mob in certain skills so they can appear as part of law enforcement. Pseudo-lawyers, judges, cops, FBI agents, all well trained, are planted as sleepers until needed.

"The various crime families behind this have been convinced to work together for the betterment of all. Once these mobsters build reputations for success at taking down organized crime members — arranged with the blessing of the mob — then they are accepted as, not only part of the establishment, but also as members with special talent when taking on the syndicate. Each replacement becomes a solid member of that team and will carry out his tasks within that job until orders are given from the man behind the plan.

"What we have been trying to do, is go through all these cases of law enforcement deaths covering the last ten years, to identify who moved in to replace the person who'd been killed or even just to fill out that team. The new guy is the key."

"Kate, should we gather these new hires into a database?" Maeve asked.

"Good idea. First, let's gather the names. There are six boxes of cases. You each take a pad and make a list of anyone who fits this modus operandi. We need to know five things: victim, date of the murder, case in which they were involved, the place, and who replaced them or was added to their team."

"Kate, I know people think of me as a kid, well, because I am a kid," Jordy said. "But I have the skills to work as part of this team,"

Kate leaned forward and looked him in the eye. "You can join the team, provided that you're not connected with the mob."

Rufus began to sputter, taking offense, but Jordy just grinned and yelled, "Deal!"

"I know you studied statistics last semester, so look over Maeve's data and see what you can predict."

"I'm on it."

Kate took orders for tea while Harry covered those who wanted coffee.

Within a few minutes, they had all settled in, with the only sounds being some calls for clarifications on certain crimes as

Search

to whether they qualified, or cheer when someone found a direct and obvious connection.

By one o'clock, they were ready to take a break for lunch. Will quickly whipped together sandwiches for everyone along with hearty minestrone soup.

They all stood and stretched. Maeve, Jordy, and Kate went out to play with the dogs for a few minutes. The snow had disappeared from the yard for the most par, but it hadn't gotten so warm as to turn the ground into a mud pen. Kate divided up the balls among the players and a five-minute free-for-all commenced. Once, the game was over and the dogs had been suitably exercised, the exercise yard was quickly policed and cleaning up. No sooner had they headed back inside when a bunch of trucks pulled into the yard followed by Agnes.

Chapter Thirty-Three

Kate, remembering what was spread out on the kitchen table, made a dive for the door. However, once she got inside, she found the kitchen was empty of any sign of their research. Shouts were coming from the living room, and she noticed all the men watching a soccer game from England and heard Jordy explaining the trajectory of the ball on the last kick which guaranteed the goal.

Agnes strode in the front door accompanied by Bob, one of the workers who had installed her security system a few months ago.

"Sorry to leave everything to the last minute," she said, "but this was the only time the security people had. You have a security system, Kate, I know, but it needs to be beefed up for the wedding. We are going to have a lot of important people attending your wedding and Sal told me that the camera in the woods had been knocked out.

"Tom, go with Harry and work with Bob to figure out possible weaknesses and plug them. There is no way any of the designers or visiting government nabobs are going to be endangered at a wedding Agnes Forester is running.

"Your mother and Ann have just returned, by the way, so I'm off to talk to your gran about displaying the gifts at the reception." With a backward and somewhat royal wave, she dashed out the door.

"Sound the all-clear. Hurricane Agnes has left the building," Seamus shouted. Everyone grinned.

Bob shook hands with Harry and all the men followed him outside. Kate turned to see Maeve snagged Padraig's arm to hold him back as she smiled at Jordy.

"Why don't you go find your father and Cathy. I'm sure that Kate's mom would love to take you on a tour of the math department at Yale. Then we might tour Wooster Square. Some of the best pizza places in the world are there."

"Pizza, great! Is that okay, Kate?"

"Perfect. We can work on this stuff tomorrow. Remember, as part of the team, you are sworn to secrecy."

"Yes, ma'am." He ran past Maeve and headed toward the group of men.

"Agnes told the company to come in unmarked trucks so your mother won't become curious. I'll tell her it's just last minute work on the reception." Her great-aunt smiled and after accepting her coat from Padraig, who had already grabbed Jordy's jacket and Rufus's coat. They waved goodbye.

Kate stood alone in the middle of her house, listening to the silence and feeling frustrated. The workmen would be in and out all afternoon, so all work had to stop on any of the research. With a sigh, she turned toward Harry's room. This might be a good time to organize some of his dad's stuff. Many of the boxes were opened but looked as though they'd only been checked to see what was inside.

In order to get comfortable, she pulled an overstuffed chair closer to the box pile and started emptying the first box onto the one next to it. This seemed to be clothing. She found two suits, several sports jackets, and about a half dozen dress shirts. Noting the length of the sleeve and width of the shoulder, she realized Harry was way too large to use any of these. In fact, none of the men outside were that small. Pete must have been about five foot eight. Harry had probably been taller than that by the time he'd come back from California as a teenager to attend MIT.

Neatly folding everything back into the first box, she grabbed the marker she had used to label the boxes when they arrived and made a list of the box contents, folded down the lids and went on to the next. Four boxes later, she had a stack of boxes containing sweaters, shoes, socks, underwear, and tee shirts all neatly organized. No sooner had she opened a box containing his uniforms when Harry stuck his head around the door-jam.

"Hey, there, I've been looking for you. What are you doing?"

"Since we can't work on what we should be doing, I thought I'd start getting some of your dad's stuff organized and labeled. Your mom must have just grabbed piles of stuff and put them into boxes. The shoebox on the nightstand has the tie clasps, cuff links, spent cartridges, and money I found in his pockets."

"It was a habit of his to take things off and stuff them in his pockets. I'm still looking for his watch."

"How are they doing outside?"

"Well, they finished the area around the studio and the barn, but I wanted to ask you for advice about the area surrounding the kennel and dog yard."

"Wouldn't the dogs set that off all the time."

"That's why we need you to figure angles which will cover the area but will be out of the range of the motion detector."

"Okay. let's go into the exercise yard. I'll need a height measurement for my tallest dog standing on top of the oversized cable spool. That would be Rory. Let's go. The dogs will all be wide awake with all these people to check out."

"Did I see Maeve taking Rufus, Cathy, and Jordy up toward the main house?"

"Yes, she got the brilliant idea of having my mom show them around her department at Yale and then promised Jordy pizza. I'd rather my mom didn't know we were ramping up security, she'd want to know why and probably wouldn't buy Agnes telling her it's to protect A-list celebrities at the reception."

They walked into the yard, and were immediately surrounded by the dogs. Kate signaled Rory to jump up onto the spool. Quinn and Shelagh immediately joined him. She stood next to the stool and measured where the tips of Rory's ears were in relation to her shoulder. She gave Bob the calculation for what the lowest setting for the motion would be on the outside cameras. Since she had the workmen here, she got an idea and asked him to add two lights which would go on if the dogs entered the yard from either the house or the kennel. That way, as soon as she let a dog out, the entire yard would be lit up as well as the surrounding areas. This way, if some animal tried to sneak up on her dogs, she'd be warned. It also meant that when they went out before the crack of dawn, they would automatically turn on the lights, leaving her to dive back under the covers. When they started back inside, she stopped.

"Bob, don't forget about the camera on the trail being shot out."

"Don't worry, Kate, I'll adjust its location to an evergreen tree so it wouldn't make such a good target. We should be done by supper time, so you'll be protected tonight."

When they went back inside, she noticed that her team had dispersed.

"Let's see. Tom took Des over to K&K to do some research. Seamus and Satu went to her house for supper. Tim had basketball practice. So with the rest of them off to New Haven, we have the place to ourselves."

The amount of time they'd spent alone since he got back was almost nonexistent. Harry took her hand, and when they reached the middle of the kitchen he stopped, pulled her into his arms, and said, "I suggest we have a date night, beginning now. We can watch a movie on Netflix, have an intimate candle-lit dinner for two, followed by another movie or maybe just a chance to sit and snuggle on the sofa."

She leaned in and kissed him and then pointed up to the top shelf of the cupboard. Harry grinned and soon a bag of microwave popcorn was being poured into a large mixing bowl.

Arms around each other, they were headed toward the living room, when Bob knocked at the back door.

"Hey, Kate, sorry to do this, but we're going to turn off the power. Hopefully, it will only be for a couple of hours. But it may be until morning if the guy I sent to track down the part that just burned out isn't back in time. But I'll definitely have you up and going by morning."

A feeling of unease came over her and the grip she had on Harry's hand tightened. He looked down at her and nodded.

"Well, Bob, you should know that this job is about more than a wedding. Someone is trying to kill both Kate and me. If you leave us security blind, whoever it is would have the perfect opportunity to finish the job. And," Harry reached out and put a hand on his shoulder, "if they succeed, you won't be paid. Under no circumstances are you leaving us without power overnight—understood."

"Uh, Agnes didn't mention that."

"Agnes doesn't know."

"Got it. We'll figure something out. You'll have power and full security in forty-five minutes."

"Thanks, Bob."

As soon as the door closed she hugged him and said, "I love it when you go all 'Dirty Harry' tough guy."

"Well, since he installs security systems for a living. I think I can take him," he said as he wandered over to the counter and grabbed a fist full of popcorn.

"Don't tell anyone I said this," she told him, "but I miss having a well-armed crowd in the kitchen. You might want to arm yourself, just in case."

"Not a bad idea but it may complicate things if we're snuggling on the couch."

"The thought of possible death tends to throw cold water on my urge to snuggle. We might as well go organize more of the boxes in your bedroom."

Kate stepped up behind Harry, as he loaded the dog dishes into the dishwasher, and wrapped her arms around him.

Resting her head on his back, she said, "With all that has been going on here, we haven't been paying attention to what's been happening in the world. The answer to this whole thing might have been in the evening news for the last few days and we wouldn't have had a clue. Maybe, if she has time, that would be something Sadie would be able to check for us once she's packed for her trip here. Why don't you call her before we leave and ask?"

"Okay, but do me a favor. Don't go outside by yourself," he said as he turned and moved to gather her in his arms. "They're getting desperate and I don't want you to be a target."

"Okay." She headed for her room to put on a warmer sweater, wash her face and comb her hair so that she'd look decent at dinner. When she came out, she found Harry sitting at the kitchen table staring at his phone. He didn't look up or move when she entered.

Search

Kate finally asked, "Is Sadie going to do our research and find an event which is happening that might fit?"

"She doesn't have too. She already knows. Apparently, the President of the United States has just nominated Aldo Ranno to be the next Attorney General."

"Isn't he the Acting Attorney General in Delaware?"

"Yup. But that's not the only thing he is. He's one of the people our list of replacements. He was put in place when the healthy forty-two-year-old Attorney General died of a sudden heart attack while riding the train home from a meeting with the Justice Department in D.C. The trip was made, specifically to share some information on organized crime with a task force. I think we have enough information to be pretty sure the nominee is an undercover plant installed by the mob, and if confirmed, the most powerful man in law enforcement in the country, will be a mobster."

Chapter Thirty-Four

Kate was up before sunrise baking the desserts for the Thanksgiving feast and to keep people happy on Friday. She had her oven filled with pies and had three kinds of cookies laid out on cookie sheets. Flour was everywhere — thank goodness for white dogs. The tiny house had taken on the air of a bakery, and she was getting a sugar rush without even having eaten anything. She had just finished frosting the turkey cookies, piping delicate feathery wings and a bright red wattle on each when hands snaked around her waist, and she found herself being pulled back and getting a kiss on her flour-covered nose. "Happy Thanksgiving! Did I wake you?"

"Not you, just that enchanting smell," Harry said, breathing in and sighing. One of the timers dinged, and she grabbed a pair of oven mitts from the counter and flipped them over her shoulder.

"Take the pies out of the oven and put them on the cooling racks. I've got to finish frosting the pilgrim cookies and get the pumpkin ones baked."

Harry opened the oven and began transporting pies. The table filled with pumpkin, mincemeat, blueberry, strawberry-rhubarb, and lemon meringue pies.

Kate began loading the oven with huge baking sheets filled with cookies and said after resetting her second timer, "While you're waiting for those too cool, go into the whelping room and get the metal cart. Once they are cool, they can be transferred to the whelping room, and we'll load them into pie baskets to be carried up to the main house."

"Should I let the dogs in for their breakfasts?"

"You do and you die. Chocolate, walnuts, and other things that are delicious but toxic to dogs are still on the counter. Once the cookies are done and in the whelping room, they can come in and eat.

Except for the puppies, they all know the holiday baking drill. When my kitchen smells like this, they know it is either Easter, Thanksgiving or Christmas, and they'll eat eventually. Baking and Sams don't mix. They either try to steal the treats or they shed white hair all over the food. The AKC might consider dog hair a condiment, but my non-dog relatives do not."

Harry was just moving the last of the pies and Kate was taking batches of cookies out of the oven when Jordy walked into the kitchen. "Wow. This place smells like heaven. How much food have you fixed? Can I have a cookie? Every day should begin with cookies before breakfast."

"Those are too hot. If you go into the whelping room, you'll find some that are cooler. If you promise not to eat them all, you can help box them up to go to the main house for Thanksgiving dinner."

Jordy yelled from the other room, "How many people are you expecting for dinner? This is enough food to feed an army."

"There is a modest size group this year because of the wedding, with only about twenty-five people. A couple of years ago, we had more than fifty because more of the cousins came plus both Tom and Will brought friends from college."

"Where are you going to put everybody? I've seen that huge table at the big house, but it doesn't seat that many."

"Magic! Just watch. Everyone will have a seat at the table. Okay, this is the last batch of cookies to go into the whelping room. Put them in there to cool and be sure the door is shut. If you go in or out, be sure that the door stays closed. I'll start feeding dogs and Harry can start breakfast. Oh! And get a couple of dozen eggs out of the fridge in there."

Rufus wandered in looking sleepy and went immediately to the coffee machine. He plunked himself down at the table, but once he had some coffee in him, was able to glance around. He spotted Harry cooking eggs and bacon. His son walked in carrying a couple of dozen eggs, with a cookie sticking out of his mouth and another one in his hand. Harry took the eggs and handed him a loaf of fresh baked bread, a knife, and pointed toward the toaster and the boy nodded and got to work.

Kate had all the bowls filled and let in the dogs. Quinn immediately ran to Jordy, then jumped up and sniffed the edge of the counter. "Quinn, get over here or I'm going to give your breakfast to Shelagh." Kate shouted. The dogs waited until all the dishes went down, then ate. They were soon back out in the yard with their biscuits. Harry took the stack of bowls to put in the dishwasher and handed Kate a plate of food. Jordy put a couple of slices of toast on her plate and a cup of tea appeared in front of her as she dug into her meal.

As she finished eating, she checked the clock. They would need the food moved to her mom's house by nine-thirty, so she had an hour to relax and change her clothes. Rufus seemed to be awake now. "What did you and Cathy do yesterday?" she asked.

"We went to the beach and it was wonderful being there when there weren't any people around. At the end of our walk, we found a lighthouse and a closed up Merry-Go-Round. For lunch, we had lobster rolls that were delicious, at some little hole-in-the-wall diner, then went in and explored Yale, and later had pizza at a place over on Wooster Street. The day was fantastic. I was amazed that we polished off two large pizza between us."

"Well, you ate some of the best food in the world, I guarantee you. However, Thanksgiving at Chez Killoy is definitely five stars. Will has never cooked a bad turkey and it's the time when we each get to show off our specialties. Right now I know all my brothers are in the kitchen hard at work.

We'll eat at approximately one o'clock. Then there is the choice between watching football, napping if you're over-stuffed with turkey, or join me while I give the kids dog sled rides. We've got enough snow that I had Sean drop off his uncle's toboggan for the older kids to go sledding on the hill."

Jordy grinned. "That sounds cool. I've got to try that."

Kate stared at him for a second. "Why don't I put you in charge of the toboggan. As a college man, you're mature enough to make sure nobody gets hurt and the kids won't think they are being supervised by grownups."

"That's sneaky. I like it. You're on."

An hour later her brothers walked in ready to help her move all the food. With Harry, Rufus and Jordy helping, they were able to get everything in one trip. The kitchen should have been chaotic, but Will had everything flowing. The smell of turkeys cooking filled the air. Kate led the way with her desserts and walked straight into the pantry where temporary shelving was set up. In under two minutes, everything was put where it belonged, and she led the way to the dining room where a stack of six-foot-long folding banquet tables was lined up against the wall and started giving directions.

"Okay. First, all these tables need to be opened up here except the first one, which goes to the other end of the table to be opened up." She stuck her head back into the kitchen to ask Will, "What's the final number?"

"Should be twenty-five adults and six kids, not counting babies and counting Jordy as an adult, unless people bring their guests in which case, it will be more." Everyone pitched in flipping down the legs. She put the table at the far end of the family's dining room table and positioned it perpendicular to the table. Then going to the other end, she began sliding tables into place extending the length of the dining room table so it flowed all the way under the archway that led into the living room. Then, she placed a final table perpendicular at that end. She set up the final folding table and pulled it off to the side.

Without pausing, she began doing table cloths. The guys pitched in and quickly the room was a sea of white. Next, she went to the double glass doors of the china cabinet and began pulling out plates. "We've got fourteen brown turkey plates and twelve of the green pilgrim plates. Arrange them so that you don't have two matching next to each other. Jordy, take these funny turkey plates and put them on the kids' table.

"Now, try to make the butter plates, cups and saucers, and salad bowls, match each plate. Harry, help me with the silverware. There are three chests in the drawer of the sideboard. Each place-setting gets a dinner knife, butter knife, dinner fork, salad fork, dessert fork, and teaspoon, including at the kids' table.

"Des, you and Tim can get out the crystal, putting a wine glass and a water glass for each adult place setting. Jordy, these silver mugs go at each of the kids' place settings. The kids get the same silverware as adults because it makes them feel grown up, plus it's how they learn."

Finally, she moved the three centerpieces to the long table and put the turkey centerpiece which was full of games on the kid's table. With everything done, Kate checked her watch. "Twenty-six minutes! A full minute under the record. Hooray!"

Jordy stood looking around the room. "Wow, Kate. That was magic. This is fabulous."

"You guy's were great. There are still forty-five minutes until dinner, so those wanting football, head for the rec room through that door and down the stairs. Those wanting to play video games, they are set up in the den, through that door, and include a new one that Satu is trying out in beta. Have fun. Maeve and I are going to help with the food and organizing serving bowls and platters."

Once in the kitchen, Kate began grabbing bowls from the pantry when Maeve stopped her. "Enough, do not touch anything else. By going non-stop since before dawn, and you're running on nerves. The smile you have on your face may fool the others, but it doesn't fool me and it's getting a little scary. Something is bothering you. What is it? Are you afraid this monster is going to succeed and your wedding will be your funeral?"

Maeve pulled her back into the kitchen, pushed her onto a bench by the window, and sat down next to her. Kate sat in silence staring at her now idle hands. Without a constant push to get things done, she felt lost. Her hands began to shake, and she quickly slapped them on the bench and sat on them hoping Maeve wouldn't notice.

Maeve reached out and pulled her hands out from under her leg and held them saying, "You need rest, reassurance and a plan. The rest you are going to take right now. Everything is in place and William will tell you when he wants the vegetables placed in bowls. You are going to sit here and let yourself stop. No running around, no solving things, no trying to save the world--just sit. Once you've been sitting doing nothing for a while, you may finally accept the fact that nobody has more backup than you do. This guy will be stopped, I promise.

"Now, let's discuss more pressing annoyances, such as your mother meeting Harry's mother. According to the phone call I got from Agnes last night right before I fell asleep, she is doing her maid-of-honor bit at my sister's home. Your mother, your grandmother, my sister Sybil, Mrs. Foyle, Sarah, and her husband along with their toddler, Sal, Agnes, and Cathy are all gathering for breakfast. The entire group will leave in time to be here for dinner. Agnes felt it was safer if both women met on neutral ground, in a crowd, with a cute little girl, plus Sal and his son, and nowhere near you or Harry. This way they can snipe and be nasty to each other, without the two people who would be hurt most by being present. I'm told that Agnes plans to threaten to ban both of them from the wedding if they are not supportive of the bride and groom, and she'll do it. Your cousin is determined that this wedding will be perfect, even if she has to resort to kidnapping and murder."

Kate laughed. "She'd do it too. For all that she drives me nuts a lot of the time, she really wants the best for me. Having someone trying to kill us has been bugging the hell out of her."

She and Maeve sat for a minute, and then they began to laugh. "We'd better find this killer before she does or there won't be much of him left of him to go to jail."

There was a movement in the doorway, and Kate looked up. Harry walked in and sat next to her. Then he reached up and took her face in his hands. "What's wrong? This whirl you've been in since you got up this morning, long before dawn, is beginning to scare me. Don't even try to tell me it's Thanksgiving. Something is seriously bothering you. That smile is your 'I've got to keep everybody safe and happy smile' which you only use when you're close to panic. Is that the case? Have I done something wrong? Talk to me."

Nothing mattered when she stared into Harry's face. All she needed was to know he was there. Finally she began, "It's not like I haven't had someone hunting me before, but this time, the problem is here. It's at home, in my safe place. I know we've been working flat out to find this guy, but I'm scared. What if we don't find him?"

"Are you beginning to doubt your husband to be? I might begin to think I'm slipping off that white horse you have me on."

A lopsided smile began to form on her face and then turned into a giggle. "Agnes will kill me if I ruin the look of the wedding by having to wear a bullet proof vest over my wedding gown. I'm scared he'll get away with murder — ours. I don't feel like Kate, the super crime fighter today, but rather like a girl who designs sweaters and shows dogs. In this battle with the mob, I'm like an ant trying to fight an elephant."

"An ant? Lady, you are the toughest ant I know. That elephant doesn't stand a chance." He leaned in, and kissed her.

Kate relaxed for the first time in hours, lost in Harry's arms, until the moment was broken as the front door opened and the house exploded with the sound of voices and the influx of what seemed like hundreds of people.

Chapter Thirty-Five

Kate decided that Agnes either possessed magical powers or was carrying a Sig Sauer in her skirt pocket because both her mother and Harry's behaved themselves for the first twenty minutes and didn't criticize either her or Harry. Granted, they didn't speak to either of them, but she could live with that. Her philosophy with her mother was never to poke the angry bear.

Marrying Harry seemed to be making a difference in getting her mother off her back. Kate was as mathematically inclined as the rest of the family. She just didn't want to make it her life's work. That decision was the real reason behind the war with her mother which had been raging for years.

Her dad and grandfather, while they lived, served as her buffer, but with both of them dying in the last year, she hadn't been able to avoid her mother's criticism — until she got engaged. Harry stepped up and became her buffer, and in the last month or two, things seemed to be getting better.

One reason for her mother's change in attitude happened because of the fact that earlier this fall, a professor friend of Harry's and his brother-in-law came to visit. The two older gentlemen were fascinated with Kate's business and shamed her mother into visiting it for the first time. Much to Kate's amazement, her mom was impressed and that combined with bringing Harry into the family seemed to get her a temporary reprieve from the constant censure.

Dinner was progressing beautifully and the food was wonderful. Her brother was a genius in the kitchen. Harry constantly leaned into her as he chatted with Rufus across the table and his warmth was reassuring. She noticed that Jordy had chosen to sit at the children's table and from the amount of laughter and excitement coming from the group, he seemed to be the focus of all the kid's attention. During a break in the conversation at the adult table, Jordy's voice became louder with excitement.

"That was the first time someone shot at her that I know about. It was this crazy woman, and she was using a rifle. Luckily, Quinn was with her, even though he was a tiny puppy, and he saved her. However, the lady did shoot Harry and everyone was worried he would die. Then, when the crazy lady kidnapped me, Kate came after me with Dillon and Liam. When the woman pointed her gun at me, Kate and Dillon walked up to her and Kate convinced her that her partner had betrayed her. The lady yelled at him and acted weird and then Quinn burst out of the bushes, covered with mud. The lady thought he was a bear cub, and she freaked which let Kate and the troopers disarmed her, and she went to jail.

"Then last month, at the Sammy National, someone else was trying to murder Kate. Only this time, it happened as she showed Shelagh in the ring. The guy got so angry, he whirled around and pointed his gun right at her. The guy's daughter didn't realize what her dad was doing and tried to upstage Kate with the judge by stepping in front of her. Luckily for her, Kate saw gun and pushed her out of the way which meant he shot Kate instead. I was so scared. I thought she was dead. But after Harry carried her to that motor home, she woke up. She was hurt but not dead. She'd been wearing a bulletproof vest, so she didn't die. Quinn and I were really scared when she was shot. Kate is really the bravest person I know."

A blush spread, starting at her hairline and moving over her face and down. She looked at Jordy and then pivoted to look at Harry who reached his arm around her shoulders pulling her close and whispering, "You're the bravest person I know, too." She smiled as she glanced back to the grown-up table only to be met with astonished stares and silence.

Maeve finally distracted everyone by saying, "I'm going to make a toast. To Kate and Harry. I wish them an uneventful honeymoon." Everyone at the table laughed and conversation resumed.

Somehow, she and Harry survived the onslaught of questioning which followed Jordy's revelations. She was kept busy downplaying the adventures which she and Harry experienced.

The crowd managed to find room for the many pies and cookies she' d baked. Agnes stood and started the exodus deciding not to push her luck with the amiable feelings by delaying just so the kids could play. In under ten minutes, the house was emptied of most of the guests, her mother and Ann both retired to rest, and she and her brothers, plus the remaining guests made quick work of the clean-up. As usual, everyone complained about eating too much, but it was a relaxing and happy time.

When done, Harry grabbed her coat and helped her into it, and they headed down the hill along with Rufus, Cathy, Jordy, Des, Maeve, and Padraig. The group almost reached her front door when a car pulled into the driveway and stopped next to them.

"Glad I found you, Foyle, we've got a problem," said the man who stepped out of the car. Kate recognized the Agent in Charge of the FBI Washington office from his help with the killer at the Samoyed National.

"Bullock, what are you doing here now, the wedding isn't until Saturday?" Harry asked.

Search

"Have you or have you not been investigating members of organized crime families on the east coast?"

Harry was startled and glanced at Des before answering. "Yes, in relation to my father's death."

"Well, not to play down the importance of the death of your father, who I'm told was a fine police officer, but, what you are working on now, according to my source, will possibly affect the entire country."

Harry stiffened, stared at Kate and then back. "Who's your source?"

The other car door opened and a tall older woman stepped out and moved around to the front of the car. "I am. Hello, Maeve."

"Sadie." Maeve and Harry shouted at the same time.

"What are you doing here?" Harry asked.

"It's my turn to be in the front row when the bomb goes off for a change." She swiveled around and reached out to hug Kate. "We've never met face to face, my girl, but I feel like I know you better than your own mother."

"That's entirely likely," Maeve muttered, then added. "I don't know about anyone else, but I'm getting cold. Let's move this discussion into the house, and we can all get some tea or coffee. I'm sure that Kate has some more of her wonderful pies inside for those not overstuffed with Thanksgiving dinner."

They sat at the kitchen table and Harry and Kate for the next hour answered rapid-fire questions about all the discoveries which had been made. They covered the attempts on Kate's and Harry's lives and the kidnapping of Jordy.

At seven o'clock. Gurka showed up with Sean to tell Harry that the FBI filed an official request for both their prisoners. Bullock introduced himself to the trooper and asked to see the request.

"Gurka pulled out the paper.

"How did you get this today? It's a federal holiday. I would think it would have come through either yesterday or tomorrow," Harry asked.

"That's the weird thing. I found it sitting on my desk when I went in to check on the prisoners after our Thanksgiving dinner. I checked to see who delivered it but nobody saw who it was."

Bullock placed the paper on the table and looked at Kate.

"Magnifying glass?"

She opened a drawer and handed it to him. For almost a minute, he studied the notice and then leaned back. "This is good. However, the watermark is off and there is a chip out of the letter 'e' in the address. It's tiny but it's there. Also, these case numbers are out of sequence. It's well-made but it's not from the Bureau."

"Which means one of the mob's people strolled right into the barracks and my office without anyone stopping him," Gurka growled, disgusted.

Bullock asked Gurka if he could spare extra coverage on the two men he had in custody. Gurka agreed and then Harry suggested that Sean pick up a scanner from Tom and sweep his office. "If they can get access to your office for this," he said pointing at the paper, "planting listening devices allowing them to stay ahead of your security planning would be a breeze." Sean left for Tom's.

Gurka nodded and glanced at Kate. "You be careful Katie, we need you in top shape. My canine troops are the best they've ever been."

Kate smiled. Cathy peeked at the clock and suggested that Rufus take her back to Agnes' so she wouldn't worry. They stood and as he helped Cathy on with her coat, he informed Jordy he was coming too. Jordy opened his mouth to object, but the hard look from his father had him putting on his coat and thanking Kate for the pie.

Kate got out the bowls to feed the dogs. They had been very patient, but she hated to change their schedule too much. Once the food was prepared, Harry stood and let them in. Quinn went to check out the visitors while the others, after circling the table once, sat in their circle and waited for supper.

"Dinner, Quinn." Kate began putting down bowls and the puppy raced to be in his spot by the time the bowl was set in front of him. When they finished, Kate got out biscuits. Harry picked up bowls, and she opened the back door giving a treat to each dog as he went through.

Bullock stared out the door. "It's like I'm back at your National show. How many of these Samoyeds do you own?"

"Counting the veterans, brood bitches, the ones I'm showing like Dillon and Shelagh and the youngsters, it's a dozen. It's a lot, but I have the kennel facility and different dogs do different things. Several of my seniors visit nursing homes and schools in the fall and spring. This time a year, I try to keep them off any icy paths for fear old bones might break. Once the weather gets warm again, they'll be more active. Liam and Dillon both do search and rescue as well as the show. Dillon does the police dog training as a demo dog and Shelagh does both breed ring work and obedience. She'll be working in agility when I find more time. Harry is training Quinn for the breed ring now. It's never dull around here. Then, of course, there are the training classes, the boarding kennel and of course, the knitting studio where I design and produce my line of sweaters. It's a lot of work but the commute is a breeze." Everyone grinned.

"So you decided to fight crime in your spare time?"

"Well, you know, 'idle hands are the devil's playground'."

Maeve and Sadie chuckled.

"All joking aside, we're getting married in two days and I don't want to wear a bullet-proof vest over my wedding dress. These people murdered their way into the power structure of justice by systematically making in-roads into the law enforcement systems of our country more often than not by using murder. It's as though the 'inmates are running the asylum'. They are taking control and soon there won't be any justice. I know that this is way too big for us to fix overnight, but, I want to know how we can get the ones trying to kill us stopped so that we can get married."

"Katie," Sadie caught her attention by grabbing her hand, "we will make sure you can walk down that aisle. Sgt. Gurka, is your security sufficient to keep those two prisoners safe until we can question them in the morning?"

He nodded and stood. "I'll get to work on that now. When should I expect you?" Sadie glanced at Bullock and Maeve. "Seven-thirty?" They nodded and Gurka headed out, stopping only to pat Kate on the shoulder.

Harry was being quiet, letting everything play out around him, but he could see that Kate was fading fast by showing a bravado she didn't really feel. He needed her to be relaxed and sure of what they were doing.

He nodded to Padraig, and they stepped into Kate's room and grabbed the boxes which held all the information they gathered. It was going to be another late night. They need to come up with a way to clip the wings of this organization, so they could get married. He set the boxes down on the table, pulled out the photos of his father and Maurio, and began laying out everything discovered and the evidence compiled. Sadie listened, as her fingers worked her laptop keyboard. Both she and Bullock stopped him to ask questions then let him proceed with the case notes. By eleven o'clock, Harry had gone over everything, but when he noticed Kate was leaning heavily on his shoulder, he stopped.

"Kate has been up since five this morning. We all need our sleep. If you guys are going to question these two prisoners early tomorrow morning, why don't we meet here when you are done. Seamus and Satu are home for the holiday, so we'll get them up to speed as to where we are now, and we can pick up from here tomorrow.

Peggy Gaffney

"By the way, in the afternoon, at four o'clock, the wedding rehearsal is scheduled. A lot of guests will be arriving by then so things could get a little insane. Most of Kate's guests will be local, except for some dog and fashion people. I've got some people from the Bureau coming, but my side of the church will be relatively empty. I think we all need to get some sleep. Are you two set for rooms?" Bullock and Sadie nodded and soon everyone was gone.

Kate let in the dogs and Harry locked up. Then, opening her bedroom door, he gently pushed her inside along with Dillon, Liam, and Quinn. Holding her in his arms, her head resting on his chest as the dogs settled around them he said, "You get some sleep. Tomorrow is going to be crazy and I need you to be in full Kate mode." He kissed her goodnight and closed the door.

Knowing he wouldn't be getting much sleep tonight, he decided to do something about the bedroom still jammed with boxes. Kate had labeled the contents of about a third of them. He might as well pick up where she left off. He located the marking pen she used and the tape. The boxes with his father's papers and the photos were in the kitchen, so he lifted the next box in the order and pulled it open.

He wasn't prepared for the blood.

CHAPTER THIRTY-SIX

Kate wasn't sure what woke her. She lay still, listening, then opened her eyes and in the dim light from the moon shining in the window, she noticed all three dogs standing at the door. Sitting up, she listened again and heard a muffled sound. Getting up, she put on her slippers and robe. When she opened the door, the dogs raced out and turned immediately toward Harry's room. At the door of his room, she stopped.

The boxes of his father's things were open and scattered about the room. But what caused her to halt is that Harry was

Peggy Gaffney

sitting on the bed, holding some clothing in his arms, and he was crying.

The dogs rushed to him and pushed their heads into his lap, whining. He buried his head in Dillon's ruff, holding him tightly while his other hand fumbled for Quinn. Moving slowly into the room, Kate sat on the edge of the bed, and gently slipped under Quinn's head to get close. Her arm slid behind Harry and drew his shaking body to her. Time passed as she held him until the sobs lessened. Once he had stilled, she took his hand, pushed her way through all the dogs, and guided him into the kitchen. After they were seated, she told him, "When you are ready to talk, I'm ready to listen. What are you holding?"

It took him a while to ease his grip and lay the object on the table. Placing his hand on it, he finally whispers.

"My father's uniform jacket — he was wearing it when he died."

His head turned, focused on her. "If I hadn't gone to California. If I hadn't been studying at MIT. If I'd been the son he wanted...," he ranted.

"This most likely would have happened exactly the same way," she said. "You did not send yourself to California, Harry. You were a kid. You didn't abandon him. No, he sent you. It was his decision. When you came home, he told you to go live on campus instead of staying at home. Pete was the one giving directions. Do I think he loved you? Yes. But he had things to do and it was easier with you out of the way."

Kate stood and wrapped her arms around his shoulders.

"Did you think that if you had gotten closer to him, were involved in his life, the mob wouldn't have latched on to him?

Search

Sorry to tell you this, but as an outsider looking at the evidence we've found, I think your father wouldn't have allowed you to get anywhere near his life."

She rested her hand on the uniform jacket he still clutched.

"He was a cop. He was doing his job. Because of him, we have an idea of how the mob may have been using him, but we don't know what was going on in his mind at the time." Her fingers slid over the fabric but stopped when she encountered a hard, crusted surface on the wool. Easing the jacket out of his grip, she saw that the left front and sleeve were covered with a brownish stain. Blood. A slice about an inch long was in the darkest part, right above the pocket.

Harry reached out and touched the blood. "Dad would have hated that his uniform was still covered with blood. It was important for him to keep his uniform immaculate and his shoes and belt polished to such a high sheen that you could see your face in them. They buried him in his dress uniform, but I only remember him wearing this. Even as a little kid, I loved the feel of his jacket when he'd pick me up to carry me. It always made me feel warm and safe in his arms."

Kate wrapped an arm around him. "Would you like me to try to clean up the jacket? I don't know if I can get all the blood out, but I could try."

Harry nodded. "Yeah, he would have liked that."

After turning on the kettle for tea, she went into the whelping room. When she returned, she had a plastic carrier fitted to hold bottles and brushes. She had loaded it with a bunch of cloths and a stack of newspaper. After making tea, she carefully stepped over the sleeping dogs, scattered around the kitchen, and laid the jacket on the counter. She noticed that some of the buttons had gotten blood on them, which called for the addition of metal polish to her collection of cleaning tools. Opening the jacket, she examined the lining.

"I'm not sure how the lining will react to the cleaners, but I can remove the stitching and push it aside while I work on the outside. Then I'll clean the lining separately. Hmm. It looks as though the lining has been separated in spots before. The restitching has been done with a thread that is close in color but doesn't match. If I just trim these stitches it will be easy separating the lining."

Sipping her tea, she reached into a zippered canvas bag, pulled out small gold scissors that were shaped like a stork and set to work. About an inch of stitches had been freed when she saw what appeared to be interfacing stitched to the jacket. Considering the fabric of the jacket, it shouldn't have needed any interfacing. She snipped more stitches, and then stopped to pull the jacket closer so that she could study the inside. This wasn't interfacing, it was pages from a small notebook, covered with writing, gently stitched to the fabric. Without damaging the fabric, she quickly cut through the rest of the stitches holding the lining to the front of the jacket and saw that each sheet was covered with a combination of letters, numbers, and squiggles resembling some ancient middle eastern script. Both sides of each sheet were covered with the tiny script.

Holding out her find to Harry, they stared at it for a minute and then Harry raised his head, gazed into her eyes and smiled. "I know what this writing is. Dad wrote what happened on the beat in his own shorthand so that he'd remember when he had to fill out the paperwork at the end of the day."

"Can you read it?"

"No, but... What time is it?"

"Twelve-thirty."

"She's a night owl. She may not be asleep yet."

He pulled his phone from his pocket and typed a text. "If she's asleep, she'll get back to me in the morning."

The phone buzzed a minute later.

"Thanks for calling, Sadie. I know it's late, but Kate just found notes written in shorthand sewn into my dad's uniform jacket. The one he was wearing the day he died. I figure if they were hidden, they were important. You're sure? Okay, about fifteen minutes. I'll put on the coffee."

While he was calling, Kate photographed the jacket, the lining, the way the papers were attached to the fabric and photographed each page of the sheets. She sent the photos to her computer and noticed that the papers, sewn nearest the wound, had chunks of the writing obscured by blood. Kate stared at that area for a minute and then reached over to pull open a drawer, extracting a small folding light. When she opened it, the strong light showed through the paper making the squiggles under the blood show up. However, it made the squiggles from both sides of the sheet show, confusing the lines. Kate took photos of both sides using the light. Maybe Seamus and Satu knew of a program which could separate the markings so that they could find what was on each side of the sheet.

Harry set up the coffee machine, then he stopped behind her, took her phone from her hand, set it on the table, and then pulled her to her feet, drew her into his arms and held her. She rested her forehead against his and drew her arms up and down his back.

"Thank you," he whispered. Then leaning back, he smiled down at her and said, "I think you might want to get dressed before we have company."

She grinned, took a glance down at her pajamas and then stepped over the dogs who were asleep between the table and the door to her room. Twelve minutes later, there was a soft knock at the door. Harry answered. Both Sadie and Bullock entered the kitchen as Kate returned. The dogs, wakened by visitors, milled around with Quinn fishing for snuggles. But even he settled once Kate told them the go lie down.

Sadie walked to the table, lifted the jacket, and ran her hand over the bloodstain. She worked her fingers up to the spot where the weapon had cut through the fabric and studied the break. "A smooth blade knife, an inch at the hilt, I'd say. Could have been a switchblade."

Grabbing his arm she asked, "Are you all right, Harry?"

He nodded.

Turning her attention to Kate, she asked, "What is this you've found."

"When I went to clean the blood off the jacket, I had to remove the lining, because the cleaner might not work on that fabric. I cut the threads, which I had noticed had been cut and replaced before. As I eased the lining away, I saw what I thought was interfacing sewn into the jacket, except this type of fabric doesn't need interfacing. Once enough stitches were cut, I peeled the lining back and realized that it wasn't a single piece,

Search

but rather a collection of small notebook pages stitched to the fabric. I began cutting them free and went to read them but couldn't. Harry said that his dad took notes in shorthand before writing up his reports. I don't read shorthand."

"Well, it's lucky that I do. When you work your way up in the Bureau, from a job as a secretary, you end up with skills. If you have any of that pie left, I'd love a piece. Let's do this."

They all sat and Sadie went through the small pieces of soft paper, handling them gently. Kate reached for her computer. She'd sent the photos of the papers to Sadie's computer and pulled up the file which showed each sheet, enlarged so that the print was easier to read.

"Thank you, Sweetheart, that makes this much easier," Sadie said giving her a hug.

First, they had to organize the sheets. There were marks in the corner of each page that seemed familiar. After a minute, she went into the living room and came back with a history of Ireland which had been given to her by a friend. The unique thing about the book was that it was written in both English and Gaelic. Each page was also numbered in both English and Gaelic script and it was there she recognized the symbols.

"Those are dates in the corner written in Gaelic script. In fact, I think," she said as she checked one sheet after another, "all the numbers are written that way."

Once they had a way to organize the pages, Sadie began to translate the words into a record. Taking out a pad, she wrote down each word. This worked until they came to the pages covered in blood which had seeped through the fabric. That was when Kate pulled up the back-lit photos.

Bullock studied the pages and then asked if he could download a graphics program he used, and Kate nodded. Once the program was downloaded and opened, he brought up the photo of the first blood covered page. Opening various color correction and graphics interfaces, he was able to bring out the slightly more pronounced script while fading the slightly dimmer script on the back. All at once, the page became readable. Kate grinned at him. "That was wonderful. Is this new FBI software?"

"Not really," he laughed. "I do nature photography to relax. This is just an excellent graphics program for enhancing the detail in my shots. When you take a shot of an eagle in flight, and you want to enlarge it. You often need the help of a good graphics program to keep the detail of the feathers crisp and clear."

"Fascinating. I bet it would help with my photos of the dogs, especially when they are in action."

"Absolutely."

Kate's smile turned into a yawn, and she covered her mouth. "Excuse me. It's been a long day."

Harry stood, and took her elbow. "You've got to get some sleep. We're almost finished here. Go to bed. Agnes will have fits if the bride falls asleep in the middle of the wedding rehearsal. We're going to need you alert in case something else happens."

She opened her mouth to object only to have another yawn take over. Giving in to his gentle push, she went into her room and ended up only taking off her sneakers before she just rolled to the side and fell asleep. A little later though she felt jostled and a cold nose pressed against her face. She didn't wake.

The next thing she knew it was morning. The sun was shining through the window. She peeked over the edge of the bed, but there were no dogs. As she went to get up, it dawned on her that she was under the covers and her jeans were gone. Her feet had barely hit the floor before Harry's head poked around the door.

"Hey, we're about to be invaded so you'd better get dressed. Breakfast is cooking. Gorgeous legs by the way," he said looking at her bare legs hanging off the bed and wiggling his eyebrows. Kate couldn't help but grin back as she extended one leg, pointing her foot. Tomorrow they would be married. There was no way she was going to be shy now.

Minutes later, she emerged, fully dressed, to a kitchen filled with people. Des, Tom, and Bullock were off in a corner discussing something important. Maeve, Padraig, Sadie, and Sal were at one end of the table, also in deep discussion. The rest of the space was taken up with her siblings and Satu.

Since the dog dishes weren't on the counter, and the pups seemed relaxed outside, she concluded they'd been fed. Harry was cooking a massive pan of scrambled eggs as Kate slipped past him and claimed her mug to make tea.

"Did you figure out what all your dad's notes were about after I fell asleep?"

He glanced over at her and leaned in close to whisper, "This is bigger than we thought, a lot bigger. I understand why they wanted us dead. I'll tell you later."

Peggy Gaffney

He began dishing up eggs into a big covered bowl. Kate lifted the bacon from two grilling pans onto a platter and then everyone settled and began eating.

They'd almost finished when the front door opened and shut with a slam, and Agnes stomped into the kitchen. Stopping in front of Kate and putting her fists on her hips she said, "After all the work I've done to make this wedding perfect, you have to go and get killers to hunt you. Couldn't you for once be normal and throw tantrums over the flowers or the seating plan? Tell me, are you planning on wearing a bullet-proof vest over your gown?"

Chapter Thirty-Seven

The silence lasted for almost a minute before everyone, except Kate, began talking. The noise was deafening. She tried to slip a word in edgewise, but finally gave up, grabbed her jacket and slipped out into the exercise yard. The dogs were delighted. She picked up the over-sized pooper-scooper and got to work.

She'd cleaned about a quarter of the yard, when she was discovered. Her cousin came through the door and Kate waited for her to start lecturing her on the dangerous situation. Instead, she grabbed a second pooper-scooper and joined in. Without a word, they worked their way across the yard and with the two of them working, the job finished quickly. After bagging what they'd collected Kate dumped it in the trash can and put the scoops away.

Agnes grabbed her arm and pulled her down to sit on the bench next to the back door. The dogs pushed in to accept snuggles and pats. "How are you doing? You're the bride. You're the one who is supposed to throw tantrums the day before her wedding."

"I don't throw tantrums." Kate wrapped one arm around Quinn while the other held Dillon close enough to lay her head on his.

"You realize that's very annoying of you. You didn't inherit any diva genes."

"You do diva so well, I could never compete."

"That's true. So why was I not told that Harry's father was murdered? He said it's a group of organized crime families that wants you two dead."

Kate lifted her head and looked straight at Agnes. "You can't talk about this to anyone. It could put you in danger. Sean knows most of it, so he's okay, but don't discuss it where you could be overheard. This was what Harry was working on while he was away. It is vitally important that it be stopped. I don't have all the information since, by the time I found the final piece of the puzzle last night, I was falling asleep on my feet and Harry sent me to bed."

"Is that the Bullock who is Agent In Charge in the D.C. office?"

"Yes. Harry worked for him at one time and Des works for him now."

"And you're not scared of what's happening?"

"I'm terrified. However, that and ten cents won't buy you anything, so I park it beside my unused diva and try to find the murderers who are behind these attacks on us and other crimes."

"So what is the plan for keeping you from being shot when you walk down the aisle. You realize that I'm asking only because I'll be walking right in front of you, of course."

"I absolutely understand. Getting gun powder on your dress as the bullet flies by would be annoying. To tell the truth, I haven't come up with a plan but there must be one floating around somewhere. Maybe they're having better luck in the kitchen with all those brilliant minds eating my bacon and eggs. We have to leave for the rehearsal in half an hour. A few prayers wouldn't go amiss. Divine intervention may be our only hope. Right now, I need another cup of tea, so I suggest we go join everybody in the kitchen."

The gathering at the back of the church was slightly larger than usual for a wedding rehearsal and definitely better armed. Her brothers practiced escorting guests to their seats. Kate had decided they shouldn't bother to ask if the guest was a friend of the bride or groom but rather, as the church filled, just try to keep the sides even. That way there will be plenty of room for everyone. Otherwise, she would need to use her dogs to fill up Harry's side. The only ones to be in assigned seats were the immediate family.

Agnes lined everyone up and then Fr. Joe gave her the high sign. Sarah went first down the aisle followed by Cathy. Then, Agnes stepped out and moved with the practiced step of the former number one model in the country. Finally, Tom stepped forward, shifted his cane to his opposite hand, and held out his arm for Kate to take, and they slowly followed the others down the aisle. Kate smiled at her brother and then turned to look for Harry. He and Rufus stood waiting.

When she spotted him, the tension, which had been with her since she woke, slid away. Harry took her hand, smiled at Tom, and led her forward to practice the actual marriage service which would be part of the wedding mass. She only lent half an ear to what Fr. Joe was saying, focusing instead, on those wonderful green eyes which had caught her attention when they first met. Then suddenly, they were done.

Agnes and Fr. Joe went off to double check on the final arrangements and the florist came in as they were leaving. Kate stopped to ask her about her dog.

As Kate got into the car with Harry she asked, "What did you learn from Pete's information?"

"Apparently my father was working as part of a task force trying to bring down organized crime in the area. He was trying to use Maurio as a way to get close to some insiders. Someone found out or Maurio became suspicious, and that was why Dad was killed. However, his notes are a gold mine of names and crimes and connections. He laid out how they planned to infiltrate the world of law enforcement on all levels and wait until their leader was in place."

"So, why are they trying to kill us?"

"Their leader is about to be put in place."

Kate stared at him. Confused, she thought back over all that had happened but just when she was about to be pissed off and force him tell her, the penny dropped. She gasped. "The Attorney General."

Harry nodded. "He's up for confirmation on Monday. We've got forty-eight hours to figure a way to keep a mob boss from rising to the top law enforcement position in the country. Once he's in place, his people will come out of the shadows and do a lot of damage. Plus, we've got to stop it, without getting killed."

"I always like that your mind can just cut to the nub of a problem. You don't happen to have a miracle or two in your back pocket, do you? I offered up a few prayers while in church, but so far, I lack answers."

Kate leaned back, her mind blank. They had almost reached her driveway when a phrase she remembered hearing nudged her brain—coming out of the shadows.

They parked and Harry came around to open her door when a bright flash went off in front of them. Kate blinked and then yelled, "Sibowitz!" She dashed forward to hug her old friend. Andy Sibowitz was not only the number one fashion photographer in the country but was a good friend and here to photograph the wedding. Andy lifted her in his arms and swung her around.

"You know, Princess, it's not too late to change your mind and marry me." He told her as he kissed her on the forehead.

Harry stepped forward, removed Kate from his arms, and shook his hand. "Yes, it is. She's mine and you can't take her."

"You're a lucky man, Foyle." He smiled as he let go of Kate and returned her to Harry's arms.

"Believe me, I thank God for that every day. Come on inside."

They had just stepped onto the porch when Kate dug in her heels and stopped. "Light. That's the answer. Shine a light. That is perfect," and grabbing Harry's hand, she rushed inside.

All the dogs were lined up at the kitchen door barking for attention which almost drowned out the sound of the the others arriving. Agnes came through the door first and as she walked into the kitchen, she screamed, "Sibowitz!"

"Hey, Gorgeous. How's life as a banker?" He was in the middle of hugging her when a firm hand landed on his shoulder, and he looked up into the face of a tall Connecticut State Trooper in full uniform.

"Whatever you think I did, sir, I swear I didn't do it."

"Then take your hands off my fiancée."

"Engaged? You're — engaged to — him?" Andy leaned back to look at Sean.

"Agnes, Sweetheart, I must shoot your wedding. You know you're my favorite model of all time, but this guy's cheekbones will catch the light perfectly. I can already see the shots. I need to start planning the lighting. Oh, and congratulations, of course. This photoshoot will make Town and Country and Vogue battle it out for an exclusive."

Kate noticed that everyone had settled back into the seats they'd that morning. She made a mug of tea and faced them. "Light, that's what we need. If these criminals are hiding in the shadows, we need to bring them out into the light." The talking stopped and everyone stared when she said, "We've got only a few hours to do it."

Search

Maeve leaned forward, looking past Sadie and asked, "Do what? Katie, darlin'?"

"Stop the mob from killing Harry and me. I've got a plan. We need to contact the top reporters on the east coast as well as those at all the national cable news networks and encourage them to break this story wide open. We'll give them proof, every who, what, where, when and why. The clock says noon so to make their deadlines, we must deliver it to them in two hours if they're going to verify it and prepare it for broadcast."

Satu pulled out her laptop and set it on the table. "Kate, in my spare time I have been collecting contacts for every newspaper and television station news bureau with emails and cell phone numbers into my data banks. I figured that if Seamus and I are working for Mr. Harry, information is vital, so I have developed many databases."

"Fantastic, Satu. You and Seamus work on that. Maeve, if you and Sadie could work on dividing the information up into usable sized bites which will work well for breaking news blurbs, then you can gather contacts from Satu and send more details to different reporters and news desks. I took photos of the pages with the facts of the crimes, though, since I used my phone, they aren't the best quality."

Andy, who had been watching them, slowly caught on to what was going on. He reached for Kate's laptop. "It is your lucky day, lady. You need work done to make photos ready for prime time news and I'm your guy. Show me the files and what software you've got."

They ended up breaking into working groups. Harry, Des, and Bullock pulled   the details of the crimes from Harry's research, and proof which mob members were part of this takeover and fed them to Maeve and Sadie to incorporate into their story information. In the middle of the job assignments, Gurka called Sean in to help with the questioning of their two suspects. Sean told them he would call if he and Gurka got any more information.

Agnes and Cathy took off to find Will. She figured someone should work on the wedding, and she would make sure Sarah ran interference with her mother if she caught the newscast about her late husband. What had been a house full of shouts and excitement, settled into one of the quiet murmurs of determined people working on something important.

Kate was exhausted. She looked around and realized that though it had been her idea, it lay outside her skill set.

Pulling her coat off the peg by the door, she went out and sat on the bench in the dog yard. This was her world. She didn't fight crime. She did dog. Quinn climbed up onto the bench beside her and Liam stuck his head under her elbow looking for a hug. Dillon placed his front feet on the bench and raising himself up, then leaned his head against her shoulder. As she looked out on the dogs and bitches she had bred over the years, she sighed and smiled. This was what she did.

The click of a camera brought her out of her reverie. She turned and saw Andy, with a camera, focused on her and the dogs, taking pictures. Noticing the others were standing and milling around, Kate patted the dogs within reach and headed back inside. It had taken them two hours and ten minutes. They had finished and sent out their information with Bullock listed as the contact. Sadie had even found old photos in Boston P. D.

files of Pete's murder scene which had been given to the press at the time, as well as his formal department portrait. These she attached to each article.

Everything had been sent so Bullock, Des, and Tom headed to the office of K&K where they could connect his phone to the multiple line setup which was covered by all of them when the expected fallout hit. Bullock needed to give his boss a heads up, as well as the acting Attorney General.

Sadie walked up and hugged Kate saying, "Thanks, Kate. I haven't had this much fun in ages. It reminded me of the good old days when I worked at the Bureau. The last few weeks I've been looking forward to the wedding so that I could meet you and see your beautiful dogs. But being part of this move to bring down a crime family has made this a wedding to remember. Maeve, Padraig and I are going over to visit with your grandmother and Sal who I know like to spend time together. I realize people will argue with me but you are more beautiful than your cousin."

"Agnes says the same thing. It's not true, but I will admit, it is nice to hear occasionally."

"I must say, your brothers are quite a handsome lot and enough to make a girl wish she were forty or so years younger. It was fabulous meeting Seamus and Satu and seeing them in action. I'm already planning some projects for them this summer after they graduate from high school. Since they are both headed for MIT, it will be easy for me to work with them next fall as well.

"Ah, Padraig is waving, so I have to go. Take care of my boy. This has been an emotional ride for him, but it will hopefully give him the closure he needs. I'll see you tomorrow."

After she left, Andy stuck his head into the kitchen to say, "I will be here about seven tomorrow morning to take photos of you getting ready. Be sure to a good night's sleep." He stepped in to hug her then followed Seamus and Satu out.

Looking around her kitchen Kate was surprised that the table was clean and the dishwasher loaded. She went to search for Harry and saw his overnight bag by the front door with his tux hanging above it. He'd be spending the night at the main house in her old room. She found him in the living room sitting on the sofa with Macbeth, another of her cats, stretched across his lap. He'd turned on one of the cable news stations and was sitting with his feet up, petting the cat.

Kate walked over and sat next to him, leaning gently against his shoulder. He lifted his arm and pulled her into a hug as the commentator was interviewing a former FBI agent about the vastness of this takedown of organized crime family members.

"The fact that these arrests not only cover states from Maine to Florida, but the scope is mind-boggling. Plus the fact that there was no leak in advance is what makes it most explosive. The blockbuster news is that the Attorney General nominee, who was due to be confirmed by the Senate on Monday was arrested as one of the members of this organized crime plot and perhaps was its leader. This has the White House and the Justice Department reeling.

"It seems that Agent Bullock, Agent In Charge of the Washington Division of the FBI was in charge of this secret investigation, which I'm told, was first uncovered by Sgt. Peter Foyle, late of the Boston Police

Department, who was brutally murdered fifteen years ago. Sgt. Foyle had hidden the proof of what was taking place as this crime group was being formed, complete with names, facts, and dates, all of which have just come to light. The timing couldn't be better. Stopping a criminal from rising to the top position in our nation's law enforcement makes us wonder how this was allowed to happen. Today's revelations, I suspect, are just the tip of the iceberg."

There was a knock at the door and Agnes and Sean walked in. She reported that the last of the snow had melted so though it might be muddy, there would be no problem parking cars for the reception tomorrow.

Sean clapped Harry on the shoulder saying, "I'll be staying here to guard your bride tonight. No sense taking a chance until we have proof that the man who killed your father has been rounded up."

He moved his and Agnes' bags in and Harry stood to leave. He pulled Kate into his arms and kissed her gently. "You will need plenty of sleep tonight," he whispered smiling, "I promise you, you won't be getting much tomorrow night."

Chapter Thirty-Eight

After handing Sean sheets, blankets, and a pillow for the sofa, she said goodnight and called all the dogs into her room. The older ones who had favorite spots around the house were not happy with the change, but they eventually found space in Kate's room and soon all were sleeping. Once in her pj's, she climbed into bed, but her body had no intention of letting her sleep tonight. She reached for her Kindle and began reading the

Search

new Sheila Connelly mystery set in Ireland. Ireland was one of the places she'd love to visit if only to see some day where her grandfather, Maeve, and Sybil had grown up. She must have dozed off while reading but the sound of Quinn whining woke her. Pushing her pillows out of the way, she flattened herself so she could reach over the edge of the bed to comfort her puppy.

A noise she'd heard before whizzed by her head and barking filled the room.

"DOWN!" Kate screamed and slid to the floor amid the dogs. The door to her room banged open.

"SHOOTER!" she yelled.

Sean dropped to the floor and wiggling closer to the sliding door he spoke into his phone, "Shooter on the west side of Kate's house. Shot fired through sliding glass door." His phone squawked for a second with someone talking.

"Kate, are you all right?"

"Yeah, I'm fine." Faint sounds of sirens sounded in the distance. Quinn started to get up to head toward Sean.

"DOWN," she ordered.

Taking a breath, she rolled to the left and looked at her closet door. The hole made by the bullet was positioned to hit her when she was sitting up in bed. By reaching for Quinn, she'd literally dodged the bullet. Quinn was making a habit of saving her from being shot. The sirens grew louder. Nobody would be getting any sleep tonight.

"Sean? Kate? What's going on?" Agnes called from the hall.

"Don't come in here and stay down. Someone tried to shoot Kate. Get back into your room and stay low," Sean ordered as he started talking into his phone again.

Kate reached out, placing her hands on Quinn and Shelagh as Dillon, Liam, and Kelly snuggled against her back.

The sound of patrol cars screeching to a stop was loud but when the sirens stopped the night was filled with a scream of silence. There was a banging on the front door. Sean crawled back to the door and rolling over jumped up, telling her to keep the dogs with her. He ran to open the door, she heard the sounds of troopers racing through the house.

Outside, voices were shouting. Kate rested her head on Dillon. She might need some rest tomorrow night, wedding night or not. She lay where she was — eyes closed, feeling very tired and that's how he found her when Harry rushed in.

"KATE!" His yell had all the dogs on their feet and barking.

"I'm okay. No damage, thanks to Quinn. His record of detecting shootings before they happen remains unbroken. It's like scientists who can detect earthquakes."

Throwing himself down next to her, he pulled her into his lap, tucked her head under his chin and wrapped his arms around her. The dogs all pushed into what they decided was a group hug which is what Gurka saw when he shoved open the door.

"Kate, Sean says you're okay."

"I'm fine, Sergeant, thanks to Quinn. I'd dozed off sitting up reading, but he woke me whining. I leaned over the edge of the bed to see what was wrong and the bullet went over my head and into my closet door. It must have been a rifle fired from a distance, since it didn't smash the window glass, but just left a hole and a divot."

"You're right. Looks like he came in on the old logging road, and was standing just outside the dog yard up against the kennel when he fired. Unfortunately, though there are signs of a car parked there, he's gone. I don't think he'll try anything else tonight, but we'll pull in extra coverage until the morning both here and at the church. You try to get some sleep if that's possible."

"Didn't Bob replace the camera on the trail?" Kate asked.

"No. It was all he had left when they got us power, so he left it to do on Monday."

"Bad timing, she said. Harry, I'll be all right. Go before Agnes throws you out bodily. The troopers will be here. The dogs can go out to check the yard and will all be with me for what's left of the night. Go reassure everyone at the main house, or we'll have my mother in full panic mode. If all else fails, tell her I'm having a nighttime training exercise. She already thinks I'm crazy, so she'll believe it."

Pushing herself to her feet, she pulled him up against her, kissed him and then shoved him out, gently closing the door. Opening the slider, she let the dogs out to check the yard then crossed the room and ran her fingers over the spot where the bullet pierced the door. Pulling it open, she saw part of the bullet sticking out the other side. Gurka would need to see this but it could wait until morning.

A yawn, which threatened to crack her jaw, had her fighting fatigue. Pushing opened the slider to let the dogs in, she then pulled the curtains closed to limit the draft from the bullet hole and slipped back into bed. As she pulled up the blankets, Quinn and Dillon leaped up next to her, quickly snuggling, one on either side. She started to order them off but decided she wanted their warm bodies for reassurance. The tug of fatigue grabbed her, she closed her eyes and slept.

Kate woke to the sound of a camera and Andy ordering her to rise and shine. Agnes pushed by him, wading through the mass of dogs to the sliding door, pulled the curtain back, and gasped when she saw the hole. The dogs pushed to get by her, as she opened the slider to let them out. "Andy, out. Kate, up and throw on sweats. We'll feed the dogs and then get organized. Move it, there's a cup of tea on the table for you that is getting cold."

Kate moved like a zombie grabbing sweats and pulling them on. The snow might have melted, but it was still cold. Grabbing her slippers off the shelf above her bed, she slipped them on and went in search of tea. What she found was a kitchen filled with troopers, Sal and her brothers. Will replaced her tea with a hot cup and placed a plate with a serving of a scrambled egg with ham and cheese casserole, along with a vase containing a single white rose in front of her.

"The food is from me, but your intended sent the rose. Des and Rufus are keeping him from coming over. I think handcuffs are involved. I've already texted him that you are fine. Agnes says you have four minutes to finish eating and then you need to get into your shower. She says that she and Ellen will be here with the dress in ten minutes and you are to be ready."

"The dog meals…"

"My job," said Tim. "You go do your bride thing. We'll take care of everything else."

She glanced at the clock hurriedly shoveling in the casserole; regretting not being able to savor the herbs and three kinds of cheese that blended with the eggs. Taking her tea with her, she dashed into her room, told the female officer who was prying the bullet from the door that the room would be bride central in three minutes, and grabbing her robe, dashed into the shower, locking the door just in case. Minutes later, Agnes banged on the bathroom door.

"Room's clear of cops. Come out and get dressed."

Kate stepped out wearing only her lacy panties and her robe. The room was filled with women. Maeve, Sadie, Cathy, Ellen, and Grandma Ann, all dressed for the wedding, were holding the dress and train while Agnes pulled the robe off and slipped a lacy corset over her head and tied up the back. Next came the silk slip which was cut low in both the front and back and fell lightly to the floor. Then, the women in unison lifted the dress high and gently passed it from one hand to another as Agnes supervised slipping it over her head and letting it slide down to the floor. Agnes reached into a pouch resting on her dresser and quickly applied lip gloss and blush to her face, ran a quick comb through her curls and taking the veil from Ellen, set it on her head and hitched it down with almost invisible hairpins.

A voice from the kitchen announced Sarah's arrival carrying the box containing the bouquets. "The florist gave me these when I arrived and then headed to the main house to do the guys."

Peggy Gaffney

Kate looked at her attendants and smiled. She hadn't had any idea what they would be wearing, but she couldn't be more delighted. The cocktail length silk dresses were beautifully cut, each slightly different to flatter the wearer. They were in the colors of fall and the flower bouquets were tied with streamers which matched all three dresses. They looked beautiful. As soon as Agnes had started lowering the dress over her head, she'd signaled Andy who came in and photographed the whole process. Kate slipped on her shoes and finally turned around so that she faced everyone.

"God, Kate, you're beautiful." He murmured. Then he had the women gather around her so that he could get a group shot.

Ann attached a gold and green cloisonne shamrock pendant around her neck. "Your grandfather gave this to me on our twenty-fifth anniversary. It is your 'something borrowed'."

Maeve stepped up and fastened a diamond-studded paw print pin to her dress. "This is the pin your grandfather gave me when I won the National with Liam's great grandfather. It's your 'something old' and yours to keep."

Sadie moved forward and said, "I was going to get for your 'something new' a replacement bulletproof vest. It was to take the place of the one that took a bullet last month, but I decided that your mother wouldn't understand. So, instead I got you this gold filigree bracelet that looks delicate but contains a tracking device with a range of forty miles so Harry will never lose you."

Ellen finally stepped forward and said, "Your 'something blue' is the garter that Juanita knit for you to wear under your dress." She lifted the hem of the dress and slipped it up Kate's leg. By the way, your mother was given the job of being at the church to greet all the visiting professors and family. The sentiment isn't something she handles."

There was a tap at her bedroom door and Padraig stuck his head in. "The cars are here. It's time to go." Kate reached for her down parka, but Agnes pulled it out of her hand and pushed her into the kitchen where a large box sat on the table. She opened it and lifted out a faux-fur lined satin cape which she settled over Kate's shoulders.

"My God, she's the Snow Queen," Andy said as his camera clicks escorted them to their rides. The limousines had the benefit of police cars front and rear for security. It had the added benefit that they were able to glide through-traffic as they approached the church. When they reached the front door of the church, her brother Tom was waiting in his tux with his cane on the top step. Will and Seamus came down to escort them with Gurka's men lined up to give coverage.

Andy took a bunch of shots of her in her dress and cape going up the steps and then dashed to the top to get more of Tom hugging her and escorting the bridal party into a small room off the entrance. This cleared the doorway as more wedding guests arrived at the last minute.

Agnes stepped back out to talk to Tim and then returned. Satu, looking very lovely in a shimmery rose knee-length dress stuck her head in to report that Harry and company were more than ready, and they had better get started, or he'll be running down the aisle to grab her. Agnes nodded and told the two troopers who were manning the doors to close them. Then she signaled pressed a button on the wall that had the music changing. Then she lined up the bridesmaids. Tom grabbed his cane which he'd set aside, offered Kate his arm then nodded to Agnes.

As they stepped out of the anteroom toward the main aisle, Kate spotted Sal, Tim, and Seamus on the other side of the door. But what made her gasp was what they had. As Sarah turned and started down the aisle, Liam and Shelagh, perfectly groomed on pure white leads stepped into heel position beside her, and she tucked their leads under her bouquet. This was repeated with Cathy as Dillon and Quinn moved into position. Agnes stepped forward and turned down the aisle. Then she and Tom stepped forward. "I would give anything for Dad and Gramps to be in my place right now," he whispered, "but I've had the feeling for the last half hour that they are here with us."

Kate looked at him with tears in her eyes. "They are here. Thanks to all of you for including the dogs."

"It was Jordy's idea."

Kate looked down the aisle to see Sarah step into her place in the front row of seats using a hand signal to get the dogs to sit, dropping the leads. Cathy did the same thing. Agnes stepped into position and signaled all the dogs to hold when Harry stepped forward ready to take her hand.

Fr. Joe asked "Who giveth this woman in marriage to this man."

Tom's voice was clear when he said, "My grandfather, my father and I do."

Harry took her hand. Agnes moved the dogs into position behind them and then took Kate's bouquet.

Search

The ceremony was beautiful. Kate was amazed she could respond correctly since her brain was caught up in a swirl of emotions. Harry must have realized it since his grip on her hands and his gaze grounded her. He was well on board when Fr. Joe said, "You may kiss the bride."

Agnes stepped forward to hand Kate her bouquet and to reach down to hand two leads to each of them so that the dogs could proceed them down the aisle. Andy was everywhere taking pictures and dashed up the aisle. Kate's brain suddenly clicked into full gear as she looked out at the friendly faces of their guests.

They had passed most of the family and were approaching the members of what Kate called 'The long arm of the law club' when Quinn growled softly and Dillon's hackles began to rise. They'd almost reached the row where most of the FBI was standing when Kate saw a face she recognized staring back from someone she'd never met. Planting a smile on her face, she forced herself to wave to her dog friends and then, still smiling, leaned into Harry to whisper, "Maurio is standing at this end of the aisle next to Bullock and Des."

She watched as the man looked up and made eye contact. He reached into his jacket and pulled out a gun.

Kate yelled, "Stick."

Dillon leapt up at the command and ripped the gun from the man's hand as Quinn jumped against his chest knocking him onto the floor. A second later, Dillon, his tail wagging, sat up in front of her and held up the gun. Kate took it, handed it off to Harry, then praised Dillon and told all the dogs to heel as Des and Bullock grabbed the man.

Peggy Gaffney

As they continued down the aisle, they heard a voice behind them say, "Maurio, I didn't know you were coming to Harry's wedding. Pete would have loved to have you here."

CHAPTER THIRTY-NINE

Kate and Harry moved into the reception line at the back of the church. Soon Harry's mother and Kate's joined the group. Kate stood, holding tightly to Harry's hand, fighting the effects of shock at once more seeing a gun pointed at her ready to take her life. Taking strength from her husband, and he finally was, she worked to smile as they accepted congratulations from those heading off to the reception.

After a few minutes, Kate leaned past Harry and asked his mother if the person she spoke to was the man in the photo Kate had shown her.

"Yes, he was the young man that Pete was teaching about the department. It looks as though he did get into law enforcement. Pete would have been proud. Your dogs, however, were vicious with him, Kate. One of them bit him. I hope he doesn't sue you."

Kate felt Harry's arms circle her waist and pull her close whispering, "How did you know it was Maurio?"

"I've been staring at his face in the photos so much, I think you could have put him in a clown wig and I'd have known him. He was the terror in my nightmare which came to life when he pulled that gun. My only thought was, I had not come this far and finally marry you only to die at the wedding. Thank God Dillon has a hair trigger."

"I love that dog, almost as much as I love his owner," he whispered as he leaned in to kiss her.

At last, the line came to an end and they moved to leave the church. They turned to get their coats before heading for the reception when Bullock and two other agents moved to the door holding Maurio. The dogs reacted with growls as he passed by.

Des stepped to Harry's side, "Bullock wanted me to apologize for bringing our newest agent, Mark Cross, or Boston as he likes to be called, to the wedding. He's only been with the team for a month and with the buzz cut hair and thinner face, I didn't make the connection."

Kate looked at him. "M.C. He didn't even change the initials. You never think to look right under your nose."

"Sorry, Kate."

"You should thank Dillon," she said, and turned away as Harry put her cape over her shoulders and they went out to the limo.

"Why did you shout 'stick?'" Harry asked.

"It is his command to go and grab a flag from a person holding a pointy object out in the audience when we do our obedience performance. He usually brings the flag to me as a finish to our musical obedience demonstration. I told him the same thing when he saved my life from the killer last February, so he now he associates the word with disarming killers. It is a handy command."

The barn resembled a beautiful ballroom, with gauze fabric hanging in swaths from the beams above a polished dance floor surrounded by linen covered tables. A band was playing and broke into a jazzy version of *Here Comes the Bride* as they entered. Laughter filled the room and Kate, who had spent part of the drive from church giving in to a mini-meltdown, managed to double down and was able to smile and greet everyone.

Jordy rushed up and claimed the ribbon leads, telling her that Sal had given all the kids permission to escort the dogs back to the exercise yard for naps after each of them had an extra biscuit to celebrate the wedding. Kate handed him Quinn and passed the leads for Dillon, Liam, and Shelagh to three of her cousin's children. She noticed that Jordy ensured that the dogs made a circle greeting everyone prior to heading out.

Maeve, Padraig, Ann, and Sal all approached looking for hugs. Maeve said, "I had only just stepped into the aisle when I saw that man reach for his gun. I didn't have time to go for mine or to get a clear shot. Thank God for Dillon. Who was he?"

"He was the newest agent added to Bullock's team. His name is Mark Cross. His nickname is Boston."

She grabbed Harry's arm. "He is your father's killer."

Harry nodded as Des stepped up. "It's even worse. Bullock filled in the whole team on what we'd done and who had come up with the idea while he was dealing with the press from the hotel last night. He was praising Kate for her brilliant idea, never realizing he was setting her up as Cross' next victim. Mark, sorry, Maurio blames her for destroying their entire plan."

Sadie, who had joined the group as Des spoke, reached out and slapped him on the back of his head saying, "Idiots. While these two are on their honeymoon, you and I are going to go through every personnel file with a fine-toothed comb and make sure nobody is still hiding in the system. You and Bullock need to park your egos and learn to look at what's right in front of you."

"Harry?"

They turned to see Sarah, Cathy, and Agnes with their significant others standing behind them. Sarah suddenly surged forward and hugged her brother and then Kate. "I know that we haven't gotten along much, and I blame myself. If anything had happened to you, I couldn't have stood it. When I saw that gun pointed at you and Kate, it suddenly occurred to me that you're just like dad, fighting for justice and having to take on killers. What I don't know was why that man was trying to kill you. He looked vaguely familiar. I think I've seen him before, maybe a long time ago."

Kate reached for Sarah's hand. "Do you remember Maurio, the boy your father was trying to help?"

"Yes, oh, that's who it was. But what was he doing at your wedding?"

Kate looked at Harry. He nodded and she told Sarah what had happened. "Maurio is the person who murdered your father. Harry has been trying to find him for years and when your mother sent the boxes of his things to Harry for storage, we found the final clues to his murderer and the mob members who were involved.

"You probably didn't see the late news last night, but your dad is being given credit for bringing down a massive organized crime operation involving mob families up and down the east coast. Maurio wanted to kill us for setting the take-down of these men in motion who were bent on destroying the country.

"Since we have guests to see to, you could help us by being the one to tell your mother that Pete's killer has been found and arrested. You are good with her and I'm sure she'd rather hear it from you than from Harry."

"I'll do it. But, I think that mom needs to apologize to you Harry as do I. She's been cruel to you ever since dad died, and I was as well. We behaved the way we thought dad had, by resenting you. But you became just the person he wanted you to be — in spite of all that math. I think he would have been proud of you. I'll go talk to mom now."

Cathy and Rufus stepped forward to hug them. "We've decided, after what we saw today, that life is to short to put off doing what we want," Rufus said, slipping his arm around Cathy's waist and said, "We're going to get married. I'm going to accept a post at the university in Spokane, a reasonable commute to Cathy's place. She's got the big house and the set up for the dogs, and Jordy loves the ideas of there being wildlife nearby.

"He'll be with Seamus and Satu at MIT and I'm told Tim will be just across town at Boston College. The flight into Seattle is actually easier than the one to Denver. So we will be sending you the date next July for you to come west and be part of our wedding." Jordy came rushing in to tell them they had to go watch a trick he'd just taught Quinn, so they left.

Agnes came forward to hug her. Kate kissed her cheek and said, "Thank you so much. The wedding and this reception were perfect. Having the dogs in the wedding party was not only fitting but life-saving. You are the best wedding planner ever."

"I must admit," she answered, "you two were correct. Having a small wedding with a dress designed by you was absolutely right. Your dad and granddad would have been thrilled, especially with Dillon taking out the killer and saving your lives. And in spite of the fact that there were guns involved and many adjustments had to be made to work around the plans of a killer, it all turned out beautifully."

Sean wrapped his arms around Agnes and spoke to them. "Do me a favor, you two, when we get married next summer, could you make sure you don't have any killers hunting you while you're in the wedding party." They all laughed but realized how close the day had come to be one of tragedy.

Kate and Harry spent the next hour circulating among the guests and sharing the day with each. They found Lily Peters and Joyce Marks who had been so involved in the trouble they'd had when they traveled to Texas to get Quinn as a puppy. They both enjoyed the fact that he was looking so good and seemed to have Dillon's instinct to fight crime. Joyce congratulated Harry about not being shot this time. They mentioned that they had met Sal and Kate's grandmother and planned to spend time with them later.

Harry got to know her aunts, uncles, and cousins better, though he told her she'd better not quiz him later because he was sure to get them mixed up.

Finally, they stopped to eat some of the delicious food Will had made.

Kate looked out over the reception hall filled with all the people she cared about and smiled. Jordy had settled with her cousins at a table of their own and was chatting and eating. It was wonderful to see him being a kid for a while. She knew that Harry had been lonely growing up as a child in an adult world. Jordy, maybe because of knowing about Harry's experience, seemed to have fewer problems with the transition. Harry's friendship seemed to have a lot to do with it.

Scanning the room, she noticed most of the FBI agents who had been at the church as wedding guests and former colleagues of Harry had finally arrived at the reception and were eating and chatting with Sal and some of the troopers. She leaned against Harry, realizing she could finally relax. Rufus and Agnes both gave toasts and Harry then stood and led her to the center of the dance floor.

The musicians began playing a waltz and they danced, the dress swirling out as she hoped when she designed it. Kate stared into Harry's loving gaze, and remembered the day they met, and how the sparkle in those beautiful green eyes had attracted her. Their meeting and courtship may have been unusual, with them being engaged before they had their first date, but as far as she was concerned, it was all perfect. This courtship had been tested many times, including when their lives were threatened, but as they moved in unison around the floor, all she felt was joy.

She was vaguely aware that Andy had been both present and invisible while taking photos all day. These they would treasure. She did wonder, though, if he had gotten a shot of Dillon saving their lives. He and Quinn had been quite a pair, father and son working in unison.

Suddenly she became aware that the floor had filled with other dancers including the wedding party, all her brothers, Sal and Ann, and Padraig and Maeve. Her heart was full.

As they headed back to their table, they saw Bullock entering the building. Harry steered her in his direction, neither man smiling.

"Kate, Harry, I am so sorry. You were right telling Des that ego had kept us from looking at what was right under our noses. I remembered interviewing Cross for the job and thinking he was absolutely perfect."

Kate told him, "You were meant to. He'd studied how to win that place in the bureau from the time Pete Foyle showed him around. Did he say why he tried to kill us? It was a stupid thing to do because it blew his cover,"

"He did it as revenge. You two had destroyed what they'd been working on going back to the time when Harry's father died. Apparently, your father, Harry, had given information to his police team, leading to the shootout which killed Maurio's father.

"The mob told him he could only find revenge if he took out the man behind that raid. He managed to befriend and use Pete to gain knowledge which he passed on to his mob family and then to finally prove himself, he killed your dad. That earned him a place in their plan to infiltrate law enforcement and destroy it from within."

"He didn't realize he was up against an opposition which was stronger, smarter, faster, and much hairier than he'd ever encountered—Dillon and Quinn," Harry added with a smile.

"Your photographer got the whole thing on film, and two of your cousins who were taking a video of the recessional did as well. We will probably need you to testify if he doesn't plead out, but it won't be that soon, so there will be time for your honeymoon. Where are you going?"

"It's a secret," Harry said. "Nobody knows."

"Not even me," Kate told him. "I'm hoping he'll tell me enough to know what to pack in the way of the right clothes tonight. We leave first thing in the morning."

Harry turned to her and said, "I gave Agnes a list yesterday and she and Cathy packed your things while you were doing the photo shoot with the dogs. Your suitcases are in the van along with dog crates and their food. Agnes said she has traveled with you to so many dog shows over the years she knows exactly how you pack and what you'd want to take with you."

Peggy Gaffney

Eventually, they left and walked back to the house while the party continued in the barn. Ellen texted her that she'd be by in twenty minutes to get the dress and take it back to the studio to keep it safe. They changed their clothes and after Ellen left, curled up on the living room sofa to take advantage of the peace.

Harry turned on the television and found that their wedding was the top story on the news. The fact that the murderer of Pete Foyle had been captured while trying to murder Sgt. Foyle's son and his new bride was made even more exciting by the fact that it was the bride's dogs who stopped the crime by grabbing the gun from the killer. It went on talking about Kate, who they said was not only was a well known fashion designer, but who ran a training school for dogs, to do everything from obedience to police work. They even mentioned that Harry, following in his father's footsteps in working to fight crime, owned a cyber security company.

Harry clicked off the television and looked at her. "When our kids ask about our wedding, they're going to think we made all this up."

"Hopefully by then, criminals will stop shooting at us and our friends will stop needing us to step up to keep the country safe."

"The number of times we've been involved this year alone, makes me doubt that, but one can hope."

Harry stretched. "We didn't get much sleep last night. I could use a nap." As he glanced at her, he raised one eyebrow. She smiled and stood pulling him to his feet. The dogs, who were milling around the house, went to follow them into

Harry's room, but found themselves shut out and Kate learned, there were very enjoyable moments in her new life that didn't involve dogs.

Author's Note

Dear Reader,

I hope you enjoyed *SEARCH*, the fourth book in the Kate Killoy Mystery series. This book gave you a chance to visit Kate's home and find out a little more about what goes on day to day and about both her and Harry's hopes and dreams.

This book took a little longer to finish. During one afternoon, while a nor'easter raged I was writing, deep in the story when I heard a bang which shook the house. Since branches had been falling on the roof since the winds got really high, I stood up and looked out the window. I saw a branch hanging down over the kitchen window. However, since the lights were still on and I still had internet, I just made a cup of tea and got back to work, waiting for the storm to end so I could call someone to get the branch down. An hour later, my son ran into the house shouting. "There's a tree on the roof."

It turned out, that an 85 foot hemlock tree had fallen on the roof of my hundred year old house. The branch was somewhat larger than I'd thought. So Dillon, Quinn, one of the cats, my son and I had to go spend three days in a hotel while huge cranes and men with saws removed the tree. Then the roof had to be replaced and the deck repaired. With all these distractions, my writing got interrupted. But finally I got back on track and finished the story.

Search
357

For the last two weeks, as I went through all the processes that come in wrapping up a book and getting it ready for press, I let my imagine wander on ideas for the perfect honeymoon for our pair. They had to go somewhere which would allow the dogs, at least three of them, to be with them. Plus it should be somewhere which would be special to both Kate and Harry. I knew just the place. Needless to say, I am already writing the honeymoon story so while their new home is being built, they are building fantastic memories of this wonderful time together.

We've had the remaining trees that were near the roof removed, so hopefully I'll be able to finish this next story without interruptions and Kate, Harry and the dogs will be able to enjoy the honeymoon peacefully—or not.

Thank you for reading my books, and for visiting Kate, Harry, and their wonderful family and friends. If you have the time, I would love for you to post a comment about what you enjoyed on Amazon or Goodreads. I'm writing quickly so that you will have more stories of these this adventurous pair and their dogs.

Enjoy,
Peggy

OTHER BOOKS BY PEGGY GAFFNEY

The Crafty Samoyed Knits

The Crafty Labrador Retriever Knits

The Crafty Golden Retriever Knits

The Crafty Bernese Mt. Dog Knits

The Crafty Newfoundland Knits

The Crafty Welsh Corgi Knits

The Crafty Poodle Knits

The Crafty Cat Knits

The Crafty Llama and Alpaca Knits

Knit a Kitten, Purl a Puppy

Do It Yourself Publishing Nonfiction In Your Spare Time

***

On the website kanineknits.com, there are over one hundred
different dog breeds represented in picture knit sweaters
designed by Peggy and available as patterns for any of you who
knit to enjoy.

Visit peggygaffney.com to keep posted on the further adventures of Kate and Harry in their next exciting adventure--a not quite relaxing honeymoon.

Love and play with your dogs.

CPSIA information can be obtained
at www.ICGtesting.com
Printed in the USA
FSHW011958011219
64652FS

9 780999 387801